'Have you forgotten the circumstances of our previous acquaintance?'

'Why, yes, of course!' Marcus replied.

Francesca, the wind taken somewhat out of her sails, stared at him.

'I thought that would please you. You said you wished me to forget the lot,' he said earnestly.

Francesca pressed her lips together firmly. He would not make her laugh; she would not let him—that was how it all started last time. And this man had a talent, it seemed, for reaching that other Francesca of long ago. She must regain control of her emotions—she must!

Sylvia Andrew taught modern languages for years, ending up as Vice-Principal of a sixth-form college. She lives in Somerset with two cats, a dog, and a husband who has a very necessary sense of humour, and a stern approach to punctuation. Sylvia has one daughter living in London, and they share a lively interest in theatre. She describes herself as an 'unrepentant romantic'.

Recent titles by the same author:

SERAFINA

FRANCESCA

Sylvia Andrew

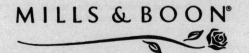

MILLS & BOON®

*First published in Great Britain 1997
Harlequin Mills & Boon Limited,
Eton House, 18-24 Paradise Road, Richmond, Surrey TW9 1SR*

© Sylvia Andrew 1997

ISBN 0 263 80380 5

*Set in Times 10 on 11 pt. by
Rowland Phototypesetting Limited
Bury St Edmunds, Suffolk*

04-9709-76884

Printed and bound in Great Britain

Chapter One

Lightning was flickering over the hills ahead, and every now and then came a distant roll of thunder—another storm was on its way. The field workers had given up for the day and were hurrying home before the storm broke, the children clinging to their mothers' skirts, fathers carrying the littlest ones on their shoulders. But they smiled at the shabbily dressed young woman who passed them on the outskirts of the village, and greeted her with respect.

Miss Fanny was on her own way home to the Manor, where she lived with her aunt, Miss Cassandra Shelwood. Though she was wearing an old dress and a tattered sunbonnet, though all the world knew that her mother had run off with a well-known rake and had never been seen again, all the same, Miss Fanny was the late Sir John Shelwood's granddaughter. She and her aunt were the last of a long line of Shelwoods who had owned most of the land round about for as long as anyone could remember.

Miss Shelwood had a heart of stone—everyone was afraid of her—but Miss Fanny was usually very friendly. Today she seemed preoccupied. Perhaps what they were saying about her aunt's health was true after all. There were long faces at the possibility, for what would happen to the estate if—when—Miss Shelwood died? It was well known that Miss Shelwood wouldn't give her niece the time of day if she could help it. So what was going to happen to the Shelwood estate?

Francesca Shelwood had been so deep in thought that she had barely noticed the lightning and was only faintly aware of the thunder rumbling ominously round the valley. The villagers were upon her before she had noticed them. But she smiled at them as they bobbed and nodded their heads, and turned to watch them as they hurried on, anxious to reach shelter before the rain came. They would have been astonished to learn how much she envied them.

Few would claim they were fortunate. Their days were hard and long, they were under constant threat of disaster—sudden accident or illness, the failure of the harvest, the whims of a landowner, or the caprices of the weather. But they laughed and joked as they went back to their modest dwellings, and the ties of affection, of love and family, were obvious.

She would never know such ties. Nearly twenty-five years old, plain, without any prospect of fortune, and with a shadow over her birth—who would ever think of marrying her?

Now the problem of her future was becoming more urgent with every day that passed. That her aunt was seriously ill could no longer be in doubt, though this was never admitted openly at Shelwood. Miss Shelwood refused to discuss the state of her health with anyone, least of all with her niece. But her attacks had been getting worse and more frequent for months, and yesterday's had been the worst yet, though no one dared dispute Miss Shelwood's assertion that it was simply a result of the excessive heat.

Francesca sighed. Years ago, when she had first come to Shelwood as a bewildered child, snatched away from everything she loved, she had looked to her aunt

Cassandra, her mother's sister, for consolation. What a mistake that had been! How often she had been snubbed, chastised, ignored, before she finally realised the harsh truth. Her aunt disliked her, and wanted as little as possible to do with her. Why this was so she had never been able to fathom. As a child she had asked her grandfather, but he had merely said that she was too young to understand. She had even screwed up her courage one day and had asked her aunt directly.

But Miss Shelwood had given Francesca one of her cold stares and replied, 'A stupid question, Fanny! How . could anyone like such a plain, naughty, impertinent child?'

One of the older servants, who was now dead, had once said cryptically, 'It's because you're your mother's daughter, Miss Fanny. Miss Cassandra never wanted you here. It was the master who insisted. You can understand it, though.' And she had then maddeningly refused to say anything more.

It had not been so bad while Grandfather was alive. He had loved her in his fashion, had tried to make up for the lack of affection in his elder daughter. But he had been an old man, and since his death Aunt Cassandra's animosity had seemed to increase—or at least become more obvious. Francesca knew that only her aunt's strong sense of duty persuaded her to give her niece a home, for she had been told so soon after her grandfather's funeral. She had been eleven years old at the time, and had been very surprised to receive a summons to her aunt's room. The scene was still bitterly vivid, even after all these years. . .

'I have something to say to you.'

Francesca was frightened of her aunt. She looked like a great crow, perched behind the desk, hair scraped back under a black lace cap, hooded dark eyes, black dress, black shawl. . . And, though her aunt was motionless, the child could sense a seething anger behind the still façade. There was a chair in front of the desk, but Francesca knew better than to sit down without an invitation, so she remained standing.

'Mr Barton has been acquainting me with the terms of your grandfather's will.'

Francesca shifted uneasily and wondered what was coming. Mr Barton was the Shelwood family lawyer, and Aunt Cassandra had been closeted with him all day after the funeral, and most of the day after. What was her aunt going to do about her? Was she going to send her away—to school, perhaps? She rather hoped so—it could hardly be worse than staying alone at Shelwood with her aunt. Her hopes were soon dashed, however.

'Your grandfather has left you a sum of money, the interest on which will provide you with a small allowance—enough to pay for clothes and so on. It is not intended for school fees, since he wished you to remain at Shelwood for the time being. I have been asked to give you a roof over your head during my lifetime, and will obey my father's wish. You have, after all, nowhere else to go.' Her tone made it clear how much she regretted the fact.

'Perhaps I could go back to St Marthe?'

'That is out of the question. There is no place for you there. You will remain here.'

The young Francesca had looked with despair on the prospect of the future stretching out in front of her, alone at Shelwood with Aunt Cassandra. She offered another solution. 'I might marry someone, Aunt—as soon as I am old enough.'

'You might, though that is rather unlikely. . .'

*   *   *

Francesca's lips twisted in a bitter little smile at the memory of what had followed. Her aunt had gone on to make it clear just why marriage for Francesca was practically out of the question.

'Very unlikely, I should say, in view of your history.'

'My history?' Francesca cast her mind over her various small misdemeanors and found nothing in them to discourage a suitor. 'What have I done, Aunt Cassandra?'

'It is not what *you* have done.' She paused, and there was a significant silence. Francesca felt something was required of her, but what?

'Is there something I should have done and haven't?' she asked. She knew that this, too, was frequently a source of dissatisfaction.

Miss Shelwood's expression did not change, but Francesca shivered as she waited for her aunt to speak. Finally, she said, 'It has nothing to do with your activities. The damage was done before you were even born. Did your grandfather not tell you about it in all those cosy little chats you had with him? When he talked to you about your mother?'

'I. . .I don't think so. He was often sad when he talked about her. He said he was sorry he never saw her again before she died.'

'He was always very fond of her.'

'He said she was beautiful—'

'She was quite pretty, it is true.'

'Everyone who met her loved her—'

'She knew how to please, certainly.'

'He used to tell me stories about when she was a little girl. She used to laugh a lot, he said. And she did.' Francesca was so nervous that the words came tumbling out. Normally she would have been silent in her aunt's presence. 'I remember her laughing, too. She used to laugh

a lot when we all lived together on St Marthe. She and
Maddy used to laugh all the time.'

'Maddy?'

'My. . .my nurse. The one who brought me here. The
one you sent away.'

'The native woman.'

'Maddy was a Creole, Aunt Cassandra. She and Mama
were friends. I loved them both. Very much.'

'A most unsuitable woman to have charge of you. Your
grandfather was right to get rid of her. So your mama
laughed on St Marthe, did she? I am surprised. But then
she always found something to amuse her. I daresay it
amused her to run off with your father. Whether she was
quite so amused when you were born, I do not know.
You see, Fanny. . .' Miss Shelwood paused here as if she
was wondering whether to go on. Then her lips tightened
and she said slowly, 'Tell me your name.'

Francesca wondered why her aunt should make such a
strange request, but she took a deep breath and answered
quietly, 'Francesca Shelwood.'

This time the pause was even longer. 'Fanny
Shelwood,' said Miss Shelwood in a voice which boded
no good for Francesca. 'Fanny. Not. . .Francesca.
Francesca is a ridiculously pretentious name. An absurd
name for such a plain child.'

Francesca remained silent. This was an old battle, but,
though everyone else now called her Fanny, she would
remain Francesca in her own mind. Her mother—the
mother she only dimly remembered—had called her
Francesca, and she would never give it up. Her aunt
waited, then went on, 'Where did the name, Fanny
Shelwood, come from?'

'You said I had to be called Fanny, Aunt Cassandra.'

'Are you being deliberately obstructive, Fanny, or
simply very stupid? I refer to your surname.'

'Grandfather said I was to be a Shelwood. After I came here.'

'Quite so. Have you never wondered why?' The little girl had been pleased that her grandfather wanted to give her his name. It made her feel more wanted, more as if she belonged. She had accepted it, as she had accepted everything else. She had never questioned his reasons. She shook her head.

'It was because, Fanny, as far as we could tell, you had no other name to call yourself.'

'I. . .I don't know what you mean, Aunt Cassandra. I was called Francesca Beaudon at home on St Marthe.'

'Francesca. . .Beaudon.' Her aunt's lip curled as she pronounced the name. 'What right had you to such a name, pray?'

Francesca was completely puzzled. What did her aunt mean? She shook her head. 'I. . .I don't know. Because Papa's name was Beaudon?'

Miss Shelwood leaned forward. 'You had no right whatsoever to the name of Beaudon, Fanny Shelwood! None at all! Your father's name is not for such as you. Richard Beaudon never married your mother!'

'Of course Papa and Mama were married!' cried Francesca in instant and scornful repudiation. What did this woman know about life on St Marthe? 'Of course they were married,' she repeated more loudly. 'Everyone called Mama Lady Beaudon.'

'Do not raise your voice to me, Fanny. I will not have it!'

There was a silence while Francesca wrestled with her sense of anger and outrage. Finally she muttered, 'They were married. It's not true what you say!'

'Are you daring to doubt my word?' A slight pause, then, 'You must accept it, I'm afraid. And, unless you learn to control your feelings better, I shall wash my hands

of you, and then where would you be? You might well go
the way your unfortunate mother went—with disastrous
consequences to herself and you.'

'It isn't true,' said Francesca doggedly. She sounded
brave, but deep down she felt a growing sense of panic.
She was not sure of the exact significance of what her
aunt was saying, but there was nothing good about it.
There was a girl in the village who had a baby though
she wasn't married. Everyone was very unkind to her and
called her names. They called the baby names, too. It was
impossible that her darling mama had been like Tilly
Sefton! 'It's not! It's not!' she said, her voice rising again.

Miss Shelwood said sharply, 'Do stop contradicting me
in that ridiculous way! What does a little girl like you
know about such things? People called your mother
"Lady"—' Aunt Cassandra's voice dripped contempt
'—"Lady Beaudon", because they did not wish to offend.
It was merely a courtesy title!'

When Francesca remained silent she went on, 'Deceive
yourself if you wish—but tell me this if you can, Fanny.
What happened after your mother died? Did your father
keep you by him, as any real father would? He did not.
He packed you off to England as soon as he could and
we, your mother's family, were more or less forced to
give you a home and a name! And what have you heard
from your father since you left the West Indies? Nothing!
No visits, no letters, no money, no gifts—not even on
your birthday. Why is that, Fanny?'

Once again Francesca was silent. She had nothing to
say in defence of herself and her father. She had been
hurt that she never heard anything from him, had tried to
find out why, but her grandfather had always refused to
mention the Beaudon name.

Satisfied that she had made her point, Miss Shelwood
went on, 'So you see, Fanny, a marriage is most unlikely

for you, do you not agree? What have you to offer a
respectable man? A girl without fortune, without name
and—you have to admit that you are hardly a beauty. But
you may stay here with me as long as I am alive.'

Even fourteen years later, Francesca still resented the cruel
manner in which her aunt had told her of her situation. It
had been like crushing a butterfly. For months afterwards
she had cried herself to sleep or lain awake, thinking of
her life with Maddy and her mother in the West Indies,
trying to remember anything at all which might contradict
what her aunt had said. But she had found nothing.

Her father had always been a dim figure in the background, especially after Mama had fallen ill and most of
her time had been spent in the pretty, airy bedroom with
fluttering white curtains and draperies. It was Maddy who
had been the child's companion then, Maddy who had
sworn never to leave her young charge.

But, of course, Maddy had been forced to go when
Aunt Cassandra dismissed her. Aunt Cassandra, not
Grandfather. Francesca's heart still ached at the memory
of their parting. She had clung to Maddy's skirts, as if
she could keep her nurse at Shelwood by physical force,
had pleaded with her grandfather, even with her aunt. But
Maddy had had to go.

As Francesca grew older, she came to accept the hard
truth about her birth, if only because she could not see why
her aunt should otherwise invent a tale which reflected so
badly on the Shelwood name. The rest of it—that she
was poor and plain—was more easily accepted. It wasn't
just what her aunt said—everyone seemed to think that
she was very like Miss Shelwood, who was tall, thin and
pale, with strong features.

Francesca, too, was tall, thin and pale, and though she
didn't have the Shelwood eyes—the Shelwood eyes were

dark brown, and hers were a greyish-green—her hair was
very much the same colour as her aunt's, an indeterminate,
mousy sort of blonde. How Francesca wished she had
taken after her small, vivacious mother, with her rich
golden curls and large pansy-brown eyes, who had always
been laughing!

A sudden rumble of thunder quite close brought
Francesca back with a start to the present. She glanced
up at the sky. The clouds were gathering fast—which
direction where they travelling? Then a horn blared behind
her and she nearly leapt out of her skin. She turned and
was horrified to see a chaise and four bearing down on
her at speed. She leapt for her life to the side of the road,
but lost her balance, skidded into the ditch, and ended up
in nettles, goose grass and the muddy water left over from
the previous night's rain.

The chaise thundered past, accompanied by shouts from
its driver as he fought to bring his team to a halt. At first
she made no attempt to move, but lay there in the ditch,
content to recover her breath and listen to crisp orders
being issued some way down the road. It had taken a
while to stop the chaise. Footsteps approached the ditch
where she lay and came to a halt beside her.

'Are you hurt?' Betsy's old sunbonnet had tipped
forward and covered her eyes, so that all she could see
when she looked up was a pair of long legs encased in
buckskins and beautifully polished boots.

'You were well clear of the coach, so don't try to
pretend. Come, girl, there's sixpence for you if you get
out of that ditch and show me that your fall hasn't done
any harm. Take hold of my cane.'

That voice! It was cooler and more authoritative than
she remembered. And the undercurrent of mockery was
new. But the rich timbre and deep tones were still familiar.
Oh, it couldn't be, it *couldn't*! Fate would not be so

unkind. Francesca shut her eyes and fervently hoped that memory was playing her false. Then the end of an ebony cane tapped her hand, and she grasped it reluctantly. One heave and she was out of the ditch and standing on the road. A exquisitely fitted green coat and elegant waistcoat were added to her vision of the gentleman.

'You see? You're perfectly unharmed.'

Francesca was not reassured by these words. She listened with growing apprehension as he went on, 'There's the sixpence—and there's another penny if you'll tell us if this lane leads to Witham Court. We appear to have taken a wrong turning.'

Francesca swallowed, tried to speak and uttered instead a strangled croak. Fate was being every bit as unkind as she had feared! He had not yet recognised her, but if he did. . .

'What's the matter? Cat got your tongue?' The gentleman pulled her towards him and, before she could stop him, was running his hands over her arms and legs. 'Yes, you're quite sound,' he said, drawing a large handkerchief from his pocket and wiping his fingers fastidiously on it. 'So stop shamming—there are no more sixpences, Mary, or whatever your name is. Nothing more to be got out of me, until you tell me where Witham Court is.' His movements had been impersonal—rather as if he were feeling the legs of a horse—but Francesca's face flamed and she was seized with a sudden access of rage.

'You can keep your money,' she said, pushing her hat back from her face, and glaring at him. 'An abject apology would be more in line, though I doubt it will be forthcoming. The last thing any of us expect is decent behaviour from the owner of Witham Court, or his guests.'

His eyes narrowed, then he said slowly, 'I appear to have made a mistake. I took you for one of the village girls.' He eyed her shabby dress and bonnet. 'Understand-

ably, perhaps. But. . .' he eyed her uncertainly again
'. . .it can't be. Yet now I look. . .we've met before,
haven't we?'

'Yes,' said Francesca stonily, wishing she could lie.

'Of course! You were wet then, too. . .we both were.
Why, yes! How could I have forgotten that glorious
figure. . .?'

He laughed when Francesca gave an involuntary gasp
of indignation and then pulled himself together and looked
rueful. 'I'm deeply sorry—that slipped out. I do beg your
pardon, ma'am. Abjectly.'

Francesca was unreconciled. He didn't sound abject.
'The details of our previous acquaintance are best forgotten, sir. All of them. And if you offer me an apology, it
surely ought to be for knocking me into the ditch.'

'We did not knock you into the ditch. You jumped and
fell. No, I was apologising for not recognising you.' He
regarded the wet and bedraggled creature before him. 'Not
even for a gentlewoman. As for our previous meeting—
it shall be erased from my mind, as requested. A pity,
though. Some details have been a most pleasant memory.'
He raised a quizzical eyebrow.

How dared he remind her of such an unfortunate and
embarrassing interlude! Had he no shame? Of course he
hadn't! He was a rake and a villain, and she was a fool
to be affected by him.

'You surprise me,' she said acidly. 'But are you suggesting you would not have practically run me down if
you had realised I wasn't one of the villagers? What a
very strange notion of chivalry you have to be sure! As
if it mattered who or what I was!'

'Forgive me, but I did not practically run you down.
My nephew, who is a trifle high-spirited, gave us all an
uncomfortable time, including my horses, in his efforts
to prove himself a notable whip. I shall deal with him

presently. But allow me to say that you were standing like a moonling on that road. You must have heard us coming?'

'I thought it was thunder— You're doing it again! How rude you are to call me a moonling!'

'It wasn't your good sense that attracted me all those years ago, Francesca! And standing in the middle of a highway is hardly the action of a rational being. Nor is it rational now to stand arguing about a trifle when you should be hastening to change out of your wet clothes.'

The justice of this remark did not endear the gentleman to Francesca. She was about to make a scathing reply when they were interrupted.

'Marcus, darling! Have you taken *root*, or something? We shall be caught in the storm if you don't hurry.'

The speaker was picking her way delicately along the road, holding up the skirts of an exquisite gown in green taffeta, her face shaded by a black hat with a huge brim. As a travelling costume it was hardly suitable, the hat a trifle too large, the dress a touch too low cut, but Francesca had never seen anything so stylish in her life. Under the hat were wisps of black hair, dark eyes, red lips, a magnolia skin with a delicate rose in the cheeks—an arrestingly vivid face. But at the moment an expression of dissatisfaction marred its perfection, and the voice was petulant.

'I'm not coming any further—the road is quite *dreadful*—but do make haste. What is the delay?' The dark eyes turned to Francesca. 'Good Lord! What a *filthy* mess! What on *earth* is it?' She stared for a moment, then turned to the man. 'Really, Marcus, why are you wasting time on such a wretch? Pay her off and come back to the coach. And *do* hurry. I shall wait with Nick. No, don't say another *word*—I refuse to listen. Don't forget to get her to tell

you the way—if she knows it,' she added, looking at
Francesca again with disdain.

'You mistake the matter, Charmian. Miss Shelwood's
accident has misled you into thinking she is one of the
country folk. In fact, her family own much of the land in
the district.'

'Really?' The dark eyes looked again at the shabby
dress. 'How very odd! Don't be long, Marcus.' Then
the vision turned round and picked her way back to the
carriage.

Francesca felt her face burn under its streaks of mud.
She was well used to snubs from her aunt, but this was
different—and from such a woman!

The gentleman tightened his lips, then said gently, 'You
must forgive Lady Forrest. She is hot and tired—Nick's
driving is not a comfortable experience.'

'So I have observed,' said Francesca. 'I am *sure* the
lady has had a quite *dreadful* time of it. *Pray* convey my
sympathy to her—my *abject* sympathy.'

He acknowledged this sally with a nod, but said
nothing. Then he appeared to come to a decision. 'You
must allow us to take you home. Shelwood Manor, is
it not?'

'Are you mad?'

'I fail to see why Lady Forrest's manners, or the condition of your clothes, should prevent me from doing my
clear duty. No, I am not mad.'

'My concern is neither for Lady Forrest nor for the
state of your carriage! I can perfectly well walk home—
indeed, I insist on doing so. To be frank, sir, I would not
go with you in your carriage to Shelwood, nor to Witham,
nor anywhere else, not even to the end of the lane! I am
surprised you should suggest it. Have you forgotten the
circumstances of our previous acquaintance?'

'Why, yes, of course!'

Francesca, the wind taken somewhat out of her sails, stared at him.

'I thought that would please you. You said you wished me to forget the lot,' he said earnestly.

Francesca pressed her lips together firmly. He would not make her laugh, she would not let him—that was how it had all started last time. She said coldly, 'I suggest you rejoin your friends—they will not wish to miss any of the. . .pleasures Witham Court has to offer.'

'Of course—you know about those, don't you?' he asked with a mocking smile.

'Only by hearsay, sir. And a brief and unwelcome acquaintance with one of its visiting rakes some years ago.'

'You didn't seem to find the acquaintance so unwelcome then, my dear.'

Francesca's face flamed again. She said curtly, 'I was very young and very foolish. I knew no better.' She started to walk along the road. 'I suggest you turn the carriage in the large drive about a hundred yards ahead and go back to the village. The road you should have taken is the first on the left. This one does lead to Witham Court, but it is narrow and uneven and would need expert driving.'

'You don't think I can do it,' he asked, falling into step beside her.

'Nothing I have seen so far would lead me to think so. Good day, sir.'

'Very well. I shall take your advice—my horses have suffered enough today, and this road surface is appalling.' He took a step, halted and turned to her. 'You are sure there's nothing I can do for you?'

'I think you've done enough! Now, for heaven's sake, leave me in peace!'

The gentleman looked astonished at the violence in

Francesca's voice. And in truth she had surprised herself. Such outbursts were rare. The child's impulsively passionate nature had over the years been subdued under her aunt's repressive influence. Nowadays, she exercised a great deal of self-discipline, and Miss Fanny's air of calm dignity, of lack of emotion—a defence against the constant slights she was subjected to at the Manor—was no longer totally assumed.

But this man had a talent, it seemed, for reaching that other Francesca of long ago. She must regain control of her emotions—she must! The little interlude years before had meant very little to him, that was obvious, or he would not now be able to refer to it in such a light-hearted manner. She must not let him even suspect the profound effect it had had on her. She would apologise for her outburst in a civilised manner, then bid him farewell.

But he forestalled her. The teasing look had quite vanished from his eyes as he said, 'Forgive me. I did not mean to offend you.'

Then, without another word, he turned on his heel and strode back to the chaise. Francesca found herself hoping he would trip on one of the stones that had been washed loose by the previous night's storm. She would enjoy seeing that confident dignity measure its length in the dust. But, of course, it didn't happen. Instead, he got into the chaise and exchanged some words with the young man who had remained with the horses.

There was a slight altercation which ended when the young man—his nephew, she supposed—got down and strode on up the lane. A few minutes later, the chaise passed on its way back to the village, the driver giving her exaggerated clearance and an ironical salute of the whip as he went.

Chapter Two

Lady Forrest saw the incident and felt a little spurt of irritation. Marcus was impossible—acknowledging a wretch like the girl on the road! Of course, he was just doing it to annoy her. He hadn't wanted to come to Charlie Witham's—it was not the sort of gathering he enjoyed and all her wiles had at first failed to persuade him to accept the invitation. But she had won in the end! And now he was showing his displeasure by teasing her.

'Are you so very displeased, Marcus?' she asked, looking at him sideways as the carriage turned into the village street.

He negotiated the tight left turn before replying. 'About Nick's driving? Not any more. Nor do you need to suffer any disquiet about him, either. By the time he's found his way to the Court, he'll have got over his fit of temper.'

Lady Forrest had forgotten Nick. 'That's not what I meant. You didn't want to come to Charlie's, when I first mentioned it. Are you regretting having changed your mind?'

'Not at all. You produced a master card and played it.' When she raised her eyebrows, and feigned surprise, he went on, 'Come, Charmian. You don't usually underestimate my intelligence so badly. You are quite ruthless in pursuing your wishes. When it became obvious I had no intention of escorting you to Witham Court, you beguiled Nick into performing the office. You counted on the fact that, although my nephew's capacity for getting into trouble seems to be infinite, I am fond of him. You knew that I was most unlikely to abandon him to the mercies of Charlie Witham's rapacious cronies.'

He looked at her with the quizzical smile she always found irresistible. 'But tell me, what would you have done if I had called your bluff? It would hardly have enhanced your reputation to arrive at Witham Court in the company of a lad half your age.'

The smile, then the rapier. He could be a cruel devil when he chose! Lady Forrest coloured angrily. 'You exaggerate, Marcus. In any case, the question did not arise. You have come—as I knew you would.' She changed her tone. 'Now, be kind. You have had your fun pretending to be concerned over that creature on the road, and attempting to introduce her—'

'You were quite ruthless there, too. Did you have to give the girl such a snub?'

'Why are you so concerned? If she were pretty I could understand it, but she is quite remarkably plain!'

'Plain? How can you say so?'

'Stop making fun of me, Marcus. Of course she is plain. Too tall, too bony, too sallow, a hard mouth— Really!'

'Her mouth is not hard, it is disciplined. And I suppose the streaks of dirt on her face disguised from you the loveliest line of cheekbone and jaw I think I have ever seen.' When Lady Forrest regarded him with astonishment, he added, 'Oh, she is not your conventional Society beauty, I agree. She lacks the rosebud mouth, the empty blue eyes, the dimpled cheeks. Her conversation is less vapid, too. But plain she will never be—not even when she is old. The exquisite bone structure will still be there.'

'Good Lord! This is news, indeed! What a sly fellow you are after all, my dear! When are we to congratulate you?' He gave her an ironic look, but refused to rise to her bait. She went on, 'Perhaps you will allow me to lend the girl a dress for the wedding? I can hardly think she owns anything suitable—nor, from the look of her, any dowry, either. Still, you hardly need that, now.'

There was a short silence and she wondered whether she had gone too far. Then he said calmly, 'Don't talk nonsense, my dear. I can admire beauty wherever I find it—I don't necessarily wish to possess it! Thank God—here are the gates. I suppose it is too much to hope that Charlie Witham has learned moderation since I was last here. So I warn you, you will have me to reckon with if you lead Nick into trouble, or make him miserable. My nephew is the apple of my sister's eye, God knows why!'

They were received warmly by their host, who could hardly believe his good fortune in snaring one of London's most elusive bachelors as a guest. Marcus Carne tended to move in circles of Society that Lord Witham and his friends, who would never have been admitted to them, apostrophised as devilish dull, riddled as they were with clever johnnies—academics, politicians, reformers and the like! But they found Carne himself perfectly sound. In fact, they termed him a Nonpareil.

He belonged to all the right clubs, was a first-class, if rather ruthless, cardplayer, and could hold his wine with the best of them. His skill with horses was legendary, and his life as an officer under Wellington had provided him with a fund of good stories, though he never bored his company with talk of the battles.

And, though he was what was generally called 'a proper man's man', he was equally popular with the ladies—not only with the frail beauties such as Charmian Forrest, who lived on the fringes of society, but with perfectly respectable dowagers and debutantes, too. His good looks and lazy smile, his air of knowing what he was about— such things appealed to the ladies, of course.

And he had another virtue that even outclassed his looks, his charm, his manliness, his straight dealing and all the rest. Marcus Carne was quite disgustingly rich. Once his cousin Jack fell at Waterloo, it was inevitable that Marcus would inherit the Carne title—his uncle had, after all, been in his seventies when his only remaining son was killed. But who would have thought that old Lord Carne would have amassed such a fortune to leave to his nephew—especially as Jack and his brothers had, in the short time allotted to them, done their best to disperse it!

However, Marcus was a different kettle of fish altogether from his wayward cousins. Though frequently invited, he was seldom seen at the sort of gathering Lord Witham enjoyed. And though he was not afraid to wager large sums at the gambling table, he had a regrettable tendency to win. In spite of this, however, his reputation was such that he was welcomed wherever he went.

So Lord Witham paid Marcus the compliment of conducting him personally to one of the best bedchambers, indicating with a wink that Charmian was lodged close by. Marcus waited patiently till his host had finished listing the delights in store and had gone to see to his other guests, then he summoned his valet, who had arrived with the valises some time before, and changed.

Suter busied himself discreetly about the room, obviously expecting his master to go down to join the company. But Marcus was in no hurry to meet the ramshackle bunch Charlie Witham had undoubtedly assembled for several days of cards and drinking. Instead, he went over to the window, which overlooked the park behind the Court.

It was nine years since he had last been at Witham. At

that time there had still been three cousins available to inherit their father's title. He himself had been an impecunious junior officer on leave, with no expectations except through promotion on the battlefield. His room then had been much less imposing—what else would he have expected? The view from its window had been the same, though. And the signs of neglect and decay, which even then had been evident, were now greater than ever. He wondered if that bridge had ever been repaired. . . Probably not. Nine years. . .

Nine years ago Francesca Shelwood had, for a brief while, filled his thoughts to the exclusion of everything else. Curious how one could forget something which had been so important at the time. Seeing the girl again had brought the memories back, memories which had been swamped under the horrors of the campaigns he had fought, and the turmoil and sea-change in his fortunes which had followed.

He had never expected to succeed his uncle. But first Maurice and Ralph, Lord Carne's twin elder sons, had both been killed in a coaching accident, then Jack had fallen at Waterloo. Lord Carne himself had followed them soon afterwards, and Marcus had, against all the odds, succeeded to the title.

Francesca had changed surprisingly little. How well he now remembered that intriguing surface air of discipline, the tight control of her mouth and face, which might lead the uninitiated to believe her dull—hard, even. He knew better. The real Francesca's feelings could suddenly blow up in rage, or melt in passion. . . His blood quickened even now at the memory of her total response to his kisses.

How absurd! Nine years of living in the world, three of them as a very rich man, had provided many more sophisticated affairs. None had been permanent, but few had lasted for as short a time as one day—yet he remembered none of them with half as much pleasure. How could he have forgotten?

From the first moment, he and Francesca had felt no constraint in one other's company. Their initial encounter had effectively done away with the barrier she customarily put up to protect herself from the rest of the world. It was difficult to retain an air of cool reserve when you have just sent a perfect stranger flying into the river! But he rather thought that, even without that sensational beginning, he would have found the real Francesca. From the first he had had a strange feeling of kinship with her that he was sure she had felt, too.

He pulled a chair up to the window and sat down, his eyes fixed on the untended lawns of Witham Court without seeing them. The years faded away and what he saw was the sun, glinting through the leafy branches of the trees down on to the stream which formed the boundary between the Witham and Shelwood lands. He had come with his cousin Jack—he would never in those days have been invited for himself. Jack's father had begged Marcus to go with his son, for the play there was deep, and Jack a compulsive gambler. It hadn't worked.

Heedless of Marcus's attempts to restrain him, Jack had wagered vast sums, more than he possessed, and had lost to everyone, even including his cousin. After a disastrous night of yet more hard drinking and gambling Jack, quite unable to honour his debts, and mindful of his father's words the last time he had asked for more money, had attempted to shoot himself—a dramatic gesture, which his cousin and friends had fortunately frustrated.

Marcus smiled wryly. Jack had survived the attempt to take his own life, but it hadn't done him much good. Just a few years later he had fallen at Waterloo along with so many other, better men. Marcus blanked out the thought of Waterloo—the memory of that carnage was best forgotten. He got up and went to the door.

'There you are, Marcus! I was just about to send some-one to look for you. Charlie's waiting for us.'

Marcus suppressed a sigh, then smiled. 'How charmingly you look, Charmian. That dress is particularly becoming. Do you know where Nick is?'

Later that night, when the company was relaxing over an excellent supper, he was reminded again of Francesca. Charmian brought up the incident on the road that afternoon.

'And then we met this *scarecrow* of a girl! Nick pushed her into the ditch, and I swear it seemed the best place for her!'

She looked magnificent in a wine-red silk dress, her black hair piled high and caught with a diamond aigrette given to her by Marcus in the heyday of their relationship. An impressive array of other jewels—trophies from her many admirers—flashed about her person, but they glittered no more brightly than her dark eyes. She was in her element, flirting with Marcus, making the others laugh with her wicked comments on London life, and teasing a besotted Nick about his driving, laughing at him over her fan.

Nick flushed and muttered, 'The horses were scared of the thunder. And she just stood there. I didn't know what to do.'

'Oh, but, Nick darling, you were *marvellous*, I swear! Then Marcus got down and went to see what had happened—the wretched girl had vanished. Just the odd boot waving in the air, *covered* in mud. Pure rustic farce. Marcus insisted on going to see if she was all right, and of course she was, once he'd pulled her out. But what a *sight*! There she stood, draped in mud and weeds, a quiz of a sunbonnet stuck on her head. But Marcus seemed quite taken with her. I began to think he had fallen in love at first sight with this farmyard beauty.' She paused dramatically. 'I was almost jealous!'

There were shouts of disbelief and laughter and Charmian smiled like a satisfied cat. 'But I haven't finished yet—you must hear this—it beats all the rest. She wasn't a village girl at all, it seems. Marcus said she owned most of the land round about. A positive *heiress* in disguise, looking for a prince. So which of you is going to rescue her, muddy boots and all?'

Marcus walked over to the side and helped himself to more wine. He said nothing.

'I wager it was Fanny Shelwood,' said Lord Witham.

'Shelwood?' said one of the others. 'Of Shelwood Manor?'

'Yes—her mother was Verity Shelwood. Now, ask me who her father was. . . No? I'll tell you. Richard Beaudon.' There was a significant pause. 'D'you see? The girl was sired by Richard Beaudon, but her name is Shelwood. Not Beaudon. Adopted by her grandfather. You follow me?'

Having ensured by sundry nods and winks that his guests had indeed followed, Lord Witham went on in malicious enjoyment, 'I don't suppose many of you know about the Shelwoods. They keep quieter now than they used. But when the old fellow was alive, he was always boring on about the company I invited down here. As if it was any of his business! A bunch of killjoys, the Shelwoods. I told him more than once—a chap can have a few friends in his own house if he wants, can't he? Have a bit of fun?

'But Sir John never liked me—a real holier-than-thou johnny, he was. And then—' he started to grin '—and then old Sir Piety's daughter kicks over the traces with Rake Beaudon, and runs off to the West Indies with him. All without benefit of clergy.'

'You mean that girl is a...a love-child?' breathed Charmian. 'The poor thing! So very plain, too. It hardly seems fair. But who was Rake Beaudon?'

'You never met him? A great gun, he was. Played hard, rode hard, had more mistresses than any other man in London. Didn't give a damn for anyone.'

'I don't think I'd have liked him,' said Charmian.

Lord Witham smiled cynically. 'Oh yes, you would, my dear. The ladies found him irresistible. That's how he managed to seduce the daughter of old Straight-lace Shelwood himself. Didn't profit from it, though. Sir John disinherited her. Refused to see her again. That's probably why Beaudon never married her.'

'Then why is this Fanny girl here now?'

'Father packed her off when her mother died. Didn't want to be saddled with a bastard, did he? Cramped his style a bit.'

'If she's coming in to the Shelwood estate, I wouldn't object to making an offer and giving her a name myself. Tidy bit of land there,' someone said. 'I could do with it, I don't mind telling you. Shockin' load of debts to clear.'

'Don't think of it, Rufus, old dear. Waste of time. Charmian's wrong to say the girl owns the land. She don't own anything, and, what's more, she never will. The estate belongs to her aunt, and she wouldn't leave her niece her last year's bonnet. Hates little Fanny.'

'I find this all quite remarkably tedious,' said Marcus, yawning. 'I don't mind gossip—Lady Forrest's latest Society *on-dits* are always worth hearing—but...what one's neighbours in the country get up to...really! The last word in boredom.'

'Don't stop him, Marcus! I've finished my fund of stories, and I find this quite fascinating!' said Charmian. 'Come, Charlie. Tell us the rest. It's just the thing for a good after-supper story. What did this Fanny do?'

'Oh, it wasn't Fanny who dished Cassandra Shelwood. It was her mother. Verity Shelwood stole her sister's beau—the only one the poor woman ever had.'

'*Rake Beaudon* was going to marry Cassandra Shelwood? I don't believe it,' said the man called Rufus.

'It hadn't got as far as that. But he was making a push to fix his interest with her. He wanted the Shelwood money, y'see, and Cassandra was the elder sister. But when he saw Verity, he lost his head, and ended up running off with her. Not surprised. The elder Miss Shelwood was always a hag, and Verity was a little beauty. Tiny, she was, with golden curls, brown eyes—a real little stunner.'

He paused. 'Y'know, it's damned odd—she was a beauty, Rake Beaudon was a devilishly good-looking fellow, but Fanny, their daughter, is as plain as they come. And when Auntie kicks the bucket, which, from what I've heard, could happen any minute, the poor girl will be looking for a roof over her head. Shame she don't take after her ma—a pretty face might have helped to find one, eh, Rufus? But she must be well into her twenties; she don't even know how to begin to please. Never been taught, d'y'see?'

'I thought we were here to play cards,' said Marcus coldly. 'Or is it your intention to gossip all night?'

'Don't be such a spoilsport, Marcus,' said Charmian. She turned to Witham. 'Marcus doesn't think she's plain.'

'You may ignore her, Witham. I made the mistake of saying something complimentary about one woman to another. It is always fatal, even to someone as beautiful as Lady Forrest. Are we to play?'

Marcus was angry, but taking care to conceal it. His first impulse had been to rush to Francesca's defence, to tell them to stop their lewd, offensive gossip about a girl who had never done any of them any harm. But second thoughts had prevailed. To enter the lists on her behalf would do more harm than good—it would merely give them more food for speculation. Better to keep calm and distract their tawdry minds. They would soon lose interest now they had got to the bottom of Francesca's story, as they thought. Cards would soon occupy their thoughts, once they were back at the tables.

But he himself found concentration difficult that evening. From all accounts, Francesca's life was no happier now than it had been nine years before—and there was every reason to fear that it might get worse. He had been angry at her rudeness on the road, and with some justice, but looking back, surely there had been desperation in her tone? She had looked. . .ridiculous, standing there covered in mud as he drove past. Ridiculous, but gallant. Endearingly so.

Francesca had refused to gaze after the chaise as it disappeared in the direction of the village. Instead, she had turned to walk briskly back to the Manor, for as the mud dried her clothes were becoming stiff and uncomfortable. She had no wish to compound her discomfort by getting caught in the storm. But she was in a state of quite uncharacteristic agitation.

She was normally a philosophical girl. She had learned over the years to endure what she could not change, to find pleasure in small things instead of pining for what she could not have. She had gradually taught herself to be content with her friendship with Madame Elisabeth, her old governess, who lived in the village, to find pleasure in her drawing and sketching, and to abandon childish dreams of encountering love and affection from anyone else and of having a home and family of her own.

But just this once, she found herself wishing passionately that she was powerful, rich and beautiful enough to give this oaf the set-down he deserved! The awareness that she still felt a strange attraction to the oaf was impatiently dismissed. Her conduct during their earlier acquaintance was a dreadful warning to any girl—especially one in her precarious situation. Twenty-four hours only, but from beginning to end she had behaved like a lunatic, like a . . . like a lightskirt! She pressed her hands to her cheeks in an effort to cool them. If only she could treat it as casually as he had! If only she could forget it as easily as he seemed to!

She reminded herself angrily that she had been not yet sixteen at the time, still hoping vaguely that one day someone would rescue her from life with Aunt Cassandra. There had been some excuse for her. But for him? It was true that she had lied to him about her age. . . Nevertheless! He had been old enough to know the effect his kisses would have on her. And all to relieve a morning's boredom—or perhaps to revenge himself for the loss of dignity she had caused him? Though he hadn't seemed angry after the first few minutes.

It all started because of that stupid conversation. It hadn't been meant for her ears, and now she wished passionately that she had never listened to it. But what else could she have done? She had been so engrossed in her sketching that the gentlemen had been within earshot before she noticed them. And then, aware that she was trespassing on Witham land, she had deliberately concealed herself. . . Francesca walked on towards the Manor, but she was no longer aware of her dirty clothes, nor of the threatening storm. She saw herself as she had been nine years before—half child, half woman—peering nervously through the bushes. . .

Francesca peeped through the bushes at the two figures walking along the banks of the stream that ran down between the two estates—they were both in shirt sleeves, but were quite clearly gentlemen. However, they were decidedly the worse for wear—cravats loose, hair all over the place, and the older, shorter one had half his shirt hanging out. The other. . . She caught her breath. The other was the most beautiful man she had ever seen in all her life. He even eclipsed her dimly remembered father. Tall, dark-haired, with a powerful, athletic build, he moved with natural grace, though he was carrying himself a trifle carefully, as if his head hurt. They came to the bridge just below her and stopped.

She knew instantly that they were from Witham Court. Lord Witham must be holding another of his wild parties. The parties had been notorious for years, even as far back as her grandfather's time. He had fulminated about them, but had never been able to stop them. It was universally known that they were attended by rakes and gamblers, a scandal and danger to every decent, God-fearing neighbour! The village girls would never accept a position at the Court if they valued their virtue, for these lecherous villains found innocence a challenge, not a barrier.

So, in spite of the fascination the young man had for her, she withdrew a little further into the bushes to avoid being seen. But she was unable to avoid overhearing their conversation.

'Freddie,' the tall, handsome one solemnly said. He sounded as if he was experiencing difficulty in speaking clearly, but the timbre of his voice was very attractive—rich and warm and deep. 'I'm in despair! What th' devil am I goin' to say to m' uncle? He trusted me, y' see, and I've failed him.' He paused, gave a deep sigh, then added, 'Failed him c'mpletely. Absolutely. Devil's own luck with th' cards last night. Never known an'thing like it! Ruined, both 'f us.'

'Course you're not, Marcus! Rich as Croesus, your uncle.'

'He trusted me, I tell you! And he's sworn not to pay 'nother penny for any more gambling debts! Said he'd die first. Ruined. I'd be much better dead myself, I swear.'

'Don't talk like that, Marcus. It will be all right, you'll see. Look, hate to interrupt—don't want to sound unsympathetic—but we ought to turn back, old fellow. Been out long enough—ought to get back to poor old Jack. Coming?'

'No,' Marcus said moodily. 'I'll stay here. Think things out before I see'm again. How 'm I goin' to tell m' uncle?'

From her bushes, she saw Freddie walking uncertainly away up the hill on the other side, and then her curiosity got the better of her. She crept forward to see what 'Marcus' was doing.

He was standing on the bridge, leaning on the thin plank of wood that served as a balustrade and gazing moodily down into the waters. He banged his hand down on the plank and, with a groan, repeated his words of a minute before. 'I'd be better dead myself! Drowned! Oh, my head!'

Francesca gazed in horror as he put one leg over the plank. Convinced that this beautiful young man was about to drown himself even while she watched, she jumped to her feet and launched herself down the hill. A second later, unable to stop, she crashed into the unsuspecting young man on the bridge and sent him flying into the water. She only just managed to stop herself from following him.

Francesca gazed, horrified, while he picked himself up, shook himself like a dog and pushed his hair out of his eyes. The shock of the water seemed to have sobered him up.

There was an ominous silence. Then, 'What the devil did you do that for?' he roared. 'Are you mad?'

'I. . . I. . .' Francesca had a cowardly impulse to run away, but she suppressed it. 'I wanted to save you.'

'Wanted to save me? From what?'

'From drowning.'

'I don't think much of your methods—' He stopped suddenly and looked down. The stream was unusually low—the water barely came up to his knees. 'In this?' he asked. The irony in his voice was gall to Francesca. She blushed and hung her head.

'I. . .I didn't think,' she confessed. 'I just ran down the hill without pausing to consider—then I couldn't stop, so I. . .I . . . er. . .I pushed you in. I'm sorry.'

'Sorry? I should think you might be, indeed!' He took a step towards the bridge, then said irritably, 'Damn it, my boots are full of water, I can hardly move. Help me out, will you? I need a pull up.'

'But I'll get wet myself!'

'So you will. Now give me your hand—just to give me a start, so I can get a hold on the post there. It won't take much once I'm moving.' He looked up and said impatiently, 'Come on, girl—stir yourself! What are you waiting for?'

She extended a reluctant hand. It wasn't just that she was afraid of getting wet. To get too close to a perfect stranger—especially one who was staying at Witham Court—was a touch foolhardy. And anyone so handsome was almost certainly a rake!

'For God's sake, girl, give me your hand properly! What are you? The village idiot?'

Francesca was noted in the neighbourhood for her withdrawn manner, and most people found her almost unnaturally reserved. But at these words, she forgot years of self-restraint, and flamed into anger. Handsome or not, this oaf's rudeness had gone too far! He needed a lesson. So, without a thought for the consequences, she let go of his hand and shoved him back into the water. 'I don't think I want to help you after all,' she said coolly, and walked away across the bridge.

Chapter Three

With a roar of fury, Marcus struggled to his feet, waded clumsily to the side, scrambled up the bank and caught up with her halfway up the hill.

Francesca gave a cry of fright as he grabbed her by the arm and swung her round. 'Now, you little wretch, you'd better explain yourself before I give you what you deserve.'

'Let go of me!'

'Not till I have an explanation. And you'd better make it a good one. Or are you the sort of Bedlamite who does this as a regular sport?'

'I'm not the lunatic!' Francesca cried. 'I tell you, I was trying to stop you from drowning—you said you wanted to.'

'But I didn't mean it, you. . .ninny!' he said, giving her a shake.

Francesca lost her temper yet again. She pulled herself free, but though she took a step back, she made no attempt to escape. 'How was I to know that?' she blazed at him. 'You stood on that bridge, draped over the water like a. . . like a weeping willow, and said you were going to drown yourself! How was I to know you were playacting?'

'A weepi—a weeping willow!' he said, outraged. 'You

don't know what you're talking about! I wasn't feeling quite the thing—I had a headache! A hangover, if you must know. But I wouldn't be such a clunch as to do away with myself. Why on earth should I?' He had glared at her. 'And if I did, I'd find a better way than to try to drown myself in two feet of water! What rubbish!'

'Then why did you say you would?'

'I didn't, I tell you.' She opened her mouth to contradict him, but he held up a hand and said slowly and distinctly, in the tones of one talking to an idiot, 'I was expressing unhappiness. I was just unhappy.'

'Well, you deserve to be! People who are rakes and who gamble all their money away deserve to be unhappy!'

'Gamble all my money aw— You are a lunatic! An impertinent, lunatic child! What on earth do you mean? I'm not rich enough to gamble any money away! Anyway, I won last night, damn it!'

'A fine story! If that's the case, why are you so worried about facing your uncle?'

The young man's eyes narrowed and he said slowly, 'You little sneak! You were eavesdropping—that conversation was private!'

Francesca was instantly abashed. 'Yes, I'm sorry. I couldn't help hearing it—I certainly didn't do it intentionally. I really am very sorry. Please, please forgive me. I meant well, really I did.' She looked up at him beseechingly. 'I promise I shall forget all about that conversation, now that I know you don't really mean to. . .to— you know.'

He was staring down into her eyes, seemingly fascinated. Francesca's heart thumped, but she didn't— couldn't move. He muttered, 'A lunatic child, with witch's eyes. . . I've seen you in paintings. . .' and he slowly drew his finger over her cheekbone and down her jaw. He held her chin and lowered his head towards her. . . Then he jerked back, and said in astonishment, 'I'm going mad. It must be the hangover.'

Francesca was not sure what he meant, but said nervously, 'And. . .and now I shall go home.'

'No, don't!' He took her by the arm once again and marched her into a patch of sunshine. 'I still want my explanation. . . You're shivering!'

Francesca thought it wiser not to explain that this was due to nerves and reaction to his hand on her arm, rather than to feeling cold. She said nothing.

'Sit in the sun here—you'll soon be warmer. Now, where were we?'

'I was telling you I'd heard you say you wanted to drown yourself because you'd gambled away all your money. And I was trying to stop you. But I forgot how steep the bank was, and I got carried down the slope and. . .and I pushed you in.' Francesca was gabbling, as she often did when nervous.

'I suppose it makes some sort of inverted sense,' he said doubtfully. 'I suppose I ought to be grateful that you meant well—though I still think I'd have been better off without your help.' He looked down thoughtfully at his sodden clothes. . .

Francesca tried, and failed, to suppress a giggle. 'I think you're right,' she said. 'Much better off. You squelch when you walk, too!' and, after another vain struggle with herself, she went off into a gale of laughter.

For a moment he looked affronted, but as she laughed again at his face he smiled, then he, too, was laughing. The atmosphere lightened considerably.

'Look, let's sit down here for a moment, and you can help me with my boots while you tell me the story of your life.'

'Well, that's a "blank, my lord",' she said, as he sat down on a fallen tree trunk and had stuck his foot out.

'Where do you live?'

'Down there, at Shelwood. With my aunt.' Francesca
tugged hard and the boot came off, releasing a gush of
water over her dress. She gave a cry. 'Oh, no!'

'It will dry. Now, the other one.' She cast him a
reproachful look, but gingerly took hold of the second
boot. She took more care with this one but, when it came
away with unexpected ease, she lost her balance, tripped
over a root and fell flat on her back. The second boot
poured its contents over her. She got to her feet hastily.
'Just look at that!' she cried.

'I am,' he said. Francesca was puzzled at the sudden
constraint in his voice. 'I. . .I seem to have made a mistake. I thought you a child.' He swallowed. 'But it's clear
you're not. You may be a lunatic, but you're all woman—
and a lovely one, too!'

She looked down. The water had drenched the thin
lawn of her dress and petticoat, and they were clinging
to her like a second skin. The lines of her figure were
clearly visible.

'Oh, no!' Desperately she shook out her dress, holding
it away from her body. 'I must go!'

'No! Please don't. Your dress will dry very soon, and
I won't stare any more. Look, if you sit down beside me
on this log I won't be able to. We could. . .we could have
a peaceful little chat till your dress dries. I'd like to explain
what I meant when I was speaking to Freddie.'

She looked at him uncertainly. He was really very handsome—and he seemed to be sincere. Perhaps not everyone
at Witham Court was a rake. But. . .'Why did you call
me lovely,' she asked suspiciously, 'when everyone else
says I'm plain?'

'Plain? They must be blind. Sit down and I'll tell you
why I think you lovely.' This sounded like a very dangerous idea to Francesca. So she was at something of a loss

to understand when she found herself doing as he asked.
She kept her distance, however—she was not quite mad.

'Is Freddie the man you were with?'

'Yes—we were talking about my c— about someone
we both know. He lost a great deal of money last night.
He. . .he wasn't feeling well this morning, and we're
worried about him. But you don't really want to talk about
this, do you? It's a miserable subject for a lovely morning.
Tell me about yourself. What were you doing when you
saw us? On your way to a tryst?'

'Oh, no! I. . .I don't know anyone. I was drawing—
oh, I must fetch my book and satchel! I dropped them
when I ran down the hill. Excuse me.'

She jumped up, glad to escape from the spell the deep
voice and dark blue eyes were weaving round her.

'I'll come with you.'

'But you haven't anything on your feet!'

'So? I've suffered worse things than that in the army.
And I want to make sure you don't disappear. You're my
hostage, you know, until we are both dry.' She looked at
him nervously, but he was laughing, as he got up and
took firm hold of her hand. 'Where is this book?'

They soon found the orchid plant she had been drawing,
and her sketch pad and satchel were not far away. He
picked the pad up, still holding her with one hand, and
studied it. 'This is good,' he said. 'Who is your teacher?'

'Madame Elisabeth.' She blushed in confusion. 'I mean
Madame de Romain. My governess.'

'Let's get back into the sun. My feet are cold.' They
collected the satchel, then went back to their tree trunk
and sat down. This time it seemed quite natural to sit next
to him, especially as he still held her hand in his. 'Will
you show me some more of your work?'

Francesca coloured with pleasure. 'Of course!' she
said shyly.

From then on, he directed his considerable charm towards drawing her out, and Francesca found herself talking to him more freely than she had with anyone for years. Sometimes, she would falter as she found his eyes intent on her, looking at her with such warmth and understanding. But then he would ask a question about some detail in one of the pictures and she would talk on, reassured.

There came a moment when she stopped. 'I. . .I haven't anything more to show you—not here,' she said. When he didn't immediately answer, she looked up, a question in her eyes.

'Why did you say you were plain?' he said slowly.

'Because I am! Everyone says so.'

'No, you're not, Francesca. You're like your sketches—drawn with a fine, delicate grace.'

'It's kind of you to say so,' she said, nervous once again.

'I'm not flattering you!'

'No, I'm sure you mean to be kind. But it isn't necessary. I'm really quite used to my looks. Please—if you carry on talking like this, I shall have to go. My dress is dry now. Your things are dry, too.'

'How old are you?' he asked abruptly.

She hesitated. Then, 'Seventeen,' she lied. When he looked sceptical, she had added, still lying, 'Almost.'

'It's young. But not too young. Have you ever been in love?'

'Me?' she asked, astounded.

He laughed at her then, and let go of her, but only to put both of his hands on her shoulders. 'Yes, you,' he said.

'Certainly not!'

'There's always a first time,' he murmured. He drew her closer. 'What about kisses? Have you ever been kissed?'

'Not. . .not often,' she whispered, hypnotised by the

blue eyes gazing into hers. 'My grandfather, sometimes.'
She swallowed. 'I suppose my father did. I. . .I can't
remember.'

'That's not quite what I meant. I meant. . .this.' He
lowered his head and kissed her gently. Francesca felt as
if she had just had been hit by lightning. The strangest
feeling overcame her, a feeling compounded of fear and
pleasure, chills and warmth, a feeling that she ought not
to be doing this—and an urgent wish for more.

'That was nice,' she breathed, bemused and hardly
knowing what she said.

They were now standing up, face to face. 'Put your
arms round my neck,' he said softly. She took a step
forward and slowly lifted her arms. 'That's right. Then I
can put mine round you—like this.' He pulled her closer
and kissed her again, not gently this time. Francesca gave
a little cry and he relaxed his grip immediately. 'Did I
hurt you?'

'No. I. . .I didn't expect. . .I didn't know. . .' She tightened her arms and pulled his face down to hers. 'Kiss me
again,' she said.

A world of unimaginable delight opened now for
Francesca. Absurd though it was, she felt safer than ever
before in this man's arms, and more alive than ever before.
He was in turn gentle, then passionate, charming, then
demanding. He called her his idiot, his love, his witch,
but she didn't hear the names—only the warmth and
feeling in the deep voice. He laughed at her lack of guile,
but tenderly, as if her vulnerability had disarmed him.

And, just occasionally, he sounded uncertain, as if he,
too, was unable to understand what was happening to
them. They were both lost in a world of brilliant sunshine
and glinting shadows, of whirling green and gold and
blue. . .

Perhaps it was as well that they were recalled to their

senses before the situation went beyond recall. Shouts in the distance proved to be those of Freddie, looking for Marcus. Marcus swore, then whispered, 'Tomorrow? In the morning? Here?' Then he kissed her once more, got up and turned down the hill. 'Here I am,' he had shouted. 'What do you want?'

Once again, Francesca listened to their conversation from her hiding place.

'It's Jack. He's asking for you. And your uncle's coming down to Witham. Thought you'd like to know. What the devil have you been doin' all this time, Marcus old fellow?'

'Er. . .nothing much,' Marcus said. . .

Francesca was startled out of her memories and brought back to the present day by a brilliant flash, followed almost immediately by a crash of thunder. The storm was now imminent. She quickened her pace. But her thoughts were still on the girl she had been nine years before.

'Nothing much'—she ought to have taken warning. But at the time she had been totally dazzled, bewitched. It had been so easy, she thought, for a man of his experience and charm. And she had been so gullible. She had met him the next day, of course, pleading to Madame Elisabeth that she was ill, so that she was excused her morning lessons. And this had not been so far from the truth—she had been ill, gripped by a fever, a delirium which suppressed all her critical faculties, all thought of self-preservation. She winced now as she remembered how eagerly she had run up the hill to meet him again all those years ago.

She had to wait some time before Marcus appeared; when he arrived, he seemed preoccupied. She felt a chill round her heart—did he despise her for being so open about her feelings the day before? They walked in silence for some time, she waiting for him to say something—anything to break the constraint between them.

'You're very quiet, Francesca,' he said finally.

Francesca was astonished. He was the one who had not spoken! And now he was accusing her, in such a serious voice...he *did* despise her! 'I...I'm not sure I should have come,' she said.

'Why?'

Francesca hesitated. She didn't know the rules of this game, and accustomed though she was to rejection, she was afraid to invite rejection from this man. It would hurt too much.

'I didn't behave well yesterday.'

'When you pushed me into the stream? I've forgiven you for that.'

'No—afterwards.'

He stopped, turned and took her hands. 'You were... wonderful. But I was wrong to kiss you.' He fell silent again.

After a while, she asked timidly, 'Why?'

'Because you're far too young. Because you're innocent. Because Jack's father arrived this morning to take him home, and...and, Francesca, I have to leave with them. I was only here in the first place to look after my cousin. And I failed.'

For the life of her, Francesca could not hold back a small cry. He swore under his breath, and said, 'I ought to be whipped. I failed him and I've hurt you, and that was the last thing I wanted. Believe me.'

Francesca pressed her lips tightly together. She would not plead, she would not beg. This was the very worst rejection she had ever suffered, but she had hidden her distress before, and she would not show it now. But it was taking all the resolution she had.

'You needn't feel too badly,' she said finally. 'I knew you were staying at Witham Court, after all, but I still let you kiss me. That's only what rakes are expected to do, isn't it?'

'Rakes!'

Francesca hardly heard the interruption. She continued, 'You needn't feel sorry for me—I enjoyed it. And they were only kisses. I daresay I shall have many more before I am too old to enjoy them. When. . .when I make my come-out and go to London.' She had even managed a brilliant smile. 'My father will fetch me quite soon, I expect. He said so just the other day in one of his letters.'

'Francesca.' He said her name with such tenderness that she was almost undone.

'So you can kiss me again, if you like. Just to show that it doesn't mean very much.'

'Oh, Francesca, my lovely, courageous girl! I know just how much it meant to you. God help me, but how could I not know? Come here!'

He kissed her, at first gently, as he had the first time. But then he held her so tightly that she could hardly breathe, kissing her again and again, murmuring her name over and over again. But gradually the fit of passion died and he thrust her away from him.

'It's no use,' he said, and there was finality in his voice. 'My uncle is right—I have nothing to offer you. And even if I had, you are too young. We both have our way to make. It's no use!'

Then he kissed her hand. 'Goodbye, Francesca. Think of me sometimes.' He strode off down the hill, but Francesca could not see him. Her eyes were burning with tears she would not allow to fall.

But that was not the end. Hard though it was, she could have borne that much, could have cherished the memory of his care and concern for her, the thought that someone had once found her beautiful enough to love. But this consolation had not been for her.

Some days later she was standing on the bridge, looking down at the stream, when Freddie's voice interrupted her unhappy thoughts. 'You must be the little goddess Marcus spent the morning with the other day,' he said. 'He was very taken with you, give you my word! Wished I'd seen you first. Missing him, are you?'

Something inside Francesca curled up. She hated the thought of being a subject of conversation at Witham Court. Surely Marcus couldn't have done such a thing?

'I don't know what you mean, sir,' she said coldly, not looking at him.

'Don't you? Marcus seemed to know what he was talking about. Never seen him so much on the go, and he's known a few girls in his time, I can tell you. Very good-looking fellow. But he did seem taken with you. We were all no end intrigued, but he wouldn't tell us who you were. It was Charlie who said you must be the Shelwood girl. Are you? Marcus was right about the figure, though I can't see your face. Why don't you turn round, sweetheart?'

Francesca shut her eyes, bowed her head and prayed he would go away.

'Don't be sad, my dear! Ain't worth it! It wouldn't have lasted long, you know, even if he hadn't had to leave with Jack and his father. It never does with these army chaps. Off and away before you can wink your eye. And if you cast an eye around you, there's plenty more where he came from.'

She would have left the bridge, but he was blocking the way.

'Cheer up, sweetheart! It's always the same with the army. Rave about one woman, make you green with envy, and then before you know it they're over the hill and far

away, making love to another! Seen it m'self time and
again. Mind you, I'm surprised at Marcus—leaving Jack
lying there in misery while he pursues his own little game.
And a very nice little bit of game, too, from what I can
see. Come on, sweetheart, let's see your face.'

When Francesca shook her head and turned to run back
to the Manor, he ran after her, caught her hand and pulled
her to him. 'You shan't escape without giving me a kiss.
You were free enough with them the other day, from all
accounts. One kiss, that's all, then I'll let you go, give
you my word. Give me a kiss, there's a good girl.'

'Fanny!' For the first time in her life, Francesca was
glad to hear her aunt's voice. Miss Shelwood was standing
a few yards away, with Silas, her groom, close behind.
Her face was a mask of fury. Francesca's tormentor let
her go with a start, and took a step back.

'Come here this instant, you. . .trollop!' With relief,
Francesca complied. Her aunt turned to Freddie. 'I assume
you are from Witham Court, sir. How dare you trespass
on my land! Silas!' The groom came forward, fingering
his whip.

Freddie grew pale and stammered, 'There's no need
for any violence, ma'am. No need at all. I was just passing
the time of day with the little lady. No harm done.' And,
within a trice, he disappeared in the direction of
Witham Court.

'Take my niece's arm, Silas, and bring her to the
Manor.' Miss Shelwood strode off without looking in
Francesca's direction. Silas looked uncomfortable but
obeyed.

Francesca hardly noticed or cared what was happening
to her. All her energies were concentrated in a desperate
effort to endure her feelings of anguish and betrayal. She
had believed Marcus! She had been taken in by his air of
sincere regret, had thought he had been truly distressed

to be leaving her! And while she had lain awake, holding the thought of his love and concern close to her like some precious jewel in a dark world, a talisman against a bleak future, he had been joking and laughing at Witham Court, boasting about her, making her an object of interest to men like Freddie. It was clear what they all thought of her.

Oh, what a fool she had been! What an unsuspecting dupe! She had fallen into his hands like a. . .like a ripe plum! Her aunt could not despise her more than she already despised herself. She had been ready to give Marcus everything of herself, holding nothing back. Only Freddie's timely interruption had prevented it. She had indeed behaved like the trollop her aunt had called her. Occupied with these and other bitter thoughts Francesca hardly noticed that they were back at the Manor.

Miss Shelwood swept into the library, then turned and said coldly, 'How often have you met that man before?'

Never. Francesca said the word, but no sound came.

'Answer me at once, you wicked girl!'

'I. . .' Francesca swallowed to clear the constriction in her throat. 'I have never seen him before.'

'A liar as well as a wanton. Truly your mother's daughter!'

'That's not true! You must not say such things of my mother!'

'Like mother, like daughter!' Miss Shelwood continued implacably, ignoring Francesca's impassioned cry. 'Richard Beaudon was at Witham Court when he first met your mother. Now her daughter goes looking for her entertainment there. Where is the difference? No, I will hear no more! Go to your room, and do not leave it until I give you permission.'

Exhausted with her effort to control her feelings, Francesca ran to her room and threw herself on her bed.

She did not cry. The bitter tears were locked up inside, choking her, but she could not release them.

In the weeks that followed, she castigated herself time and again for her weakness and stupidity. She, who had taught herself over the years not to let slights and injuries affect her, to keep up her guard against the hurt that others could inflict, had allowed the first personable man she met to make a fool of her, to destroy her peace of mind for many weary months. It would not happen again. It would never happen again.

Her aunt remained convinced that Francesca had been conducting an affair with Freddie. Francesca was punished severely for her sins. She was confined to her room on starvation rations for days, then kept within the limits of the house and garden for some weeks. It was months before she was allowed outside the gates of the garden, unaccompanied by her governess or a groom. She was made to sit for long periods while Mr Chizzle, her aunt's chaplain, expatiated on the dreadful fate awaiting those who indulged in the sins of the flesh.

This last Francesca endured by developing the art of remaining apparently attentive while her mind ranged freely over other matters. Since she felt in her own mind that she deserved punishment, though not for her escapade with Freddie, she found patience to endure most of the rest.

But the worst of the affair was that Miss Shelwood took every opportunity it offered to remind Francesca of her mother's sins. That was very hard to endure. And, in her mind, the distress this caused her was added to the mountain of distress caused by one man. Not Freddie— she forgot him almost immediately. No, Marcus What-ever-his-name-was was to blame. She would *never* forgive him.

*   *   *

The first few drops of rain were falling as Francesca found, to her surprise, that she had reached the Manor. She slipped in through the servants' door—it would never do for Aunt Cassandra or Agnes Cotter, her maid, to see her in her present state. Betsy was in the kitchen.

'Miss Fanny! Oh, miss! Whatever have you been doing?'

Francesca looked down. The mud from the ditch had now dried and the dress was no longer plastered to her body. But she was a sorry sight all the same.

'I fell,' she said briefly. 'Help me to change before my aunt sees me, Betsy. I'll need some water.'

'The kettle's just about to boil again. But you needn't fret—your aunt won't bother with you at the moment, Miss Fanny. She's had another of her attacks. It's a bad one.'

Suddenly apprehensive, Francesca stopped what she was doing and stared at Betsy. 'When?'

'Just after you went out. And. . .' Betsy grew big with the news '. . .Doctor Woodruff has been. Didn't you see him on your way to the village?'

'I went through the fields. Did my aunt finally send for him, then? What did he say?'

'They wouldn't tell me, Miss Fanny. You'd better ask that maid of hers. Miss Cotter, that is,' said Betsy with a sniff.

Worried as she was, Francesca failed to respond to this challenge. Agnes Cotter had been Miss Shelwood's maid for more than twenty years and jealously guarded her position as her mistress's chief confidante, but Francesca knew better than to quiz her. If Miss Shelwood did not wish her niece to know what was wrong, then Agnes Cotter would not tell her, however desperate it was. So, after washing, changing her clothes and brushing her hair back into its rigid knot, she presented herself outside her aunt's bedroom.

'Miss Shelwood is resting, Miss Fanny.'

'Is she asleep?'

'Not exactly—'

'Then pray tell my aunt that I am here, if you please.'

With a dour look Agnes disappeared into the bedroom; there was a sound of muted voices, which could hardly be heard for the drumming of the rain on the windows. The storm had broken. The maid reappeared at the door and held it open. 'Miss Shelwood is very tired, miss. But she will see you.'

Ignoring Agnes, Francesca stepped into the room. The curtains were half-drawn and the room was dim and airless. Her aunt lay on the huge bed, her face the colour of the pillows that were heaped up behind her. But her eyes were as sharply disapproving as usual, and her voice was the same.

'I expected you to come as soon as you got in. What have you been doing?'

'I had to change my dress, Aunt,' said Francesca calmly.

'You were here before the rain started, so your dress was not wet. There's no need to lie, Fanny.'

'My dress was muddy. How are you, Aunt Cassandra?'

'Well enough. Agnes has a list of visits for you to make tomorrow. I've postponed what I can, but these are urgent. See that you do them properly, and don't listen to any excuses. I've made a note where you must pay particular attention.'

Miss Shelwood believed in visiting her employees and tenants regularly once a month, and woe betide any of them who were not ready for her questions on their activities. During the past few weeks, Francesca, much to her surprise, had been required to act as an occasional stand-in, so she knew what to do. Since both she and her aunt knew that she would perform adequately, if not as ruthlessly as Miss Shelwood, she wasted no time in questions or comments. Instead she asked, 'What did Dr Woodruff say? Does he know what is wrong?'

'How did you know he'd been? Betsy, I suppose.'

'She told me, yes. I am sorry you were so unwell.'

'I'm not unwell! Dr Woodruff is an old woman, and I shan't let him come again. I don't need him to tell me what I am to do or not do. Don't waste any time before seeing those people, Fanny. I shall want an account when I am up. You may go.'

Against her better judgement Francesca said, 'Can I get you anything? Some books?'

'Don't be absurd! Agnes will get me anything I need. But you'd better see the housekeeper about meals for the rest of you. Agnes will let her know what I want. Agnes?'

Francesca was given her aunt's list, then she was escorted out and the door shut firmly behind her. She made a face, then walked wearily down the dark oak staircase. It was not easy to feel sympathy or concern for her aunt—not after all these years. But she was worried. Whether her aunt lived or died, her own future looked bleak indeed. If no post as a governess was forthcoming, where could she look for help? In spite of her brave words to Marcus, her claim on her father was non-existent. She had not heard a word from him since she had left the West Indies nearly twenty years ago, and had no idea where he might now be.

The world would say that her aunt ought to do something for her, there was no doubt about that. But Francesca had every doubt that she would. Shelwood was not an entailed estate—Miss Shelwood could dispose of it as she wished—and whatever happened to Aunt Cassandra's money, her sister's child would see none of it—nothing was more certain. Her duty, such as it was, would end at her death.

Francesca came to a halt, thinking of the cheerless years since her grandfather had died. She had always been required to sit with her aunt at mealtimes, though the meals were consumed in silence. She was adequately clothed, though most of that came out of her allowance. She had a bedroom to herself, though it was the tiny room allotted to her when she had first arrived as a child of six. She had been taken to church twice every Sunday, and forced to join in her aunt's weekly session of private prayers and readings with the Reverend Mr Chizzle. But there was nothing more.

Was it that Miss Shelwood could not tolerate the evidence of the shame that her sister had brought on the family? But Sir John Shelwood had never shown any sense of shame. Regret at not seeing his daughter again before she died, at not telling her that she had been forgiven, perhaps, but there had been no sense of shame. There had never been anything in his attitude towards his granddaughter that even hinted at the shocking truth. Strange. . .

The next morning Francesca rose early; by midday, she had completed her round of visits. She had made notes of complaints and requests, and, in order to satisfy her aunt, had written down one or two criticisms—nothing of any consequence—together with some recommendations. She attempted to see her aunt, but was denied access, her civil enquiries about Miss Shelwood's health being met with a brusquely indifferent reply from Agnes Cotter. Resolving to see Doctor Woodruff for herself when he called that evening, she left the papers and escaped from the house.

At the end of an hour, she found she had walked off

her frustration and anger and was enjoying the woods and open ground above Shelwood. The air was still heavy, however, and swallows and martins were swooping low over the swollen expanse of water left by the storm, catching the insects in the humid air. Francesca watched them for a while, marvelling at the speed and skill with which they skimmed the surface.

But even as she watched, one bird's judgement failed disastrously. It dipped too low and, as it wheeled round, its wing was caught below the water line. Francesca drew in her breath as it dropped, then rose, then dropped again. By now both wings were heavy with water, and the bird's struggles to fly were only exhausting it further. It would soon drown.

Without a second thought, Francesca hitched up her skirts, took off her shoes and waded in. The water was very shallow—it shouldn't be difficult to scoop the bird out.

'I never knew such a girl for water! You must have been a naiad in your previous existence.'

She recognised the voice, of course. But she said nothing until she had captured the bird and released it on dry ground. Then she said calmly, 'And you seem to be my nemesis. I lead a very dull, dry life in the normal course of events. Excuse me.' She bent down and put on her shoes. 'Let me wish you a pleasant walk.' She wanted to take polite leave of him, but realised that she had no idea what to call him other than 'Marcus'. That she would never do again. She started off down the hill without saying any more.

'Wait!'

She pretended not to have heard, but he came striding after her.

'I was hoping to learn how you fared.'

'Thank you—very comfortably. But my aunt is not

well—I must get back to her. I know you will understand and forgive my haste. Goodbye.'

'Not so fast! I want to talk to you.'

The pain in her heart was getting worse. He was still as handsome—more so! The years had added one or two lines to his face, one or two silver strands to the dark hair, but this only increased his dignity and authority, and the blue eyes were as alert, as warm and understanding as ever. The villain! The scheming, double-dealing villain! Where was the lady from the carriage?—if 'lady' was the right word! He should be using his charm on her, she might reward his efforts—probably had done so long before now. But she, at least, was old enough to see through him. She was well past the age of innocence!

But none of these uncharitable thoughts showed in her expression as she said coolly, 'That is a pity. I have no wish to talk to you. I doubt that we now have very much in common. You must find someone else to amuse you.'

'Is your aunt as ill as everyone says?'

He blurted this out with none of the polish she expected of him. What was he thinking of? Had he heard the rumours and was daring to be sorry for her? Francesca fought down a sudden rise in temper, then said in measured tones, 'I am surprised that Lord Witham's guests indulge in village gossip. I would have thought they had other, more interesting, pursuits.'

'Don't be such a awkward cat, Francesca—tell me how your aunt is.'

He had no right to sound so anxious. It weakened her, made her vulnerable once again to his charm.

'I don't know why such a thing should concern you,' she said, maintaining her usual air of colourless reserve as she lied to him once again. 'But if you insist on knowing, my aunt is suffering from the heat. I am sure she will be quite well again in a few days.'

'That isn't what I have heard.'

They must have been discussing the situation at Witham Court. Once again she had been made the subject of gossip there. It was intolerable! 'You must think what you choose, sir. However, I am sure my aunt would not welcome speculation by strangers. And nor do I.'

'Strangers, Francesca?'

Francesca had been avoiding his eye, but now she looked directly at him. She did not pretend to misunderstand. 'Whatever happened nine years ago, sir, we were, and are, strangers. Of that I am certain. Now please let me go!' In spite of herself, her voice trembled on these last words.

He took a step forward, hesitated, then bowed gracefully. 'Very well. Good day to you, my dear.'

She felt his eyes on her as she set off again down the hill. She hoped he could not see how her hands were trembling, or hear how her heart was pounding.

Chapter Four

Marcus was astonished to discover that, even after nine years, the strange line of communication between Francesca and himself was still there. The horrors of war, the problems and anxieties of peace, the totally absorbing task of learning to run a huge and prosperous estate had caused him to put her out of his mind, but no sooner had they met again than he was once more caught in a strange web—a curious feeling of kinship with her. It was as infuriating as it was inexplicable.

He stood watching her as she went down the hill, and knew, though he didn't know how, that, in spite of her gallant attempt to deceive him, she was lying about her aunt, just as she had lied to him all those years ago about her future with her father. Francesca was desperately worried about the future. And if the gossip last night had any foundation, she was right to be worried. The impulse to run after her, to shake her till she admitted the truth, then to reassure her, swear to protect her from harm, was almost irresistible.

It was absurd! It had been absurd nine years ago, when he had been a penniless and inexperienced officer in Wellington's army. At that time, he had been convinced that Francesca was the love of his life, and only the intervention of his uncle had stopped him from making what would have been a disastrous mistake. His uncle had been right—he had indeed forgotten the girl once he was back with the army!

But to find, now, that he had the same impulse to protect Francesca nine years later was ridiculous. A man of thirty, rich, sophisticated and, not to put too fine a point on it, extremely eligible. . .how London would laugh! He must take a grip on himself, before he did something he would later regret. Shrugging impatiently, he strode off down the other side of the hill.

When Francesca got back to Shelwood Manor she found Agnes Cotter waiting for her. The woman was clearly distressed.

'Miss Shelwood has suddenly got much worse. But she won't hear of sending for Dr Woodruff. I don't know what to do, Miss Fanny.' The situation must be grave indeed—this was the first time ever that Agnes had appealed to anyone for help.

'We must send Silas for him straight away,' Francesca said calmly.

'But Miss Shelwood will—'

'I will take the blame, Agnes. Go back to my aunt but say nothing to her—it would only cause her unnecessary agitation. Stay with her till the doctor comes, then I shall take over.'

Dr Woodruff came with a speed that showed how grave he thought the situation was. 'I knew this would happen. It is always the same in cases like these.'

'Cases like what, Dr Woodruff?'

'You mean you don't know that your aunt is dying, Miss Fanny? No, I can see she hasn't told you.'

'You mean she knows?'

'Of course. I warned her some months ago, but she

refused to believe me. A very determined woman, your aunt, Miss Fanny. I'm afraid that very little can be done for her, except to ease the pain. I prescribed laudanum yesterday—perhaps she will accept it now. Take me to her, if you please.'

Francesca went up the stairs with a heavy heart; when she entered her aunt's room, she was shocked at the change she saw in her. Miss Shelwood was a ghastly colour, and gasping for breath. Agnes was bathing her mistress's forehead, but when the doctor came in she glided away.

'What are you doing here?'

Francesca was not sure whether her aunt was speaking to the doctor or to her. She went up to the bed and said gently, 'It's time you had some medicine, Aunt Cassandra. Dr Woodruff has something to make you feel better.'

'I don't want his morphine! If I'm going to die, I want to die in my right senses! But you can stay. I have something to say to you. A-ah!'

'Drink some of this, Miss Shelwood. You won't feel less alert, but it will take away the worst of the pain. And if you wish to be able to talk to your niece, you will need it.'

'Very well.' The voice was but a faint thread of sound.

Dr Woodruff held a small vial to the sick woman's lips, and then stood back. He said quietly, 'That should make her feel better for a while. I'll be in the next room.'

After a moment, Francesca said tentatively, 'You wished to tell me something, Aunt Cassandra?'

'Yes. Box on the desk. Fetch it.' Francesca did as her aunt asked, then on request opened the box. 'Letter. . . underneath.'

The letter was dry and yellow. It began, 'My dear Cassie'. . .and was signed 'Richard Beaudon'.

'Do you wish me to read it?'

'Later. No time now. It's from your father. Richard Beaudon. To tell me my sister had stolen him.' The dark eyes opened, and they were glittering with malice. 'Why I hated you. Still do.'

'Aunt Cassandra, don't! I have never done you any harm, you know that.'

'Never should have existed. He'd have married me if she hadn't told him...told him...' The voice died away again.

'Shall I fetch Dr Woodruff?'

'No! Not finished. It's the money. Chizzle's got to look after the money. Told him.'

'Mr Chizzle? The chaplain?'

'Don't be stupid. Who else? Do as he tells you. M'father had no right... A pauper—that's what you ought to be!' Miss Shelwood raised herself and stared malevolently at her niece. This time she spoke clearly and with intense feeling. 'You'd better do what Chizzle tells you—you needn't think anyone will marry you for love! A plain, dull child, you were. Plain, like *me*! Not like...' She sank back against the pillows, and her words were faint. 'Not like Verity. You'll never be the honeytrap she was.' The lips worked, then she added, 'Seen your father in you, though. The eyes.' A dry sob escaped her. 'God damn him!'

Francesca was appalled. 'Please, don't—I'll send for Mr Chizzle. He ought to be here—he'll help you.'

A grim smile appeared on her aunt's pale lips. 'I won't be here myself. Remember what I said, Fanny. Plain and dull, that's you. She called you Francesca—what a stupid name for such a plain child... Rake Beaudon's child...'

The voice faded away and Miss Shelwood closed her eyes.

Francesca ran to the door. 'Dr Woodruff!'

But when the doctor saw his patient, he shook his

head. 'It won't be long now,' he said. 'I doubt she'll be conscious again.'

'But. . .' Francesca gazed at the figure on the bed. 'She didn't have time to think! She didn't have time to make her peace with the world, to forgive those who had hurt her! And those who hadn't,' she added forlornly.

'Miss Shelwood is dying as she lived. A very unhappy woman,' said Dr Woodruff, adding drily, 'But God will forgive her. It's his job, after all.'

These were the most sympathetic words Francesca was to hear about her aunt. Words of respect, of conventional regret, of admiration for her energy and devotion to duty—all these were paid to her memory. Madame Elisabeth came, but her sympathy was for Francesca. Only Agnes Cotter truly mourned Cassandra Shelwood.

Following her aunt's death, Francesca underwent a time of confusion and shock. Mr Chizzle was much in evidence, though she wished he wasn't—his attempts to provide consolation were misplaced, to say the least. The funeral was well attended, and though Francesca was surprised at first, on reflection she decided it was to be expected. Although Miss Shelwood had been something of a recluse, she had, after all, been one of the great landowners of the district. But the biggest shock of all came after the funeral, after her aunt's will had been read.

The will was very much on traditional lines. Various small sums had been left to the servants, in proportion to their length of service. Mr Chizzle, as the local curate and Miss Shelwood's chaplain, received a modest sum, Agnes Cotter quite a large one. The rest of Miss Shelwood's estate was left to a fund for building and maintaining almshouses in a neighbouring town. Francesca's name was not mentioned in the document.

Gasps of astonishment came from the servants—Betsy

even voiced her disapproval out loud. But Francesca herself was not at all surprised. It was a blow, but one for which she had been prepared. The question of a post as a governess had now become urgent, and she decided to consult the family lawyer, Mr Barton, on the best way to set about doing this.

The others finally went. Mr Chizzle took his leave so warmly that Francesca began to wonder whether she had been mistaken in him all these years. He was most pressing that he should come again to see her the next day and, though she was reluctant, she eventually gave in, largely because it was the only way she could be rid of him.

But when she mentioned her intention of seeking a post as governess, Mr Barton was astounded. 'My dear Miss Shelwood! What on earth for? You now have control of the money left by your grandfather.'

'It is hardly enough to keep me, sir!'

'Well, that is a matter of opinion. I should have thought that seventy thousand pounds was enough for anyone! Together with what the Shelwood estate brings in, it is a considerable fortune.'

Francesca sat down rather suddenly on a convenient chair. 'Seventy. . .? Do you. . .do you mean to tell me that my grandfather left his *whole estate* to me?'

'Most of it. He left a sum of money outright to the late Miss Shelwood, and the rest was put into trust for you until you reached the age of twenty-five, in November of this year. The arrangement was that, during her lifetime, your aunt would run the estate and receive half of the income from it. The other half was put back into the Shelwood trust, which is why it has now grown to such a handsome fortune.'

'How much did you say it was?' asked Francesca faintly.

'About seventy thousand pounds. The trust was set up for the benefit of you and your children, and has certain safeguards which are in the discretion of the trustees. But you will have more than enough to live on, nevertheless. Shelwood is a thriving concern, and should provide you with an income of about ten thousand pounds per annum. Do you mean to say that Miss Shelwood never told you of this?'

'No. I had no idea. . .'

Mr Barton looked uneasy. 'I have been remiss. I agreed with your aunt that you were too young to be burdened with it at the time of your grandfather's death, but I ought to have made sure you knew later. But I have to say in my own defence that it simply never occurred to me that she would keep it from you. Why should she?'

'My aunt. . .my aunt was a secretive woman, Mr Barton,' was all Francesca said, however. Aunt Cassandra was dead. No good would be done by raking over the past.

'Hmm. I knew of course that she was dissatisfied with the arrangement, but still. . .' He cleared his throat. 'I can see that you have had a shock and need time to assimilate the news, Miss Shelwood, so I will not weary you. I should perhaps just add that one, somewhat curious, condition of the trust is that no one else—neither your father, Lord Beaudon, as your legal guardian, nor a future husband could benefit from it. Only you or your children may have use of it.'

'Since my father has never acknowledged me, he could hardly claim legal guardianship!'

'You are now of age, of course. But until you were twenty-one, he could always have claimed it, had he wished.'

'Even though I am illegitimate?'

The lawyer was astounded. 'Whatever gave you that impression, Miss Shelwood?'

'I. . .I was told. . .that is to say, I. . .was led to believe that there is no record of my parents' marriage.'

'What nonsense! Of course there is! I have all the relevant documents in my safe. Your grandfather gave them into my care just before he died.'

'But Aunt Cassandra said. . . Did my aunt know of these documents, Mr Barton?'

'Why, yes. We discussed them after Sir John's death.'

So Aunt Cassandra had lied to her, had lied to an eleven-year-old child about her parentage. For so many years Francesca had carried a burden of shame around with her, had worried over her future, had made no effort to be received into society or make friends with the surrounding families, sure that she would be rebuffed. Aunt Cassandra had done her best to ruin her niece's life in the way that her own had been ruined. How could she?

Perhaps, in her twisted unhappiness, she had convinced herself that her lover had really not married her sister, in spite of incontrovertible evidence to the contrary. Or had she been exacting a terrible revenge on the child of those she felt had wronged her?

'Miss Shelwood?'

'Forgive me, I. . .it has been a shock.'

'A shock? But why should you think. . .?' His face changed. He said sternly, 'Are you telling me that Miss Cassandra Shelwood, your own aunt, gave you to understand that you were not. . .not legitimate? I find that very hard to believe, Miss Shelwood. Your aunt was not an easy person to know, but she was generally respected throughout the neighbourhood as a just and upright woman.'

'I am not *telling* you anything, Mr Barton,' said Francesca, forcing herself to speak calmly.

'But you have obviously been under a misapprehension—for many years. Why did you not consult me?'

'It never occurred to me to do so. I never thought I had any sort of claim on the Shelwoods, except one of charity.'

'But this is disgraceful!'

With an effort, Francesca put aside her own feelings of outrage. Her aunt was dead—it would do no one any good to reveal how badly she had treated her niece. 'Mr Barton, whatever. . .misunderstandings there may have been in the past, the truth is now clear and we will, if you please, leave it at that. The future is now our concern.'

Mr Barton nodded. 'You are very wise, Miss Shelwood.'

'Do you. . .do you know why my father has remained silent all these years, Mr Barton? Unless. . .unless he is. . .dead?'

'I have no reason to believe he is.'

'Then. . .why?'

'When your parents eloped, Miss Shelwood, Sir John Shelwood refused to have any further contact with his daughter Verity. But when she died, he asked me to write to your father, offering to bring you up in England, and make you his heir. This would be on condition that Lord Beaudon should have no further communication whatsoever with you, once you had arrived at Shelwood Manor.

'I have to say that I disapproved of the arrangement, and was surprised that Lord Beaudon eventually agreed. Of course, the inducement was a strong one. You were motherless; as the Shelwood heiress your future would be assured, and—I have to say—your father's previous manner of life was not one in which a young child could flourish.'

Francesca said slowly, 'I suppose so, but. . .'

'However, your grandfather and aunt are now both dead, you are of age, and, in my opinion, it would not be improper for you to meet Lord Beaudon, if you wished.'

'I. . .I'm not sure. . . Mr Barton, you must excuse me. I am. . .overwhelmed by what you have told me. This change in my circumstances has come as a complete surprise, as you see. But tell me, how many others knew of my grandfather's will? Why did no one ever indicate something of the matter to me, even if my aunt did not?'

'You said your aunt was a woman who kept her secrets, Miss Shelwood. She always said she was very anxious that your position as a considerable heiress should not lead others to court and flatter you. She required my silence, and led me to believe it was out of a desire to protect you. As you know, you both led a somewhat reclusive life here at Shelwood. I doubt anyone else knows.'

With this Francesca had to be satisfied. She felt she had had enough for the moment, so asked Mr Barton to come again after she had had some time to reflect on the change in her fortunes. They fixed on the morning of the next day but one.

'You have been so discreet in the past, I know that you will continue to be so, Mr Barton. I need time to think things out for myself. To decide what I am going to do about Shelwood and my own life.'

The lawyer agreed, then took his leave with a deference that demonstrated, more than any words could have done, Francesca's new importance as owner of Shelwood and all that went with it.

The fact that Miss Fanny had not even been mentioned in her aunt's will scandalised the countryside. The news soon reached Witham Court, where there was a certain amount of speculation over her fate, now that she had been left penniless, together with some ribald suggestions. But after a while the company grew bored with this and forgot her in other pursuits. Everyone, that is, except

Marcus. Once again he had the urge to seek Francesca
out and offer what help he could, but the gossip and lewd
suggestions about Francesca's likely future gave
him pause.

What could he possibly offer that would not compromise her further? A girl without money, without friends
and without respectable background would have to be
more than ordinarily circumspect. She could not afford
the risk of scandal. After some thought, he decided that
Francesca would be safe at Shelwood for a short while
until the lawyers sorted things out. Meanwhile, he would
consult his sister about her when he returned to London.
Sarah might be able to find something suitable for
Francesca—a post as a companion, or governess,
perhaps?

When they got to London, Marcus delivered Lady Forrest
to her house in Chiswick, and went on without further
ceremony to see his sister, depositing Nick on the way.
But Lady Chelford was not at home, and Marcus found
to his annoyance that she would not be able to see him
till the next morning. He spent the night haunted once
again by Francesca's image, and was relieved when morning came and he could go round to Duke Street.

But here he was doomed to disappointment. Lady
Chelford, somewhat put out at having to receive her
brother at a ridiculously early hour, was unhelpful.

'Marcus, when will you direct your considerable talent
for helping others into more suitable channels? I am sure
your family could do with your counsel, and. . .and help.'

'My dearest Sarah, you need neither! Your husband
may be a touch stuffy, but he is perfectly sound
financially, and has a great deal of common sense. Too
much so!'

'But he does not understand the children as you do! He is talking of sending Charlotte to a seminary! He says she needs the discipline of school life.'

'Since the child has had four governesses in as many months, I am not sure I disagree with him there, Sally.'

'Then there's Nick. . . He is so often at odds with his father.'

'There's nothing wrong with Nick that can't be cured by a little experience. He'll soon grow up. Indeed, he showed surprisingly good sense at Charlie Witham's.'

When his sister looked doubtful, he added impatiently, 'Sally, he's no gambler, I promise you. In any case, I'll keep an eye on him. Now, what can you do for Francesca Shelwood?'

'Why are you so anxious about this girl? She's nothing to you, is she? *Is* she, Marcus? It would never do!'

'My God, women are all the same! Your imaginations leap from a slight comment, a simple desire to help someone who badly needs it, to wedding bells and the rest. No, I have no personal interest in Francesca Shelwood. I simply wish to preserve her from a fate she does not deserve! Now, can you help or not?'

'It's all very well, but you cannot reasonably expect me to come up with instant ideas for a girl who has no experience and no. . .background! What would my friends say if I foisted Rake Beaudon's love-child on them as a governess or whatever? This is yet another of your quixotic impulses and I have suffered from these before! Ever since you were a child, you have leapt in to help those you regarded, often mistakenly, as less fortunate than yourself. Your reformed pickpocket, whom I placed as a groom with Lady Castle, ran off with a selection of her best silver, and she hasn't forgiven me yet.

'Then there was the widow of a serviceman, a certain Mrs Harbottle, whom I took on myself as an assistant housekeeper. She created havoc in the servants' quarters before I managed to get rid of her. I have no doubt there have been others, if I chose to remember them. No, I will not help you.'

'This is different, Sarah! Miss Shelwood is a lady!'

'She cannot be a lady if, as you tell me, she is Rake Beaudon's illegitimate daughter. I'm sorry for the girl—it sounds as if life has treated her most unfairly—but I cannot help you. And if you wish the girl no harm, you will stay away from her. Tongues will soon wag if you are seen to be taking an interest, however platonic it is.'

'Dammit, of course I mean her no harm!'

'Then leave her alone.' There was a short silence, then she said irritably, 'I suppose I'll have to find something—if I don't, I can see you marrying the girl out of a more than usually stupid attack of conscience. And I owe you something for looking after Nick. If you wish, I will keep an ear open for anyone who seems to be looking for a companion, and is not likely to ask too many questions about the girl's breeding. But I warn you, such a one is most unlikely to be an agreeable employer.'

Marcus left Duke Street in an even gloomier frame of mind. It was clear that Francesca was doomed either to penury, or to life as a drudge, unless something intervened. His sister's words haunted him throughout the night; by the morning, he had come to a desperate decision. He set off for Shelwood later that day.

Francesca was not given much opportunity to consider her situation in peace. First, Agnes Cotter left Shelwood after a final, mercifully brief, interview, then Madame Elisabeth called to sympathise and to renew her offer of help, though she did not stay long, either. Francesca was glad of this—her old friend would be the first to know of the change in her circumstances, but not yet.

But the other servants and people on the estate trailed in one after the other, anxious to express their concern, both for Miss Fanny and for their livelihood. It took all her ingenuity to deal with them tactfully and reassuringly, without telling them anything of the changes in store.

The morning after the funeral, Mr Chizzle arrived to keep his appointment. Francesca was still reluctant to receive him. She had never liked him. He had been unctuously ingratiating with Miss Shelwood, but had followed his patron's example in dealing with her niece. His manner to Francesca had always been either indifferent or suffocatingly condescending. And she found it difficult to forgive those hour-long sermons on the question of her moral welfare after her escapade with Freddie. But she made herself welcome him. He was probably fulfilling some duty to Aunt Cassandra, who had mentioned him that last afternoon. Was it to do with the money she had left him?

'Miss Fanny—'

'Mr Chizzle, you have known me since I was a child, so I suppose it is difficult for you to think of me as Miss Shelwood—as I now am. But if you insist on using my Christian name, I should like you to use the correct one, which is Francesca, *not* Fanny.'

Mr Chizzle was full of confusion and fulsome apologies. Then he took up a position in front of the fireplace and began sonorously, 'I hope you will not condemn me, or think me presumptuous, if I claim a certain interest in your happiness, Miss Francesca. I like to think we have always understood one another very well, and that my efforts towards providing you with spiritual guidance and comfort over the years have not been unappreciated.'

'Of course,' Francesca said, somewhat confused. This was a different Mr Chizzle from the one she had been used to. What could account for it? She was quite certain that no word of yesterday's revelations had reached any other ears. What was this about?

After some small talk, in the course of which he expatiated on the virtues of her aunt—a subject which was hardly likely to make him popular with his audience—he said gravely, 'Your dear aunt, your late and sadly mourned aunt, was much exercised in her mind about what would become of you after she had passed on to higher things— an inexperienced girl, lacking any protector, and, dare I say, with certain unfortunate propensities—' Francesca straightened up at this, and he said with a kindly smile '—though these seem to have been somewhat subdued of late. But your aunt did me the honour of confiding her anxieties to me, and I have to say that I shared her fears.'

'Your concern does you credit. But I assure you, sir, it is misplaced. I am in no need of protection or guidance.'

Mr Chizzle smiled, and he shook his head in tolerant understanding. 'My dear Miss Francesca, that is precisely the problem! You are too young, too. . .headstrong to see it. You need someone—someone with maturer wisdom— to save you from the many pitfalls that life presents. Someone such as my humble self, perhaps.'

'Well, if I should ever feel the need for a friend—' Francesca began doubtfully.

'Ah, I shall not allow your modesty to cause you to misunderstand. Nor should you let the thought of your shameful birth—or any incident in the past—give you pause, either. Let him who is without sin. . . I do not regard it, I assure you. I am here, Miss Fanny, to tell you that my dearest wish—and that of your aunt as expressed to me on her deathbed—is to share your life, to give you companionship where there is loneliness, guidance where there is confusion, wisdom where there—'

'I am not sure what you mean, sir. Can you be more plain? Are you. . .*can* you be asking me to marry you?'

Mr Chizzle, put somewhat off his stride with this blunt question, mopped his brow and said that he was.

'I see.' Francesca turned away to hide her expression. Then she turned back and asked calmly, 'Did my aunt discuss with you the terms of my grandfather's will before she died, Mr Chizzle?'

'As it happens, she did mention it, yes. We both saw the inheritance as a source of danger to you and a temptation to unscrupulous men, attracted by your riches, rather than your. . .lovely self.'

'I see,' said Francesca flatly. 'So you knew about the money.'

'But I flatter myself that you would not dream of ascribing a mercenary motive to my efforts to secure your hand and heart, Miss Fanny—'

'*Francesca*, if you please.'

Mr Chizzle got somewhat awkwardly on to one knee. The effort made his face red, and he mopped it once again before saying, 'My heart is all yours, believe me, dearest Francesca, without any taint of venality. Even had it not been your aunt's dying wish that we two should carry the burden of the great Shelwood inheritance together, had you been the merest pauper, as bereft of fortune as you are bereft of name—I should still have offered you all I have—my admiration, my heart and my life.'

'I. . .I am flattered, of course. That you should be prepared to overlook the stain on my birth means a great deal to me. And what it pleases you to call my. . .propensities. But I cannot permit you to compromise your own good name, dear sir. Why, what would less worthy people say? That you are prepared to marry a bas—love-child as long as she is rich enough? That sin can be washed out in a stream of investments? That the Shelwood gold can persuade you to overlook the Shelwood shame? It is unthinkable! No, much as I am touched by your. . .

disinterested offer, I'm afraid I must decline it.'

'But your aunt assured me—she said you would be fortunate to find a man willing to marry you—'

'My aunt is dead, Mr Chizzle. My fortune was never hers to give away. And though I am sure that you have a noble indifference to the personal possession of wealth, I should tell you that any future husband of mine will have no control of the Shelwood inheritance. Under the terms of the trust set up by my grandfather, the income remains mine and later that of my children, even after I marry.' Her suitor's jaw dropped. He looked rather like a stranded fish, thought Francesca, somewhat unkindly. She said, 'Do please get up.'

Mr Chizzle recovered himself and rose with commendable dignity. 'Your aunt warned me,' he said sadly. 'You do not have that nobility of character a man should seek in his wife. I had hoped that with precept and discipline we should succeed in subduing the baser aspects of your nature. But it is not to be. To impute mercenary motives to a man who wishes merely to protect you, to save you from the dangers that surround a young girl left alone. . .' He gave a great sigh, then turned to go.

'Mr Chizzle!'

'Yes?'

'My aunt, as patron of the living of Shelwood, had full confidence in your discretion. I trust that I may repose equal confidence?'

The chaplain drew himself up, then said coldly, 'Your threats are unnecessary, Miss Shelwood. I wish to forget an episode which has been painful in the extreme. I will not mention this matter—or you—to anyone. Anyone at all. Goodbye.'

Francesca could hardly wait for him to leave. She struggled with a wild desire to laugh at the ridiculous picture Mr Chizzle had presented, bending his spindly, black legs in a travesty of a suitor's supplication, his face scarlet with his exertions. But then she was overcome with a feeling of sadness. So much for romance! Was Mr Chizzle merely the first in a succession of such suitors?

It was clear that the Shelwood estate and seventy thousand pounds were attractions which would more than compensate for any shortcomings in herself. Well, let the suitors come! And in her own time and at her own choosing, she would take a husband—but she doubted very much that she would be in love with him, whoever he was.

The sound of a carriage coming up the drive sent her to the window. Another visitor come to commiserate! She was in no mood for yet more verbal fencing. What she needed was time to herself—time in which she could come to terms with her new situation. It looked as if she was soon going to have to learn to deal with fortune seekers, if the last half hour was anything to go by. She would escape through the kitchen, while the visitor was waiting at the front of the house.

But here she miscalculated. The visitor had taken his carriage round to the stables; as Francesca came out through the gate to the kitchen garden, she was confronted with a tall, handsome, self-assured figure. She stopped dead.

'Good afternoon, Miss Shelwood.'

'What are you doing here, sir?' she asked, ungraciously.

'I heard of your aunt's death. I want to talk to you, Francesca.'

There was a silence. 'Well?' said Francesca. 'I'm listening.'

Marcus hesitated, then said, 'It. . .it is a somewhat private matter. May we go inside?'

Chapter Five

Francesca led the way in silence to the small parlour, where the ridiculous scene with Mr Chizzle had so recently taken place. But the tall, elegant figure that followed her in presented a very different picture from that gentleman. She was puzzled. What was Marcus doing here? What did he want of her? She stole a glance at him. He looked calm enough, but there was an air of reluctance about him—as if he was being driven down a road he was not quite sure he wanted to travel.

'And now?'

'Francesca, I want you to marry me.'

Francesca sat down suddenly. Whatever she had been expecting, it had not been another proposal. A feeling of apprehension chilled her bones. Perhaps Mr Chizzle and Marcus were not so very different after all?

He went on. 'Forgive me if I express myself a little abruptly—I know this must come as a surprise to you. Though our acquaintance is longstanding—'

'Nine years,' she said expressionlessly.

'Nine years—it has been short in terms of hours and minutes we have spent with one another.'

'Very short.'

'But I have always felt a. . .a communion of spirit with

76

you, and believe we could make as good a marriage as any other I have seen.'

'Always?'

'Always what?'

'Always felt this communion of spirit, as you call it?'

'Damn it, you know we share it!'

'I thought we did, certainly. Nine years ago. But you said that you were poor, that you had nothing to offer me, that we each had our own way to make. I remember what you said, you see. I was...quite distressed at the time.'

'I know. I behaved badly, Francesca. I never intended to hurt you, but I know I did. Please forgive me.'

Francesca carried on as if he had not spoken. 'Then you disappeared for nine years. We met by chance in the lane the other day—you hadn't come to seek me out. Indeed, at first you didn't even recognise me.'

'You will allow that that was unsurprising. Your dearest friends might not have recognised you in all that mud.'

'You are right, of course. In spite of the "communion of spirit", as you called it. Er...I still don't quite understand this proposal of marriage, however. Are you now trying to say that you have loved me all this time—unknown even to yourself?'

'Of course not! Look, nine years ago you were very young, without a penny to your name, and I was an ill-paid soldier. Marriage was out of the question.'

'And now?' asked Francesca. Try as she might, she could not keep the cynicism out of her voice.

Marcus was too intent on what he was saying to notice. 'But things are different now! And I feel I could give you the protection, the support that you lack in your present circumstances. You need a man to take care of you, give you the things you never had—'

A sudden vision of Mr Chizzle saying very much the

same thing, not an hour before, flashed through Francesca's mind. 'Thank you, but I really don't need anyone,' she said. 'I have plenty of money—enough for everything I need. I see you've heard the news.'

'Yes.'

'I wonder how? Did you know that I have seventy thousand pounds, too?'

He smiled, the old quizzical, deceitfully tender smile. 'That much?' Then he came over to her, took her hand and kissed it. 'My dearest girl! Still the same, gallant spirit!'

She waited in stony silence.

He eyed her closely, then said with an air of admiration, 'Well, I admit, that puts icing on the cake. It does indeed. Seventy thousand pounds, ay? A great deal of money.'

When she still said nothing, he put his arm round her and drew her to him. 'But you know in your heart that I'd want to marry you, whatever your dowry, Francesca. I'd marry you even if you had nothing, if you were a pauper. Come, stop prevaricating. Say you'll let me look after you for the rest of your life. I swear you won't regret it.' His manner was tender, but somewhat complacent. There was no suggestion that he was uncertain of the outcome.

Francesca badly wanted to stay calm, to deal with him as she had dealt with Mr Chizzle, but, as always seemed to be the case with this man, her emotions were getting the better of her. It was obvious that he expected her to fall into his arms as easily as she had done all those years ago. That she would be so dazzled by his blue-eyed charm, so blinded by the powerful attraction he knew he could exercise, that she wouldn't see the greedy self-interest behind it, the desire to better himself at her expense. She must have given him a pretty poor opinion of her wits during their brief affair, indeed she must!

Her efforts to hide her rage and humiliation were

choking her. Mr Chizzle had been bad enough, but this was ten—twenty times worse. She suddenly lost the battle with herself, and gave vent to her feelings. 'I won't pretend to feel grateful or flattered,' she said, thrusting him violently away. 'I don't need looking after; to be honest, I think you'd marry me if I had a squint and a wooden leg, as long as I had the rest.'

'What the devil are you talking about? I'm offering you the protection of my name and all that is mine.'

'Really? Well, I wouldn't marry you if you had five hundred thousand pounds and half of England for your heritage! My father was a charmer and a scoundrel, a rake and a fortune hunter, who didn't give a damn for the hurt he caused. The last thing I want is a husband just like him!'

'Now, listen to me, young lady—'

'No, I will not listen to you!' Years of distress and resentment rose up inside Francesca as she stormed on. 'I listened nine years ago, when you charmed me off my feet and then told me you had nothing to offer me. At the time I was fool enough to believe you sincere. I soon learned differently, and it's a lesson I am very unlikely to forget.

'So, allow me to tell you, sir, that *nothing* is now what I have to offer you! Take yourself and your professions of concern, your offers of protection, back to Witham Court, or wherever your other ladies are hiding. They might listen to you, but I never will—my only wish is never to see you again!'

He stood, staring at her as if she had gone mad.

'Have I not made myself plain, sir?' she said passionately. 'Why do you not go?'

'You have made your opinion of me perfectly plain,' he said, rigid with rage. 'If you really think of me in such terms—though God knows why you do—then I understand your refusal to marry me. But I question the need to express yourself quite so offensively, with such remarkable lack of moderation. A simple refusal would have sufficed. We have obviously each been mistaken in each other. Good day, ma'am. I wish you well in your future life, and will do my best to comply with your wish that we should not meet again.' He bowed and left the room.

Francesca sat down and buried her face in her hands. She sat there a long time, listening to the sounds of his carriage dying away down the drive. . . It was strange how painful the final disillusionment was. They had been so close, and so far apart. They had fought, and made love, all in the space of one day. They had met after years of separation, and now they had quarrelled for the last time. And the strange thing was that, during all of this, she had only ever known half his name.

'Marcus!' she whispered, 'Oh, *Marcus!*' and then at last the bitter tears fell.

Marcus drove back to London in a worse temper than he had ever known before. He was furious with himself and with Francesca Shelwood. After all these years, after all the women he could have asked to marry him and who would have been more than eager to receive his proposal with delight, he had exposed himself to a refusal from a penniless nobody! He must have been mad! His sister had already told him he was too quixotic—she would think he was out of his mind, if she learned that he had actually offered to marry Francesca Shelwood to save her from life as a drudge—or even worse!

His sense of injustice grew. His motives had been of the purest. Many would say he had acted nobly in asking Francesca to be his wife—to choose a nameless pauper when he might have chosen from any number of London's most eligible debutantes. Whatever she said, he didn't for one minute believe her claim to have seventy thousand pounds. She was merely putting on a front, as she had done at least twice before. Seventy thousand pounds, indeed! What a story! She might have seventy guineas, but not much more. The depth of her ingratitude was immeasurable. . .immeasurable!

But why had she refused him so angrily? Her father's neglect had done much to sour her view of life—that was obvious. And his own behaviour in the past had not been the sort to reassure her. But to be so excessively vituperative. . . The woman was a neurotic, and did not deserve his sympathy or his regard. From this day on he would forget her. She could find her own way through life, without any further help or interest from *him*!

Unaware of her catastrophic misunderstanding of Marcus's motives, Francesca did her best during the next few weeks to conquer her personal unhappiness and concentrate on a seemingly unending series of tasks and duties. She accomplished these with grim determination, for she had formulated a plan and was now working to it.

Thanks to her aunt's behaviour, she had very little experience of estate business, but Mr Barton was an invaluable ally. He found a very well-qualified agent to look after Shelwood and, by accompanying him round the estate, Francesca made sure that it would be looked after with understanding as well as efficiency. Shelwood Manor was partially shut down for the time being, and again with Mr Barton's help she found new places for one or two servants who were no longer needed. Betsy was put in charge of the rest.

Francesca intended to visit the Manor occasionally, if only to keep an eye on its welfare, but she would soon be busy elsewhere. One piece of business she was glad to perform. A deed of gift was drawn up, and Madame

Elisabeth was presented with the cottage she had tenanted for so many years, and given an increased annuity.

Mr Barton had performed one other service for Francesca. She had told him that she would like to meet her father, if it could be arranged.

'Miss Shelwood, I shall do my utmost to find him. He has been abroad for many years, of course. It may take some time. Leave it to me.'

But only a week or two later, he came back to Shelwood. 'I cannot believe our good fortune, Miss Shelwood! As you know, I have been trying to trace your father for you for some weeks without success. I had sent a letter to him at Packards, the family home in Hertfordshire, telling him that your aunt had died, and that I was anxious to get in touch with him. Not with a great deal of hope—the house has been unoccupied these many years.

'But see! I have here a letter from your father. It arrived this morning; I have come post haste to tell you of its contents. Lord Beaudon arrived in England only a few days ago, called at Packards, saw the letter and replied immediately. He writes that he no longer feels bound by the promise he made to your grandfather, and would like to see you again. He wonders if you would care to visit him in Hertfordshire. Is that not strange?'

Francesca agreed that it was strange, and asked him to make suitable arrangements. She would do as her father had asked. Mr Barton left happily prepared to do everything necessary to re-unite father and daughter, and Francesca was left with a curious feeling of apprehension and excitement. She decided to ask Madame Elisabeth to go with her to give her support.

So it was that, in the middle of October, Francesca found herself gazing curiously around her as her carriage bore her up the long, winding drive to Packards, the Beaudon family seat. Madame Elisabeth and Carter, her new maid, sat opposite her, two grooms were outside, and her new carriage was both comfortable and stylish. Her aunt's death was still very recent, so Francesca was dressed modishly, but quietly, in black. She was aware that it did not suit her.

'You are very quiet, Francesca,' said Madame Elisabeth. 'Are you weary from the journey?'

'It hasn't been such a long one, madame. But I have not been sleeping very well.' She gave her companion a little smile. 'Meeting my father after all these years is. . . a little nerve-racking.'

'You will have so much to say to one another.'

'You think so? We shall see.'

Francesca drew a deep breath as she stepped out of the carriage in front of a wide, shallow flight of steps. She was ridiculously nervous. The steps led to a handsome doorway and in front of the doorway stood a tall figure. Her heart gave a thump, and for a moment she thought she was seeing things. But then the figure moved towards them; she saw that this man was white-haired and used a stick. He was older than she had expected—he must have been well into his forties when she was born. And, though he had once been as handsome as that other, his face was pale and lined, and he was very thin.

'Francesca! My dear child!' He descended the steps, took her hand in his and surveyed her. 'I cannot begin to tell you how happy I am to see you again.'

For years, Francesca had resented the way in which her father had abandoned her, but the chill round her heart was melted a little by the sincerity of his voice and by the warmth of the expression in his eyes. She swallowed and said politely, 'And I am glad to see you, Papa. May

I present Madame de Romain to you? My friend and companion.'

Lord Beaudon took Madame Elisabeth's hand and held it to his lips. In perfect French he said, 'Madame de Romain, what can I say? It enchants me to meet you.'

Madame Elisabeth smiled and assured Lord Beaudon that he was too kind, and the little procession moved up the steps into the house. This took some time, for Lord Beaudon moved slowly, and the steps themselves were uneven.

'Packards is not what it once was, I am afraid, Francesca. I have lived so long abroad that it has fallen into some disrepair. But I have managed to engage some people from the village, and hope to have it put back into a better state before long.'

'You've been in the West Indies? I often wondered.'

'No—I've lived in Paris for the last few years. Ever since the monarchy was restored, in fact.'

Francesca wondered what her father's establishment in Paris might be—was he married? Did he have a family? It was not the sort of thing she felt she could ask. So she smiled and asked if she and Madame Elisabeth might refresh themselves after the journey. They were given into the care of a housekeeper who took them upstairs to two very handsome bedrooms.

A short while later, refreshed and tidy once again, Francesca collected Madame Elisabeth and went downstairs to seek out her father. She found him in the library, sitting in front of the fire, but he put down his book as soon as he saw them. There was a small silence, a silence which Francesca found difficult to break. At last she said, 'You must have been working your servants hard, Papa. Our rooms look beautiful.'

'I'm glad you like them,' he said simply. Then, as he

saw that Madame Elisabeth was standing by the door, he
added, 'Come, Madame de Romain—you must join us.'

'You are very kind, Lord Beaudon but, if you don't
mind, I should like to have some fresh air before it gets
dark. And I am sure that you and your daughter have
much to say to one another. Will you excuse me?'

Francesca did not want to be left alone so abruptly with
a father she had not seen for nearly twenty years, but
Madame Elisabeth smiled reassuringly and disappeared.

Lord Beaudon seemed to find the situation just as difficult. He started by making the usual kind enquiries about
her journey, such as any host might of any guest. But his
mind seemed to be elsewhere during these exchanges, and
he seemed to be observing his daughter's movements
and gestures rather than listening to her replies. His eyes
seldom left her face.

After a while, however, they both felt easier in one
another's company and he began to talk of old Sir John
and the Shelwoods, about the district and people he had
known there. He even made her smile at his description
of Sir John's battles with the owners of Witham Court.

'And now they're all dead,' he said suddenly. 'You are
all that is left of the Shelwoods. Sir John, Cassie and
Verity—they were the last of the line. It was tragic that
Verity should have been the first to go. She was younger
than Cassie by a good ten years.'

'So much?'

'Cassie was the eldest child, then there were two boys
who died in infancy, then lastly your mother. Everyone
wanted me to marry Cassandra Shelwood, you know—
and I very nearly did. It seemed a fair exchange.'

'A fair exchange?'

He smiled kindly at her. 'I expect your head is full of
romantic notions about marrying for love—but in the
world I was brought up in, we married for advantage,

and sought pleasure elsewhere. And that is what I fully intended to do. You wouldn't have liked me in those days, Francesca—I was even more cynical than most of my contemporaries.

'I met Cassandra Shelwood just at the point when my fortunes were at their lowest, and I was beginning to feel that I ought to settle down, but was without the resources to do so. In my youth I had indulged in every folly known to man, and my reputation was such that no parents in their right mind would entrust a young girl to my care.'

'They told me you were a rake. Rake Beaudon, they called you.'

'I deserved the name. But then someone introduced me to Sir John Shelwood. Sir John didn't approve of me, but he was quite content to see me marry his elder daughter. Cassie was past thirty when I first got to know her, and he wanted to see her married. They both thought she was perfectly capable of keeping me in line.'

'You. . .you didn't ever pretend you loved her?'

'Oh, no. There was never any question of love between us. An establishment was what she wanted, and preferably a title. But then I met your mother. . . Against all the odds, I fell in love. I could never have married anyone else after that.'

Francesca kept very still. This was a very different tale from that of the heartless rake who seduced his fiancée's sister! She felt she was hearing the real story for the first time.

'Cassie was very bitter. Although I had not actually committed myself, she expected me to marry her. Nothing I said could pacify her. Sir John stormed and ranted. He was prepared to accept me as a husband for Cassie, but would not contemplate entrusting his precious little girl, his lovely Verity, to a rake and adventurer! But Verity. . .'

he gave a laugh '. . .Verity said we should have to
run away.

'Up to that point I hadn't even realised that she was in
love with me! I told her it was impossible, that I had
nothing, and that her family would almost certainly cut
her off without a penny if we eloped. She didn't care. I
was twice her age and twice her weight—but she outclassed me and everyone else I knew for courage. Gaiety,
too. She was always laughing.'

'I don't remember her very well, but I remember her
laughter. And her bedroom—it was pretty.'

'Yes, she liked pretty things. I had a rundown estate in
the West Indies. We ran off to Gretna, were married and
went out to St Marthe. Then, soon after you were born,
she became ill. . .and eventually she died. . .'

There was a pause while Francesca composed herself
to ask the question that had tormented her for so many
years. She carefully suppressed any feeling of resentment
and her voice was neutral as she said, 'Why did you send
me away, Papa?'

'I was no fit company for a child after I had lost your
mother. What else could I have done? Your grandfather
sent word to say he was prepared to give you a home—'

'But I already had a home with you on St Marthe!'

'It wasn't a home without your mother. I couldn't bear
to stay there, but I didn't know where to go or what I
wanted to do. I certainly didn't want to return to England.
I thought I was doing the right thing for you by sending
you to your grandfather. But it was a pity that they
wouldn't keep Maddy.'

'Papa, what happened to Maddy? Did she go back to
St Marthe?'

Lord Beaudon hesitated, then said, 'Yes. . .'

'I missed her so much. I'd like to think she is well and
happy. Is she, do you know?'

'I think so, yes.' The was a touch of restraint in Lord Beaudon's voice, but before Francesca could pursue the question of Maddy he went on, 'My dear, I hope you will believe me when I say it simply didn't occur to me that Cassie would be so vindictive.'

'I. . .I think you were mistaken about her feelings for you, Papa. I think she really loved you. She kept your last letter to her, even. . .even showed it to me when she was dying.' Francesca's voice trembled as she remembered that dreadful scene. 'It's possible that you ruined her life, Papa.'

'Oh, no! I shan't allow you to say that. Cassandra Shelwood's life was spoiled before I ever met her and, if we had married, it would have been hell for both of us. I have no regrets on that score. The thing I do regret most bitterly was that I let Sir John impose the ban on writing to you. I should never have agreed to that.'

Francesca remained silent. What a great deal of misery could have been avoided if she had been able to communicate with him!

'And now, my dear? What are you going to do? And how can I help you? Do you wish to make your home with me—in Paris?'

'Thank you, but I would rather stay in England for the moment. I. . .I should like to marry. Like my aunt Cassandra, I should like to have an establishment of my own. But I recognise that this will not be easy, for, like her, I suffer from certain disadvantages.'

Her father looked sceptical, but asked, 'And they are?'

'I am plain, and I am past the age of your average debutante.'

'My dear girl, forgive me, but you are talking rubbish! How old are you? Twenty-one, twenty-two? And you are far from plain.'

'Please, Papa! You are trying to be kind, and I am

touched. But you really need not pretend. I am five-and-twenty and perfectly accustomed to the notion of being plain. But my newfound wealth—'

'No, no, no! I must stop you. You are so wrong, Francesca! I will allow that you have not learned to dress to advantage. Nor have you acquired the arts women customarily employ to make the most of their looks. But these are superficialities—easily changed. A well-trained maidservant would soon deal with them. You must not believe otherwise.'

'You are very kind,' Francesca said politely, but in a tone which dismissed the possibility. 'But to return to our original topic—the time-honoured way to find a husband is to become part of polite society—London society. And that is what I would like to do. Can you help me?'

'Of course I will help you all I can, but. . .I have been away from London for too long to help you directly. You would need a chaperon—'

'I thought Madame de Romain could act as my chaperon?'

'Very well. But in that case you would need a sponsor—someone who is familiar with London ways,' he said thoughtfully. 'She would need to be part of the great world, of course. A dowd won't do. And it would need to be someone who would teach you how to make the most of your appearance. Give you a little town polish. . . Let me sleep on it, Francesca. I'm sure I can find someone.'

Lord Beaudon slept on it to good effect. The next morning he suggested that his daughter might like to make the acquaintance of a lady who would make an ideal sponsor.

'I think she would do it. Her father-in-law was a good friend of mine. The Canfields are related to half of the top families in England, one way and another, but they are no longer as wealthy as they once were. Maria Canfield's husband was killed at Waterloo, leaving her with three children to bring up, and a limited income with which to do it. Her two sons are at Eton still, but she has a daughter she would like to bring out this next season. She might be pleased to share the expenses of a London season with me.'

'You, Papa? You are kind, but I have no intention of being a burden on you,' Francesca said firmly. 'I have more than enough to meet any expenses.'

'My dear—'

'No, Papa. I would be grateful for any help you can give me in finding my way through London society. But the expense must be mine.'

Lord Beaudon regarded her with a frown. He seemed prepared to argue, but she stared back at him with cool determination. Finally, his expression of displeasure gave way to one of great sadness, and he shrugged his shoulders, merely saying, 'Shall I arrange a meeting with Mrs Canfield?'

'Please do.'

Francesca liked the Canfields immediately. Lydia Canfield was a small, dark, lively girl with a great deal of self-confidence, and a wicked sense of humour. Her mother was still a beautiful woman, but she dressed quietly, and her manner was reserved. Lydia was her only daughter, and it was obvious that Mrs Canfield's dearest wish was to see her safely established. For this reason she was prepared to take on the task of introducing Francesca to Society in return for assistance with costs.

But she was taking no risks. Though her manners were exquisite, Mrs Canfield subjected Francesca to careful inspection, and some close questioning. Far from being offended by this, Francesca understood perfectly, and answered all enquiries as frankly as she could.

'I am somewhat older than most young ladies who seek to enter London Society, I know, and I am not looking for a debutante's "come-out", such as Miss Canfield will have. I will be open with you—my aim is to find a respectable man of moderate birth and fortune who is prepared to marry me. I do not seek a brilliant match, but it is important that the person I marry is honourable and considerate.'

'That may be more difficult than you think, Miss Beaudon! London is full nowadays of men who are rich, powerful, dashing, elegant—what you will. Honour and consideration for others do not play an important role in their ambitions.'

Francesca was slightly taken aback at hearing herself addressed as Miss Beaudon, but said nothing. It was her name, though only a month ago she would have denied it. She would soon have to make up her mind how she wished to be known in London.

'Mama, do you not think that Lord Carne would be the very man for Miss Beaudon?'

'Lydia—I had forgotten you were there. You should not be listening to this.' Mrs Canfield shook her head at her daughter, then turned to Francesca. 'I am sorry, Miss Beaudon. Lydia has been such a comfort to me since her father died, that I have perhaps indulged her too much. She is a dear girl, but. . .over-enthusiastic, shall we say? I am hoping she will acquire some discretion before next year.'

Francesca smiled and said she was quite certain of Miss Canfield's discretion.

'I wish I were half so confident,' said Mrs Canfield. 'She should not have interrupted us, however.'

'But, Mama—I had to! Lord Carne is a very kind man—you have said so a hundred times. And you have said more than once that he should think of finding a wife.'

'Lydia is right to reproach me, Miss Beaudon. Lord Carne was in my late husband's regiment, and we owe him a great deal. After Peter was killed, he helped us in all sorts of ways, and he still continues to take an interest in Lydia and my sons, even though he is a very busy man.'

'We haven't seen him in an age, Mama. Will he be in London for my début?'

'I hope so. He said he would see to it that he was.' Mrs Canfield turned to Francesca with an apologetic smile. 'You must forgive my importunate daughter, Miss Beaudon. Lord Carne is a great favourite of hers. But recently he has been away in Paris a great deal of the time.'

'I wonder if my father knows him.'

'He will know *of* him, of that I'm sure. But unless Lord Beaudon mixes in diplomatic circles, he might not know him personally. Lord Carne's work in Paris is chiefly concerned with the envoys of other nations.'

'He is a diplomat?'

'Not quite. The ambassador uses his skills occasionally, shall we say?'

The irrepressible Lydia broke in. 'He's a very important man, Miss Beaudon. But you would never guess it from his manner. Oh, he would be a perfect match for you! And he's quite old, too.'

A vision of a distinguished, grey-haired diplomat, a couple of years younger than her father, floated before Francesca's eyes. 'Well. . .' she said hesitantly.

Mrs Canfield shook her head at her daughter again. 'Please, do not listen to Lydia's nonsense, Miss Beaudon. Lord Carne is in the prime of life and a very rich man. He must be considered one of the most eligible *partis* in London.'

'In that case, he is quite beyond my touch,' said Francesca, smiling. 'I must restrain my ambition.'

'No! Oh, forgive me. I do not mean to be rude. It's just that he has been a target for matchmakers for so long, and no one has yet succeeded in engaging his attention.'

'And I am not attempting to be one of the season's sensations—I must leave that to Miss Canfield. But there's something I have to confess. . .'

Mrs Canfield looked anxious, and Francesca hastened to reassure her.

'It is not very serious, and I hope can be easily remedied. You see, Mrs Canfield, my life till now has been very restricted. I'm afraid to say that I have managed to reach the age of twenty-five without having had the smallest instruction on behaviour in polite society, and lessons in deportment and dancing. Your daughter probably has no need of such things, but I must find someone to help me.'

'My daughter has every need of lessons in behaviour, Miss Beaudon.'

'Mama!'

'And she is in dire need of a few accomplishments. I am sorry to say that Lydia has never had instruction in painting, nor any foreign language. A fact I much regret.'

'There I may be able to help you! I can soon find someone to teach your daughter. In fact, I was hoping you would accept my own dear former governess as a member of our household, and Madame de Romain would, I am sure, love to instruct Miss Canfield. We shall both have time to improve ourselves, I hope, before next May.'

'Excellent! I think we may deal with each other very well, Miss Beaudon. And Lydia will have the sort of come-out I have always wanted for her.'

'Is it settled, Mama?'

'Miss Beaudon?' asked Mrs Canfield with a smile.

Francesca nodded.

'Then, if you agree, we should put the business of finding a suitable house and servants in hand. These things take longer than one thinks. Your aunt's death is of such recent date that it would not be suitable for you to mix widely in Society. But perhaps we could plan one or two modest social events before Christmas? It would give both of you an opportunity to experience London before the Season starts. We shall be able to visit dressmakers and modistes, too.'

'A delightful prospect—I can hardly wait!'

Francesca reported this conversation to her father, not without some humour at Lydia's enthusiasm, and thanked him for arranging it.

'I might pay a visit to town myself, my dear. To see you in all your glory.'

'I leave glory to others, Papa. Talking of which—have you heard of a man called Carne? Lord Carne? Do you know him at all?'

'Carne? I haven't met him, but of course I've heard of him. Everyone talks of Carne. You'd sometimes think he was the only Englishman the French regime can bring themselves to trust. His role in the Allies' campaign against Bonaparte may be small, but it's vital.'

'Napoleon? But surely that campaign was won long since! At Waterloo!'

'This is the postwar campaign. The Bourbons are not at all popular in France. There are a good few perfectly honest Frenchmen who would be glad to see the back of King Louis and his hangers-on. Some of them would fetch Napoleon back from St Helena, if they could. It's mess, Francesca!'

'I had no idea. . . But what does Lord Carne do?'

'It's not so much what he does. . .the career diplomats do the real negotiating. But Carne seems to have the confidence of the French as well as the Prussians and the rest—and the English, of course. You might call him a link. They *all* trust him, you see. Why are you so curious about Carne?'

'Mrs Canfield was singing his praises. And Lydia said he was the sort of man I was looking for.'

'Carne! My dear girl. . .my dear Francesca—he's a Nonpareil! The present top of the tree—you'd have a better chance of marrying the man in the moon! Every female in London would give her eye teeth just to be noticed by him! Dowagers, debutantes, heiresses— beauties all of them. And he ignores them all. It would be a triumph, of course. . . But, no. You must lower your sights a little. I'm afraid Carne would never think of asking you to marry him.'

Chapter Six

Francesca's life now changed radically. Her days were still as busy as ever, but she spent them, mostly in the company of the Canfields, in an orgy of shopping for silks, muslins and other delightful fripperies, looking at a selection of elegant houses in the best part of town with her father's man of business, and approving the staff which he had engaged for her.

Then she returned to Hertfordshire and spent hours learning from Mrs Canfield, or her father, the social skills that had been so lacking in her life. It was not easy. She had to learn in a few short weeks what most girls had time to absorb over years of normal family life and training, but the self-control she had learned in her earlier life now stood her in good stead. The results were astonishing. Fanny Shelwood, no one's child—shabby, dull, stiff and awkward in society—was replaced by Francesca, the accomplished daughter of Lord Beaudon.

This transformation did not happen overnight, nor was it without some difficulties. Francesca quickly found the company of the Canfields easy to enjoy—Lydia's vivacity and humour, her loving relationship with her mother and her willingness to regard the world, including Francesca, as her friend, warmed Francesca's lonely heart, and after a while she slowly began to join in the laughter and conversation which resounded through the rooms in Mrs Canfield's house.

But the relationship between father and daughter was a different matter. She still found it difficult to absolve him from all blame for her unhappy years at Shelwood. And, for his part, Lord Beaudon found it hard not to be disappointed in his newly discovered daughter. He looked in vain for a trace of his impulsive, laughing, loving wife in her. He was grieved by the formidable wall of reserve with which Francesca surrounded herself, and he regarded with some disapproval her lack of romance, her coolly cynical assessment of how to set about finding a husband.

But then he began to see that years of rejection lay behind Francesca's refusal to depend on others. He had not suspected, not for one moment, that Cassandra Shelwood would hate her sister's child, that Francesca would be the innocent victim of her desire for revenge, and was shocked to hear, chiefly through conversations with Madame Elisabeth, of Francesca's unhappiness and deprivation at Shelwood Manor after her grandfather's death. Though it helped him to understand her better, he blamed himself too bitterly to try to force her confidence, sadly accepting that the only contribution required of him before he returned to Paris was to find her a sponsor.

This he had done with great success. Maria Canfield proved to be the perfect choice. As well as learning to take her part in Society, Francesca was able to enjoy a loving, uncomplicated family life such as she had never known. And, as time went on, Lord Beaudon's patience was rewarded. He was delighted to hear her laughter with Lydia Canfield, to see her pleasure in mastering the intricacies of the dance steps he taught her, her enthusiasm for improving her skills in riding and driving.

Through these minor activities he began to see behind

his child's defences, to catch glimpses of the real
Francesca. He saw that her self-possession was only surface deep, that Francesca was, in fact, deeply uncertain
of herself. Time and time again he cursed the Shelwoods
for their part in destroying Francesca's self-esteem, for his
sister-in-law's efforts to break the child's spirit. Madame
Elisabeth answered his questions about Francesca's life
at Shelwood as discreetly as she could, but it was clear
that her own sense of loyalty to her employers had been
sadly stretched.

'Was there no one else for her to talk to, Madame
Elisabeth? No friend of her own age?' he asked one day.

'No, *milord*. Miss Shelwood paid no visits herself in the
neighbourhood, and received no one except her chaplain.
Besides. . .'

'Well?'

Madame Elisabeth looked uncomfortable. 'The neighbours were as deceived about your daughter's birth as she
was herself. It was unfortunate, I think, that Sir John, no
doubt with the best of intentions, changed the child's
name to Shelwood. It gave rise to rumours after he
was dead, which the late Miss Shelwood did nothing to
dispel.'

'From what I hear, she probably fostered them. Damn
the Shelwoods! He was an arrogant old man and she was
a cold-hearted witch. How on earth Verity came to be a
member of such a family, I shall never know. And to think
I abandoned her daughter to their untender mercies. . .'

'Sir John was very fond of Francesca, Lord Beaudon,
but he was old. He died five years after you left her with
him. It was a pity, perhaps, that he did not see fit to trust
me with all the facts when he engaged me. Though I am
not sure what I could have done. . .'

'He wouldn't have imagined it necessary. No one, no
one at all, could have suspected the depths to which Cassie

would descend. Not even I, who thought I knew her. It is a miracle that Francesca survived her treatment. With the exception of yourself, no friends at all, you say?'

'There was once talk of a man. . . He was not a desirable acquaintance, but I always thought Miss Shelwood treated Francesca with undue severity in the matter.'

'A man? From the village?'

'No,' said Madame Elisabeth reluctantly. 'He was staying at Witham Court.'

'Oh, my God! That, too?'

'Francesca always swore that he was harmless, that she had only met him once. I believe her. She was always a truthful child. But. . .'

'But what?'

'Something had made her deeply unhappy at that time. If it was not this "Freddie", then something else had caused her great distress. It took her a long time to recover her spirits. I do not know who or what it was.'

'That might explain her cool approach to marriage— I thought there must be something! Madame Elisabeth, Francesca owes you a great deal, and I too would like to tell you how grateful I am for the friendship you have shown her. I hope you will stay with her during this coming season. She needs a friend to support her.'

'Of course I will stay! But. . .may I say something?'

He nodded.

'It is you she needs, Lord Beaudon. It is your approval she seeks.'

Lord Beaudon shook his head. 'I wish I could believe that. But I fear she still blames me for what she sees as my neglect of her.'

'Perhaps a little at first,' said Madame Elisabeth, ever the diplomat. 'But no longer, I think. Her view of you has been changing, and now, for the first time in years, Francesca has someone of her own to love. Someone who belongs to her. I assure you, *milor'*, your presence at her début would give her all the assurance she needed.'

Lord Beaudon thought long and hard about this conversation. Madame Elisabeth seemed to think that he had some influence with Francesca, after all. And if it was indeed important to his daughter that he should be present during her Season in London, then he would be there, at whatever cost! He began to look at her with new eyes, to listen to her laughter with new pleasure and pride. And as he looked, he began to catch reminders of his beloved Verity in his daughter, though there was no physical resemblance.

Francesca was tall, but she moved with her mother's grace, and the timbre of her voice, which had tended to be stiff and cold, now had her mother's warmth and flexibility. Her laughter was slow to come in his presence, but when it came it was an exact echo of Verity's expression of delight with the world. Some of Francesca's former reserve was still there, but this merely gave her an air of distinction which entranced him.

'My dear child, you will be a sensation! You may have my looks, but you have all your mother's spirit! And when I hear your laughter, I can imagine she is in the room with me again.'

'*Your* looks, Papa? People always said I was like my aunt.'

'Like Cassie? Don't be absurd! They must have been blind. Look at yourself, Francesca!' He led her to the large mirror at the side of the fireplace. 'Look!'

They stood side by side in front of the mirror, a tall, distinguished man, dressed for the evening in sombre colours, and a slender girl in a dress of palest green *peau de soie*. As she stared at their reflection, Francesca could see that she was, in truth, the feminine counterpart of her father, that any resemblance to her aunt Cassandra had been pure chance. Aunt and niece had both been tall, but any possible likeness ended there.

Lord Beaudon was tall, too, and his daughter's bone structure and features, though more delicate, were those of her father. Her hair, no longer scraped back as her aunt had required, had proved to be thick and lustrous, and, dressed by an expert maid, it was coiled on top of her head in a loose knot. A few curls had been allowed to escape to frame her face, softening, but not disguising, the pure line of cheek and jaw. Her hair was still not the honey-blond she had so longed for, but its pale gilt brought out the sparkle in her gray-green eyes, and flattered the delicate colour in her cheeks.

'Papa!' Francesca turned in astonishment to her father. 'I hadn't realised. . . They all said. . .I thought. . . But I'm not an antidote, after all!'

Her father burst out laughing. 'No, you're not an antidote, my dear. Far from it.'

'And all because of a few fine feathers! How absurd! Aunt Cassandra should have tried them!'

Her father sobered instantly. 'Clothes and the attentions of a good maid enhance the picture—it would be stupid to say otherwise. But you are a delight to look at, Francesca, because something now shows in your face that your aunt never had, and never wanted. I'm not sure I can put a name to it. . .a generosity of spirit? A love of life? That's your mother's gift to you, and it's more valuable than anything the world can do for you. People call it charm.'

Francesca looked uncertainly in the mirror again. She was not sure what her father meant. 'I think you're being over-partial, Papa. But thank you.'

'Well, we'll see what your effect on Society will be. You and Lydia Canfield together will take the *ton* by storm, mark my words.'

'Now I know you're being absurd, Papa! Lydia, perhaps, but not I.'

Her father paused, then went on, 'And though I ought to be back in Paris, I have decided to spend the Season in London after all. I. . .I wish to be with you.'

'With me?' Francesca turned to look at him. What she saw in his face moved her as she had not been moved for a long time. Her own face lit up and she said joyfully, 'Oh Papa! Oh, thank you! I didn't dare to hope you would be there. Oh, this makes all the difference!' She threw her arms round her father and hugged him. It was the first spontaneous gesture she had ever made towards him.

Lord Beaudon cleared his throat and said, 'I must be there to see your triumph, Francesca. And so. . .this seems to be the moment to ask you how you intend to be known in London. You have had the name of Shelwood for so many years—and I expect you still think of yourself as one. But you *are* my daughter, my only child. . .' He stopped.

Francesca, faced with a decision she had been postponing for too long, realised that it was in fact very simple. She smiled at her father and swept him a magnificent curtsey. 'The Honorable Francesca Beaudon presents herself to you, my lord. She can't promise you a triumph. . . but she will do her best not to let the Beaudon name down.' She looked up at him, her expression, had she but known it, exactly like one of her mother's—an enchanting mixture of mischief and anxiety.

'My dearest girl!' Lord Beaudon took her hand and then pulled her to him and held her close.

The wall of reserve which lay between father and daughter had at last been breached by this decision of Lord Beaudon's to stay in London. It had only needed Madame Elisabeth's encouragement for him to do so, for he was already beginning to feel protective of this girl, this precious inheritance Verity had left him. But from the moment Francesca had spontaneously embraced her father, there was nothing and no one who could have prevented him from doing all he could to make her happy.

One result was that he showered her with presents—a fur tippet to keep her nose warm in the January frosts, an exquisitely painted fan to keep her cool in overheated rooms, books and flowers by the dozen to keep her amused and happy. When he produced a necklace of beautifully matched pearls on the evening of her first introduction to Society, she was overcome.

'Indeed, you are too good, Papa! You should not spend so much money on me!'

'My darling child, the pearls were your mother's. Who else should I give them to? And for the rest. . .' With a look of wry amusement, he went on, 'The Beaudon fortune falls short of the Sheldwood riches, I admit, but it is far from negligible. I am not the pauper your aunt undoubtedly led you to believe.'

'But. . .but they said you wanted to marry Aunt Cassandra for her money!'

'I did! And it's true that life would have been more comfortable if your mother had been given a dowry. But that is many years ago now. I have lived a fairly quiet life since your mother died, Francesca, and the Beaudon assets have increased. If you had permitted me, I would have been able to give you a London Season without the help of your Sheldwood inheritance.'

'Then I shall have no more qualms and will accept your gifts with great pleasure. You see, apart from Madame Elisabeth, no one has wanted to give me anything before.'

'Well, that situation will be remedied the minute you make your bow in Society! I prophesy that you will be showered with flowers and the rest.'

'Papa, you are a tease! I leave that sort of thing to Lydia. She is of an age to enjoy it.'

'You talk as if you were a hundred, Francesca. Twenty-five is not such a great age.'

'It is too old to look for romance. In any case I do not seek it, as you very well know.'

'My child, I was forty, and a rake past redemption, I thought, when I fell in love with your mother! But tell me. . .' Lord Beaudon paused. He was treading on delicate ground, he knew, but the temptation to gain Francesca's confidence was very strong. 'Have you never been in love?'

The response was too swift and too emphatic to be convincing. 'In love? No!'

'Not even with Freddie?'

Francesca's face was blank. 'Freddie who? Oh. . .that Freddie! Of course not. Who told you about him? Madame Elisabeth?'

'Don't blame her. I asked her if you had had any other friends, and she mentioned the episode with Freddie. She seemed to think your aunt had been unjust.'

'Well, I think so, too. I told Aunt Cassandra that I hadn't wanted to talk to him and, what's more, he hadn't spent more than five minutes in my company before she found us, but she wouldn't listen. She probably wanted to believe me wicked.'

Lord Beaudon gave an angry exclamation, but Francesca went on, 'You needn't worry, Papa. It's all in the past now; anyway, even at the time, I didn't care very much what she did—the worst part was having to listen to Mr Chizzle's sermons.'

'Why didn't you care?' He spoke so softly that Francesca found herself speaking without guarding her tongue.

'Nothing mattered very much at that time. . .'

'Were you so unhappy?'

'Yes.'

'Why, my child?'

Francesca walked away from him and stared out of the window. Her father held his breath as he watched her. If only she would confide in him!

When she finally spoke, her voice was flat and stiff, as if the words were being forced out against her will. 'I was not telling you the truth before. I did love someone once—or thought I did. A friend of Freddie's—also from Witham Court. Aunt Cassandra never knew about him. No one did.' Her mouth twisted in a bitter little smile. 'Except Freddie. Nothing of any consequence happened between us, but I thought my heart was broken. Silly, wasn't it? To break your heart over a rake—for that is what I discovered he was.'

She turned round and gave a wry smile, 'It's very rare to find a rake who really falls in love—Mama was luckier than she knew.'

Lord Beaudon smiled back at her. 'Your mama, Francesca, had her own anti-rake brand of magic. From the moment I saw her, my days of rakishness were over! And, in my opinion, you have the same magic—or could have, if you chose to exercise it. But. . .this man—how are you so sure that he was a rake?'

'He was staying at Witham Court. He gambled and drank. . .'

'He cannot be condemned on those grounds—they are not exactly unusual pursuits for a young man!'

'No, but. . . He made me believe he loved me. . .that I was beautiful. . .of value to him. Have you any idea what that meant to me, Papa? To be loved? After years of living without it?' Her father drew in his breath and shook his head in self-disgust. Francesca came over and put her hand on his arm. 'I understand now, Papa, really I do.

You mustn't blame yourself. You did what you thought
was best.'

'But I should never have agreed to lose all contact with
you, Francesca! However grieved I was at your mother's
death, I should never have abandoned you so completely.
I should have been there to help you when this man. . .
What happened, my dear? Did you. . .did he seduce you?'

Francesca flushed and looked away. She said painfully,
'No, Papa. I was spared that folly. But not because. . .
because I refused him. I was besotted enough to have
given him anything he asked of me. No, I was saved from
that last betrayal by his friend, who had come up the hill
in search of him. We had to part before Freddie found us.'

'Freddie!'

'Yes, Freddie, Papa.'

Lord Beaudon decided to leave the question of Freddie
for the moment. His daughter was talking of someone
who had been much more important to her. 'This other
man. . .?' He paused, hoping she would put a name to
him. Francesca was silent, so he went on, 'You saw him
just once?'

'No, we met the day after, too. But by then he had
decided he. . .no longer wished to continue the acquaintance. Oh, he was plausible enough. He played the part of
the romantic hero to perfection, pretending concern for
me, telling me that he could offer me nothing, that he
was poor, I was too young, that he had to go away. . . He
was very plausible. He seemed as unhappy to leave me
as I was to see him go.'

She stopped for a moment, then went on, 'And poor
fool that I was, I was completely taken in. I believed
him, Papa! I was unhappy, of course, but I was used to
disappointment. And the thought that someone had loved
me, really loved me, even if Fate and Fortune were against
us, gave me courage to bear it. A latter-day Romeo and

Juliet. . .I was really very young—and very naïve,' she added bitterly. There was a pause. 'Then a few days later I found out how he really regarded me. Freddie told me.'

She turned and lifted her head, gazing defiantly at her father. 'When my aunt found me with Freddie, I had just learned that my "Romeo" had boasted of his conquest to the others at Witham Court. I expect they repeated all the gossip to him, about my lack of fortune and. . .and all the rest. They had probably laughed about me. And after my "hero" had made his escape, Freddie came to see if he could be equally lucky.'

Lord Beaudon could restrain himself no longer. He swore comprehensively, then took his daughter in his arms and held her closely. 'My poor child! May Cassandra Shelwood rot in hell! Why the devil did I ever let her keep you?'

'She couldn't have stopped me falling in love, Papa. I did that all by myself.'

'But you wouldn't have been so vulnerable. Did you. . . did you never see him again? Not Freddie—the other man.'

'Oh, yes! As soon as he heard I had inherited the Shelwood fortune! He couldn't wait to come to see me again. I understand why—I knew he was poor, he had told me himself. But, on that occasion, even he couldn't bring himself to pretend he loved me. He talked of a "communion of spirit", was kind enough to offer me marriage as a form of protection from fortune hunters! He appeared to have no doubt that I would accept his offer. I was. . .humiliated by his assumption that I was stupid enough, still besotted enough to marry him!' Francesca's voice trembled. 'I am ashamed to remember what happened next, Papa.'

'Go on.'

'I have always tried to keep my feelings under control,

whatever the provocation. I take pride in the fact.'

'I had noticed,' said Lord Beaudon drily.

'It was the only way to survive with Aunt Cassandra. But he. . .it was strange—it was as if I had no barrier to put up with him, whatever I felt. So when he tried to deceive me yet again. . .I tried to stay calm, to dismiss him with d-dignity, but. . . He stood there, Papa, so complacent, with such confidence! And I lost my temper. I can't remember exactly what I shouted at him, but I was unforgivably rude. I don't think he'll come back. I certainly never wish to see him again.'

'My child!'

'It's all right, Papa. It hurt at the time—it even hurt when he came back, though I knew him for what he was. I'm over it now. But that is why I want to marry someone. . .kind. Safe. Someone I can respect, but not anyone who will make me so stupidly fond. . .not ever again.'

But Francesca's wish never to see Marcus again was not to be granted. And once again, even after all the lessons on deportment and correct behaviour, she discovered that Marcus possessed the power to strip away her calm veneer, to reveal the tempestuously impulsive creature beneath. It was not a comfortable sensation.

On the few occasions she was left to her own devices, Francesca took to riding or driving in the woods and lanes round Packards. She was interested to visit the various farms on her father's estate and compare them with Shelwood. This was one interest that her father did not share with her, so, after an initial introduction to his agent, he left her to her own devices. Since she was always accompanied by her groom who knew the district well, Lord Beaudon's mind was easy.

On one such occasion she drove over to Brightwells',

a large farm on the farther side of the estate, and was surprised to find that Samuel, her groom, was the younger son of the house. The family were delighted to welcome them both, especially as it was Mrs Brightwell's birthday.

When the time came for them to leave, Francesca could see that Sam's mother was disappointed not to have her son at the feast that was due to take place that afternoon, and insisted that Sam should stay. She could quite well find her way back to Packards without him. Thus it was that Francesca started off for home on her own—something she had been well used to at Shelwood.

The road was deserted, for the day was cold, though the sun was shining, but Francesca revelled in the fresh air, and the unexpected sense of freedom. In the enjoyment of her new life, she had not realised how much she missed some pleasanter aspects of her old one, when no one had been in the slightest concerned what she did. The road ran alongside the forest, and she slowed down to admire the huge trees that lined the way. She could see a small clearing off the road a little way ahead and decided to risk pulling in for a short while. But as she drew nearer, she saw that someone was there before her.

A carriage was standing on the edge of the forest, with a groom in livery in attendance. He had his hands too full to notice her—the horses were restless, and it was taking all his skill to keep them under control. Francesca was puzzled. What was such a splendid equipage—for the carriage was a handsome one, and the horses a magnificent pair of matched bays—doing here in this remote spot? She drew up behind the trunk of a large oak tree and watched.

Now she became aware that the noise of the groom's efforts to pacify his horses had been drowning other, more menacing, sounds. An altercation was taking place in the forest, and she could hear a girl's voice raised in distress.

They were coming nearer, and Francesca heard the girl cry out.

'Leave me alone! You're hurting me! Leave me alone, I say!'

Francesca started up in her seat. What was happening?

Then a man's voice exclaimed in pain, 'Ouch! You little vixen! By God, I'll make you sorry for that, Charlotte!'

Two figures came out of the trees, a tall man, half-carrying, half-dragging a young girl towards the carriage. The girl was kicking and shouting, and the man's face was black with fury, his voice trembling with rage, but even so Francesca recognised him. With horror she realised that the abductor was Marcus! It couldn't be! Oh, dear heaven, surely it couldn't be! Even he could not stoop so low!

'Please don't make me go with you! I don't want to go with you!' The girl was sobbing with fear.

'Don't be such a fool, Charlotte! You know I'm stronger than you, so why keep on fighting me? It won't be half as bad as you fear!'

'It will, it will!'

'Oh get in, girl, and spare me these histrionics!' Francesca hardly knew Marcus's voice, it was so harsh. But what was she to do? She must do something to save the girl, but what? Marcus and the groom between them could easily foil any attempt at rescue.

But at the very moment when Francesca had decided to drive forward and risk the consequences, fate intervened. Some birds, which had been roosting in the trees above the carriage, suddenly flew up in a swirl of fluttering wings. One of the bays took strong exception to this and reared up, knocking the groom to the ground. Marcus let the girl go and ran to his servant's aid, ducking under dangerously flailing hooves to drag the man clear. The girl, left unchecked for a moment, looked wildly round, obviously wondering which way to go.

'Quickly, girl! Here!' Francesca cried. With a sob of relief, the girl ran to the phaeton, and with Francesca's aid scrambled into it. Francesca gave her horses a crack of the whip and they careered off along the the high road, leaving Marcus still wrestling with his horses.

The girl sank back into the seat and burst into tears. Francesca glanced down sympathetically, but was too busy to comfort her. She was encouraging her horses to go faster than ever before, for she had seen the groom getting to his feet as they had passed the carriage. It was some miles to the next village and she must make every effort to get there before they were overtaken. It would not be long before the two men would set off after them, and her horses were no match for those bays! But as she whipped her horses to ever greater effort, her thoughts were in turmoil.

She had known that Marcus was a rogue and a fortune hunter, but this latest exploit was villainous! She could still hardly believe it. The girl was no more than sixteen— if that! But then, she reminded herself, she had been less than sixteen when he would have seduced her, a more willing victim than the girl beside her. Oh, Marcus! How could you, how could you be so wicked! And why am I foolish enough to be made so miserable by it?

She drove on, immersed in her own unhappy thoughts, till a small voice beside her said, 'I must thank you, ma'am.' The girl had recovered and was now looking at Francesca in grateful, if surprised, admiration. Francesca pulled herself together.

'I was glad to help you. . . Charlotte, is it? It was fortunate that I happened to be passing. But we are not clear yet, I am afraid. I shan't be happy till we have reached civilisation.'

Charlotte turned round and looked fearfully back down

the road. 'I can't see anyone yet,' she said. 'Oh, please drive faster, ma'am! He mustn't catch me again.'

'I'll do my best. What is your name, child?'

There was a slight pause. 'Charlotte... Johnson, ma'am.'

Francesca glanced down. The dark blue eyes were guileless, but the girl was lying. She decided to let it pass for the moment. No doubt the child was shaken by her experience—her hands were trembling. What a fiend Marcus was! 'I think you may relax a little now, Charlotte,' she said calmly. 'My home is not far away. I shall take you there and then we shall decide what to do with you. Where do you live?'

Another pause. 'In London. I was waiting to take the stage coach to London. But he took all my money away from me and now I can't pay the fare.'

'You were travelling *stage* to London?' Francesca's hands tightened on the reins, but she spoke calmly. 'Forgive me, but I find that hard to credit. You mustn't be frightened of me, my dear. I shall help you all I can, but I must know the truth. Now tell me where you really live.'

'But if I do, you'll send me back! I can't go home again, I can't! I won't!' The childish voice rose in panic.

'Will your family not be worried about you?' asked Francesca.

'They won't care! They want to send me away, anyway.'

'Send you away? Where?'

'Back to the seminary. That's why I ran away.'

Francesca began to fear that this affair was not quite as simple as she had thought. Had Marcus encouraged the girl to run off with him? Or had she asked him to help her and then changed her mind when faced with the consequences—in which case Marcus might not be quite as villainous as she had thought? She shook her head impatiently—what was wrong with her? She was mad to try to find excuses for him! Whichever way it was, that scene in the forest had been very ugly. But. . .there was something odd about the affair. She drew up and turned to face her protégée.

'Charlotte—'

'Why have you stopped?' the girl cried, her voice shrill with fear. 'They'll catch up with us!' She reached over to take the reins, but Francesca took them firmly into her own hands again.

'Before we go on, I should like some answers, Charlotte. I would like to know your real name. I would like to know why you were on your way to London on a stage coach. And I would like to know the part played in all this by the man back there.'

'But he's coming! I can hear the carriage!'

'I have been thinking—he can't harm you while I am here. I know him, you see. He won't dare try to take you away again.'

'He will! Mama asked him. Oh, you don't *understand*—'

'You are quite right. I don't,' said Francesca, and watched with foreboding as the bays swept to a halt alongside the phaeton. Marcus handed the reins to the groom with a word, and strode over.

Chapter Seven

'Get down, Charlotte,' Marcus said grimly. 'Or, by God, I'll give you the hiding you deserve.'

Francesca rallied at these threatening words. 'One moment, sir!'

Marcus turned his attention to her. 'Good God!' he exclaimed. 'Francesca! Francesca Shelwood! What the *devil* are you doing here? And what the hell do you mean by racing off with this brat? Are you mad?'

Francesca did not allow herself to be intimidated by the outrage in his voice. She said coldly, 'I understand your annoyance at having your plans frustrated, sir, but surely your language is immoderate? Is this the manner in which you usually address ladies of your acquaintance?'

'Ladies of my acquaintance do not usually romp about the countryside unattended, interfering in matters which do not concern them. Now, I have better things to do than to bandy words with a madwoman, so if you will kindly remain quiet while Charlotte transfers to my carriage. . .'

Francesca was rapidly losing her temper. He was so dismissive, so coolly confident that she would do just what he asked! A madwoman indeed! She strove to keep calm as she said, 'I shall do nothing of the kind! The matter concerns me deeply, indeed it does. You forget that I know you for what you are, sir! How could I stand by and listen to this child's screams, watch while you dragged her to your carriage, and do nothing about it? I will most certainly not remain quiet. . .nor am I a mad-woman!' In spite of herself, her voice rose on this last sentence.

She took a deep breath and went on, 'In fact, I fully intend to take her to my home and, after she has recovered from the fright she has suffered at your hands, I shall restore her to her family. You will now allow us to drive on, if you please.'

Marcus looked at her incredulously. He seemed ready to give her a blistering response, then his face suddenly softened and he burst out laughing. 'I see now what you think. . . Oh, Francesca, Francesca! Still leaping in where angels fear to tread? How refreshing to discover that the years have not changed you, after all!'

Puzzled by this extraordinary response, Francesca stared at him. The warmth of his tone, the memory evoked by these words transported her back to the day on the hill above Shelwood, to a world of sunshine and hope, of love and laughter. She gazed in fascination at Marcus, his face transformed into that of the young man of long ago. She began to smile in return, but then she remembered his betrayal so soon after, of her misery and disillusion in the weeks and years that followed, culminating in that cynical proposal at Shelwood.

'Nor have they changed you, Marcus,' she said bitterly. 'If I remember correctly, I was about this girl's age when I was unfortunate enough to meet you. But, unlike her, I had no one to protect me.'

He reddened, but said, 'Charlotte needs no protection from me.'

'That is a matter of opinion, sir! But I have no wish to waste any more time on a villain such as you. Make way, if you please!' And Francesca raised her whip.

Marcus leapt forward and took a firm hold of her wrist. They stared at one another in silence. Then he said softly, 'Charlotte, tell Miss Shelwood who you are.'

Charlotte had been gazing at them in wonderment, too interested in what was being said to attempt to run away. She said accusingly, 'She said her name was Beaudon!'

Francesca looked down at her. 'And you said your name was Johnson.' Charlotte was silenced.

'Are you going to tell Miss. . . Beaudon who you are, or shall I?'

Subdued, the girl said, 'Charlotte Chelford, ma'am.'

Marcus, still clasping Francesca's wrist, looked at her with scorn. 'Are you ashamed of your name, Charlotte Chelford? You have no reason to be. And, my girl, unless you mend your ways, it will be the Chelfords who won't wish to acknowledge *you*!' He turned his attention to Francesca. 'As for you, ma'am, I suggest you return to Packards—for that is where you must be staying if you're claiming the name of Beaudon—and be content that I don't pursue the matter further.' He dropped her wrist and turned back to Charlotte.

Francesca was bewildered. Marcus was certainly not behaving as a man discovered in a criminal act might be expected to behave. Had she indeed made a terrible mistake?

She looked at Charlotte, who suddenly clasped her hands together and exclaimed, 'Please, Uncle Marcus, *please* don't take me back to the seminary.' The expression in her eyes would have melted a heart of stone, but Francesca was too shocked to notice.

'*Uncle*!' she exclaimed. '*Uncle* Marcus?'

'Yes, madam busybody, I have the misfortune to be Charlotte's uncle.'

'Her uncle! Oh, heavens, I thought. . .'

'You thought. . .?'

'I was under the impression that you were. . .' Francesca paused, then she said miserably, 'It looked as if you were abducting her.'

'I thought as much.' He looked at her with a wry smile. 'You must tell me some time, Francesca, what I did to give you such a very low opinion of my character. Nine years is a long time to carry such a grudge, wouldn't you say?'

Francesca bit her lip and said nothing.

Marcus sighed, then looked at Charlotte, who was regarding them both with fascination. He went on, 'I would like to pursue the matter with you, but this isn't the time. My first concern must be to deliver Charlotte to her long-suffering mother—'

'To Mama? Not back to the seminary?'

'I shall see if I can persuade your mama to keep you at home—perhaps with yet another governess. You must promise to treat this one better than the others.'

'I can really go home again to stay? You're not sending me back to the seminary?'

'A ladies' seminary, however famous, is obviously even less able to deal with you than your family, you wretched child,' said Marcus severely. Then he spoilt the effect by adding, 'And I am sure your mama doesn't wish you to be unhappy. But you must promise me that there will be no more escapades, Carrie. Your mother has had enough to bear.' He waited until Charlotte nodded, and then he smiled. 'Now, get into the carriage and I'll take you home. Er. . .are you going to take your leave of Miss Beaudon?'

Charlotte took Francesca's hand and said earnestly, 'I do thank you, Miss Beaudon. Even though my uncle laughed at you, I think you were a heroine!'

Marcus laughed again. 'Things that might have been better put! Now get into the carriage, you minx!' Charlotte got down and went quietly enough across to her uncle's carriage. Marcus looked up at Francesca. 'Will you give me your hand, Francesca?' Almost without volition she extended her hand. He took it and held it while he went on, 'I apologise for my harsh words. You thought something was wrong, and you, being you, had to do something about it. Will you forgive me?'

She nodded, unable to say a word. He took a breath, hesitated, then said, 'Can't we be friends, Francesca? You are at Packards, I take it? May I call on you there?'

Francesca snatched her hand away. 'No!' she said violently. His face darkened, and she strove to speak more calmly. 'That is to say. . .I think it is better if we do not meet again. I have nothing to say to you. I may have been mistaken on this occasion, but my opinion of you remains the same.'

'This is ridiculous!'

'Good day, sir.'

He took hold of her wrist again, so tightly that it hurt. 'Take care you do not become like your aunt, Miss Beaudon! This obstinate prejudice against me is absurd, and when you are accepted into society you will discover just how absurd it is!'

'I do not expect to mix in the same circles as you, sir. Lady Forrest need expect no competition from me!'

He looked at her inscrutably, then he released her and shrugged his shoulders. He moved towards his carriage, saying, 'I do not intend to argue with you, but I must insist on one thing. We will go with you to the edge of the forest. You are not yet as familiar with this area as I am, and I assure you it is unwise for you to travel here alone. You should engage someone to accompany you if you intend to drive out much.'

Francesca did not bother to tell him that she already had a groom, nor that her father had already given her the same warning. She was desperate to escape from him. His presence was working the same old magic and she wanted none of it. She said curtly, 'Thank you. Good day, sir,' and whipped up her horses. The carriage followed her till they came to the village near Packards, then it swept past and went on its way.

Francesca found it impossible to put this encounter with Marcus out of her mind in the weeks that followed. Furthering her acquaintance with Marcus had never seemed so desirable, nor so dangerous. One moment she congratulated herself on having turned him away, and the next found her passionately regretting having done so.

For some time she had been ashamed of her extraordinary outburst at their last meeting at Shelwood. It had been unworthy of her. Hurt and angry herself, she had been unpardonably rude, had insulted and enraged him. And in the forest she had given him further reason to be angry with her. But he had seemed willing to overlook it all, to be prepared to begin again, had offered her friendship. . . Had she misjudged him?

Then Francesca would scornfully revile herself for being so spineless. Of course she hadn't! It was all perfectly simple. She had a fortune. Marcus had not. It wasn't at all difficult to see why he had been willing to overlook her mistake, had smiled instead of frowning, had offered her friendship instead of expressing justifiable anger at her interference. Not at all difficult. He was still hoping to marry the Shelwood fortune.

But, under any circumstances, friendship was the last thing she wanted from him. She could hate him for what he had done. She could, if the circumstances had been different, have loved him with all her heart. But friendship? Never! She must obliterate the little scene in the forest from her mind, and forget him. And sometimes, in the bustle of preparations for her introduction to the great world, she even occasionally succeeded.

If Francesca's introduction to Society was not quite as sensational as her fond father had prophesied, it was certainly very satisfactory. Mrs Canfield, true to her word, arranged several small gatherings during the early months of the year to give the girls some experience, and Society's approval of Miss Beaudon and Miss Canfield was immediate. Some less charitable souls wondered aloud if Mrs Canfield had offered to sponsor tall, blonde, elegant Miss Beaudon because she knew what an effective contrast the girl provided for her own lively, dark-haired daughter, but Mrs Canfield was generally so respected that these remarks were ignored.

They were invited everywhere. Mrs Canfield had the entrée to even the highest circles, and, in addition, Society was highly intrigued that Richard Beaudon should reappear after so many years with a daughter in whom he clearly took so much pride. London's hostesses were eager to learn all they could about the legendary Rake Beaudon, and Mrs Canfield was subjected to many an inquisition. She was her usual discreet self, merely saying enough to establish that Lord Beaudon was a reformed character, interested only in seeing his daughter take her rightful place in society.

'I never thought I should live to see Rake Beaudon doing the pretty at an occasion like this,' said an elderly dowager to Mrs Canfield one evening at Almack's. 'He would have died of boredom in the old days. And how he persuaded the patronesses to receive him, I cannot imagine.'

'Come, Lady Clayton, you should show more charity,' said Mrs Canfield with a teasing smile. 'I can answer for the fact that he has reformed. It must be a good twenty-five years since Lord Beaudon scandalised London society.'

'And what has he be doing since then, I'd like to know? I suppose the chit really is his daughter?'

'Most certainly she is, ma'am!'

'Well, there's no need to get on your high horse. You're too young to remember Rake Beaudon in his prime. There's nothing he wouldn't have dared. But I suppose you wouldn't be sponsoring the girl if there was anything amiss—and she is remarkably like him. Where's her mother? And who was she?'

'Lady Beaudon died some time ago, but she was a Shelwood before she married.'

'Shelwood? I've not heard of them.'

'They're quite a respectable Buckinghamshire family, but they always lived very quietly. I don't think they ever came to London.'

'Hmm. I expect the Shelwood girl was an heiress— Rake Beaudon wouldn't have married her otherwise.'

'On the contrary, I understand that Sir John Shelwood cut his daughter off without a penny when she married Lord Beaudon. He approved of his son-in-law even less than you.'

'Oh, I didn't disapprove of Beaudon, my dear. Like all the rest of us, I fell in love with him, but my mother had more sense than to let him near me. And it looks as if he hasn't lost the art of pleasing even after all these years— just look at Sally Jersey, she's positively flirting with him! He is still very handsome, of course. So is the girl—pity the Beaudon fortune is so small.'

Mrs Canfield smiled but did not contradict Lady Clayton. The world would eventually learn that Francesca's fortune was not limited to what her father could give her, but meanwhile she should be given time to find the man of consideration and honour she desired to marry. Once the extent of her fortune was known, she would be pursued by other, less noble characters.

This conversation was one of many similar ones, but since Mrs Canfield kept her counsel, Francesca and Lydia were free to enjoy the popularity which their own charm brought them, and susceptible gentlemen in Society were soon debating which lady was more worthy of their devotion—the divinely fair Miss Beaudon or the vivaciously dark Miss Canfield.

They were invited everywhere and met everyone of note. Everyone, that is, except Lord Carne. He was apparently away, for Society saw nothing of him, and it was rumoured that he was employed on some Foreign Office business in France. Lydia and Mrs Canfield were disappointed, but the name meant nothing to Francesca and, though she sympathised with Lydia, she was personally unaffected by his absence.

'I know you wish me to meet this paragon, Lydia, but surely, if he is as eligible as you say, he would regard me with indifference?'

'But Lord Carne is not like that at all, Francesca! He is the kindest of men—is he not, Mama? And whatever Mama may say, I think you would be an ideal match for him. Oh, why doesn't he come? I do so wish he were here! He promised to dance with me at my début!'

'I'm sure he will keep his promise to you, Lydia,' said Mrs Canfield with a sympathetic smile. 'But you must try for a little patience, my dear—the season has hardly started yet. And it does not become you to be gazing round every five minutes, as you were last night at Lady Carteret's, to see if Lord Carne is present.'

'No, Mama.'

Francesca took this conversation to heart, for she too had been guilty of such behaviour, though it had not been to seek out Lord Carne, nor had it been with Lydia's eager anticipation. Wherever she went, she was unable to prevent her eye from wandering through the crowds, looking in apprehension for a tall lithe figure, to stop herself from listening for the deep, warm tones of the man she had dismissed so summarily from her life. Marcus.

She smiled ruefully. Once, she remembered, she had passionately wished to be powerful, rich and beautiful enough to give him a set-down. Well, she was now rich enough, and though she would never consider herself beautiful, others admired her. But did she have the power? Could she give Marcus the set-down he deserved? She doubted it. She was not certain how to deal with him at all when they met in Society—as they surely would. But her training in difficult social situations was not put to the test. To her great relief, she told herself, she never saw him, however diligently she watched and listened.

Apart from this, Francesca found that she was enjoying London life, though after a while she began to wonder whether she would ever find the husband she sought. Mrs Canfield saw to it that she was introduced to a number of respectable gentlemen, and one or two of them seemed more than ready to regard Miss Beaudon as a future wife.

But though Francesca acknowledged their worth, she found it impossible to take any of them seriously. Mr Caughton was both respectable and reasonably rich, but the poor man was very dull! Lord Banford was more amusing, but he brayed like a horse—she couldn't possibly live with that. Sir Jeremy Sharp was handsome enough if you liked blond men, but she found his uncritical admiration definitely cloying. Though she had no intention of falling in love again, the prospect of living in intimacy with anyone she had met so far appalled her— she was apparently more difficult to please than she had thought!

Meanwhile, the approval of the world around her was balm after all the years spent as an outcast, and it was very pleasant to go to balls and routs, to walk, drive and ride in the Park, to visit the shops whenever she wished, and, above all, to be accepted for her own sake. So she decided to put aside the question of her future, and enjoy for the moment all that life in London had to offer.

This state of affairs was not to last much longer. One evening at the theatre with her father, Francesca became aware that she was being stared at by a lady and gentleman a short distance away, and when she turned to see who it was she recognised Lady Forrest and Freddie. Though it was a shock, Francesca looked away again as indifferently as she could. But apparently it was not enough to put them off.

'Forgive me, but have we not met before?' Lady Forrest had come over, followed by a reluctant Freddie. She was smiling, but her eyes were appraising Francesca, as if she could not quite believe what she saw. Then her look shifted to Lord Beaudon and the smile became more practised. This, her admiring gaze told him, was someone worthy of her attention. Lord Beaudon remained unaffected. He had taken in Lady Forrest's opulent charms and Freddie's slightly seedy air, and lost no time in removing his daughter from both.

'I rather think not,' he said coldly, and, taking Francesca's arm, led her firmly away. Francesca gasped at this snub, but was quite content to go with him.

'You didn't know them, did you?' he asked after they were safely back in their box. 'They're certainly not the sort you ought to know. Raffish, both of them.'

'We were never introduced, if that's what you mean, Papa,' said Francesca. 'I. . .have come across them when they visited Witham Court.' He gave her a sharp look, and she nodded. 'The gentleman was Freddie. Lady Forrest I met more recently when she was on her way there. I have no desire to know either of them any better. Thank you for rescuing me—I had no idea you could be so. . .so. . .'

'Ruthless? Oh, I know all the ways of dealing with undesirables, my dear. I was one of them myself in the old days! But if I'd known who that fellow was, I might have been considerably less courteous.'

'*Courteous*? Is that what you call it?' asked Francesca with a laugh that caused her father to smile in return. 'Then I'm glad you didn't know who he was. And I'd far rather forget all about both of them.' And in her enjoyment of the play afterwards, she did indeed forget the encounter.

But the damage had been done. Charlie Witham was told of the incident when Lady Forrest next saw him.

'I could *hardly* believe it, Charlie. It was Lord Beaudon with her—I asked Freddie. What a *rude* man he is, for all he's so handsome! But it *must* be Fanny Shelwood, it *must*. What a *transformation*!'

'A little beauty, give you my word,' said Freddie. 'Good mind to take up where I left off, money or no money.' This enthusiasm did not please Lady Forrest.

'She's still as skinny as a rake, of course,' she said coldly. 'And basically as plain as ever, I suppose. But her clothes! Where did she get the means to dress herself at Fanchon? And the pearls she was wearing were worth a small *fortune*. I am *dying* to know, Charlie. Didn't you say that Lord Beaudon was her father? Is he really foisting his love-child on the *ton*?'

'He's capable of it. But it don't sound like his sort of caper. I wonder whether we've been wrong all these years. . .I'll see what I can find out, Charmian. I'll put Withers on to it right away.'

Withers worked to good effect, and such details as were not available through official documents he ferreted out elsewhere. Charlie Witham could hardly wait to spread the news. An heiress loose in London, with such a colourful story behind the scenes! A long-lost father, a vengeful aunt, poverty, deprivation and the sudden acquisition of enormous wealth. . . In no time, the whole of London was humming with the details of Francesca Beaudon's past history. And, what was more to the point for some of them, her present riches.

Poor Francesca became an object of universal sympathy, curiosity, and ambition, inundated with invitations on every side, pursued relentlessly by every gazetted fortune-hunter in London. Her father was furious, and he, Mrs Canfield, Lydia and a small circle of true friends rallied round to protect her. But their powers were limited. Short of remaining indoors, there was no way Francesca could avoid the unwelcome attentions of gentlemen who had ignored her when they thought that the Beaudon fortune was all she could look forward to.

The self-control she had learned as a child helped her to remain calm, in public at least, but her simple pleasure in London life was now at an end. It was almost the last straw when Marcus reappeared in London, and she found that all her brave resolutions had not diminished in the slightest her confusion of feelings about him. And it seemed inevitable that their meeting should be just as unexpected, every bit as unconventional as their former encounters.

Francesca had had enough! It was too bad! Evenings that had been so delightful just a few weeks before were turning into nightmares. She had looked forward to visiting Carlton House ever since Mrs Canfield had described its splendours. Besides, whatever they said about the Prince Regent, he was the leader of London Society, and it was an honour to be invited to one of his balls. But she had been sadly disappointed. The atmosphere was stifling in the crowded rooms, and though the furnishings were every bit as magnificent as Mrs Canfield had said, Francesca found them slightly overdone.

The Prince himself was not at all as she had imagined him—handsome, witty, and regal. Instead she was faced with a corpulent gentleman, whose clothes were too tight and too elaborate, and who was so heavily complimentary to her that she blushed in spite of her famous cool reserve. He insisted on holding her hand for far too long, and then introduced her to a tall, saturnine gentleman who was standing near by, whose cold eyes were appraising her in a manner which caused her to feel rather like a horse complete with a price tag stuck to her forehead.

'Lord Coker has been asking who the beautiful young lady in the blue dress is, Miss Beaudon. He's a great friend of mine so—may I tell him?' the Prince asked with a roguish look.

'Of course, sir. I am honoured,' was Francesca's dutiful reply.

'Miss. . .Beaudon? Charmed t'meet you,' drawled Lord Coker with marked lack of interest. There was a slight pause then, somewhat puzzled, Francesca curtsied and moved away. She joined Mrs Canfield and Lydia, and together they went through to the ballroom.

'You look serious, Francesca. Was the Prince Regent not as you imagined?'

'It is always strange to meet someone so famous in the flesh, ma'am,' was Francesca's diplomatic reply. 'But tell me about Lord. . .Coker, was it?'

Mrs Canfield looked disapproving. 'He is a great friend of the Prince, of course. But I would regard him as an undesirable acquaintance for my daughter. He can be charming. . .'

'I did not find him so.'

'No, he did not set himself to please you, did he?'

Francesca laughed. 'Why on earth should he?'

'It is said he is in search of a wife. And Lord Coker's wives are always rich.'

'Mrs Canfield! How many has the poor man had?'

'Save your sympathy for the two first Lady Cokers. Neither of them was a happy woman. Francesca, I am very content that Lord Coker appeared to ignore you. Do not seek his acquaintance. He is a dangerous man to cross. The Prince Regent is capricious, but at the moment Lord Coker is undoubtedly enjoying his favour, and it gives him a great deal of undeserved power.'

Francesca could hardly believe that her friend, normally so moderate, so restrained in her judgements, could be so harsh. But she soon forgot Lord Coker in her enjoyment of the conversation and dancing that followed. Later on, however, when she was sitting quietly, half-hidden in one of the many alcoves, his indifference to her was accounted for.

Lord Coker and a companion came strolling through the room, observing the dancers. They did not notice Francesca behind them, and through some trick of the acoustics in the room their conversation was perfectly audible to her. Wine had perhaps made them less cautious than they might have been.

'Why on earth you've dragged me away from the best run of luck I've had in weeks, just to watch all this cavorting, I cannot imagine, Coker! What the devil are you at?'

'I need to find the demned Shelwood filly. I've been looking for her all night, but I haven't seen a trace! How can I fix my confounded interest with her if I don't even meet her?'

'Of course you've met her! Prinny introduced you not an hour ago. Damned civil of him, if you ask me.'

'When? Which one was she?'

'The tall blonde girl in blue.'

'That's Beaudon's daughter.'

'She may be Beaudon's daughter, but she's the Shelwood heiress all the same. Shelwood was her grandfather.'

'The devil he was? So she is an heiress, after all. Damn it! I was looking for someone called Shelwood, and when the Prince introduced us, I thought he was amusing himself at my expense with the Beaudon filly. You know his way. Confound it! I may have made a slight error there.'

The other chuckled. 'You were more than a touch uncivil to the lady. You'll have to exercise all your famed address to reinstate yourself when you do find her.'

'You think I can't?'

'Miss Beaudon doesn't look like your usual emptyheaded debutante. You might find it harder than you think.'

'A wager, Felton?'

'On what? That you'll marry her?'

'I intend to do so, of course. But at the moment, my aim is to get her to dance with me.'

'Oh, I shan't bet on that. All you'd have to do is to ask Prinny to present you to her as a partner—and he'd do it for you, too! You're very much in favour at the moment.'

'I won't ask him to present me, and I shall dance with the girl before the supper interval. Will you take me on?'

'That's only half an hour away... You won't do it, Coker! Five guineas that you can't.'

'Fifteen minutes would be enough, but we will leave it at the half-hour. And we'll make it ten guineas.'

'You won't do it, y'know. Miss Beaudon is well known to be difficult to please, and you started off very badly.'

'I'll do it with ease, and enjoy it. The ten guineas are as good as mine. But first we must find the chit. Getting her away from Maria Canfield will be the hardest part. You seem to know something about the heiress, Felton. Tell me about her. . .'

Chapter Eight

They wandered away and Francesca was left to fume alone in her alcove. To be the subject of such a conversation, to hear men making a wager on her future behaviour disgusted her, and she spent some minutes recovering her temper. Her first impulse was to find Mrs Canfield and then leave Carlton House, but cooler reflection persuaded her that this was impossible. What reason could she possibly give for such discourtesy to her royal host? That one of his closest friends had insulted her? Impossible!

Besides, it was said that Lord Carne was coming to Carlton House on his return from Paris and Lydia had been in high spirits all day because of it. She could not deprive the girl of her chance to meet her hero again. No, flight was not possible, so she must simply find Mrs Canfield and stay close to her for the rest of the evening— that might be protection enough.

Unfortunately, her plan was foiled from the outset. She saw Mrs Canfield at the far end of the room and got up to join her. But she had gone little more than a few paces when she was confronted with the very man she hoped to avoid.

'Miss Beaudon!'

Francesca looked coldly at him and nodded.

He smiled. 'I have looked for you everywhere. I wish to explain. . .'

'You must excuse me, Lord Coker. I am on my way to join Mrs Canfield.' Francesca made to walk past him.

'Then I will accompany you. It is hardly fitting that such an exquisitely elegant young lady should walk unprotected through these crowds.' He put up his glass and surveyed the scene with a look of contempt. 'One wonders how some of them got past the flunkeys.'

'It really isn't necessary. . .'

Taking Francesca firmly by the arm, he said, 'Come, Miss Beaudon. I see your friend only a few yards away.'

As they threaded their way through the throng, Lord Coker said, 'You are right, of course. Explanations are tedious. We will dispense with them. Ah, Mrs Canfield! I have your lovely protégée here, but I am in something of a dilemma.'

'A dilemma, Lord Coker?'

'You see, the Prince Regent, in his infinite wisdom and kindness, has asked me to look after one of your charges during the supper interval. But I hardly dare take Miss Beaudon away from you without first asking your permission. She is too modest to agree without it.'

'I assure you, Lord Coker—'

Ignoring Francesca's protest, he went on, smiling all the while with great charm at Mrs Canfield, 'Or should I offer to look after your lovely daughter, instead? The Prince would not wish me to ignore his orders entirely, you see.' He raised one eyebrow.

'But I. . . I. . . It is too much honour, Lord Coker. The Prince is very kind, but—'

'He likes his own way, too.' Lord Coker's smile grew a little steelier. Mrs Canfield threw a desperate look at Francesca as he went on, ''Pon my soul, ma'am, the choice is a difficult one. A golden goddess like Miss Beaudon here, or. . .' he turned to Lydia, who was standing by her mother looking awed at being addressed by the great Lord Coker '. . .Miss Canfield—a bewitching naiad in green. And so delightfully young.'

Lydia blushed and looked down, but she was smiling at his flattery.

Mrs Canfield stiffened and Francesca said hastily, 'I believe Lydia is already engaged for the supper interval, sir.' She looked at Lord Coker with delicate disbelief. 'But if the Prince has commanded—'

'I assure you on my honour he has, Miss Beaudon.' He looked at her, daring her to challenge his words. 'Do you wish me to take you to him?'

Francesca gave him a level look. 'I would not put you to so much trouble. I am sure the Prince is a loyal friend.'

'Then shall we go?' He offered her his arm; after a moment's hesitation, she curtsied to Mrs Canfield and took it.

Francesca was thinking hard as she walked away. She found it galling that Lord Coker was about to win his wager so easily. The minute they joined the throng on the ballroom floor he would be ten guineas the richer, and she would have helped him to it. Was there a way in which she could prevent his leading her on to that floor in the next half hour? She would certainly try.

'But, sir,' she said, smiling as charmingly as she could, 'did you not say that the Prince wanted you to take me to supper?'

He stopped and looked down at her. 'I did.'

'Then should we not go to the supper room rather than the ballroom?'

'I think not,' he said calmly. 'I am very self-indulgent, Miss Beaudon. I cannot deny myself the pleasure of a dance with you—indeed, a waltz with you. Come.' He would have walked on with her, but she removed her arm and stood where she was.

'Please, Lord Coker,' she said with another delightful smile. 'Do not indulge yourself at my expense. I am an indifferent dancer, but I love to talk—you have been described to me as one of the best conversationalists in London. And in addition, I am really very thirsty.' She looked at him under lowered lashes in what she hoped was a beguiling manner.

His thin lips twisted in a complacent smile at her pleading tones and he took firm hold of her arm. 'My dear,' he said, 'we shall talk all you wish. We have much to say to one another, I am sure.'

'Then—'

'But we shall dance first.'

Francesca felt her control slipping. 'I don't wish to dance, sir!'

His grip on her arm was cruelly tight. 'Nonsense, of course you do.' When she still pulled against his grip, he said softly, 'I can't believe you wish to make a scene here, my dear. Think what damage it would do you and your friends. . .' and without waiting any longer, he swept her into the circling throng.

Francesca endured, rather than enjoyed, the dance that followed. Lord Coker was expert enough, but, without holding her too obviously close, his grip on her waist, and in the twists and turns of the waltz, was both intimate and cruel. Nor did he release her afterwards. Before she realised it, he was leading her out of the ballroom.

'Lord Coker! Stop! Where are we going?' she cried, as they went through long doors into an apparently empty passage.

'You wished for refreshment? This is a less crowded route to the supper room. We shan't lose ourselves— I know Carlton House like the back of my hand.'

Suspicious, but unable to argue, Francesca allowed him to lead her down the passage. It was lined with furniture and *objects d'art*, but she was not allowed to linger.

They went through a hall, then along another passage and finally arrived at an entrance guarded by two flunkeys. At a nod from Lord Coker, they opened the doors and Francesca was led into one of the loveliest rooms she had ever seen. Furnished in blue velvet with touches of gold, the room was dominated by a magnificent chandelier. Forgetting her suspicions, she walked into the room, gazing at the pictures and ornaments, all in exquisite taste, which filled it. She was speechless with admiration.

'I see you like it.' Lord Coker had come up behind her and put his hands on her shoulders. Startled, she moved away and turned to face him.

'Thank you for showing me such a beautiful room, sir. Now, if you please, I should like to join the others in the supper room.'

'In a while,' he said.

'Now!'

'Come, Miss Beaudon. You surely don't imagine that I would take all this trouble to be alone with you just to show you a room! You expressed a very flattering wish for my. . .conversation. I thought we should manage better if we were private.' He took her hand and kissed it. 'The admiration you demonstrated for me before we danced has encouraged me to hope for even more.' He smiled with arrogant confidence.

Francesca moved towards the entrance. The doors were shut. Refusing to panic, she said coldly, 'Lord Coker, I think you mistake me. I am not in the habit of listening to anyone who tries to coerce me. I insist that these doors are opened immediately!'

'Admirably said! Well, I will let you go—'

With a sigh of relief, Francesca put her hand on the

ornate handle of the door. She was pulled back ungently and held in his arms.

'After you have heard me out.'

'Let me go!' she cried, struggling in vain to free herself. 'You must be mad, sir!'

'Not mad—merely in love.'

If Francesca had not been so frightened and angry, she would have laughed at the lack of any real feeling in these words. He could not have made his motive plainer. But the situation was none the less serious. Fear of this man, fear of the scandal should she be discovered in this private room with him, anger at his arrogance and conceit—all were fighting for supremacy. Anger won. She leaned back as far as she could and said coldly, 'If you do not release me this instant, Lord Coker, the world shall know you for the villain you are. I am not entirely without protectors.'

'My intentions are honorable, Miss Beaudon. I wish to marry you. And, if you were to spread tales about me, then you overestimate your influence in Society. The world saw you laughing and flirting with me in the ball-room. You came willingly enough. No, my dear. Telling the world would not harm me, and it would ruin you. Come, you shall listen to what I have to say—how much I admire you, and how ardently I wish you to be my wife. We shall forget your harsh words.' He pulled her head towards him and kissed her.

Outraged, she snatched up an ornament from the console table nearby and hit him with it. The vase shattered and he staggered with the blow. For a moment she was free. She fled to the far corner of the room, praying that the door she had seen there was not locked. It opened at her touch and she raced through and locked it from the other side, just as Lord Coker, snarling with rage, reached it. He was cursing her comprehensively and threatening her with ruin and destruction.

Francesca did not wait to hear. She fled through a
second door and a third, forced herself to walk swiftly
but calmly down a staircase thronged with people. But
though their presence offered some protection, she
doubted she could control the trembling in her limbs much
longer. She must seek out some quiet place where she
could recover. The doors at the far end of the conservatory
opened into the garden, and Francesca made for these,
desperate for fresh air and solitude. She snatched a glance
behind her.

Lord Coker was at the far end, by the staircase. He was
consulting a footman, who shook his head and pointed in
the other direction. She must escape before he turned and
saw her.

Abandoning decorum, Francesca slipped out and fled
in a panic down the garden. A bank of bushes lay to her
right. She stopped, gave another rapid glance behind to
make sure that she was unobserved, then darted to the
side—and ran straight into the tall figure of a gentleman,
who had apparently been enjoying the air, and indulging
in a cigar. The unexpected force of the collision caused
him to stagger, but he threw his cigar away and held
her firmly in his arms until they had both regained their
balance.

With no surprise at all, Francesca heard the deep, warm,
familiar tones say, 'Why! What a pleasant surprise! I
thought you never wished to see me again, Miss Beaudon.'

It was too much. Francesca gazed up at Marcus in
horror. It was humiliating enough that there had been a
witness to her unseemly behaviour and headlong flight,
but although she was somewhat overwrought by her scene
with Lord Coker, she could have controlled her feelings
with anyone else. But that she should meet Marcus again
in such circumstances. . .it was too much! She burst
into tears.

After an initial stiffening of surprise, Marcus gathered her more firmly to him and held her until gradually her sobs subsided and she was able to speak.

'You shouldn't. . .I must ask you. . . Please let me go. I'm sorry to make such an exhibition of myself.'

He released her instantly. 'What happened?' he said curtly.

For one moment Francesca was tempted to tell him. The feeling of security, of comfort she had experienced in his arms, was very seductive. But another moment's thought stopped her. If she told Marcus what had occurred in the Blue Velvet Room, he might involve himself on her behalf. Lord Coker was a powerful man. He would take it very badly if Marcus, whom he would regard as a nobody, questioned his behaviour. She had no wish to see Marcus hurt.

Even worse, Marcus himself might look embarrassed and make some excuse to leave her. That would mortify her beyond bearing. So she said, somewhat lamely, 'It. . . it was so hot in there. I was overcome.'

'Francesca, I'm not a fool. It must have been more than that. Considerably more to have so discomposed you. I have never seen you in tears before.'

The proximity of this man, and the events of the night, loosened her tongue. Her reply was almost involuntary.

'Haven't you?' she asked wryly. 'I assure you I have shed many in the past. But then, you were not there to see.'

They stared at one another, and as they looked the old magic took hold of her. When Marcus grasped her arms and drew her to him, she did not resist. And when he held her even more closely, she did not pull away, but buried her head in his shoulder. The sense of being where she belonged was immediate.

Oh, Marcus, she thought in despair, why do I feel this closeness with no other man? Is this why I have refused

all the others? Why I regard them as second-best, though
I know them to be good, kind men, so much more worthy
of my regard than you could ever be. They would never
hurt me as you have hurt me, yet I can feel nothing for
any of them. What have you done to my life, Marcus?
Why did we ever meet?

'Let me look at you, Francesca.'

She lifted her head. He was as handsome as ever, but
in the dim light reflected from the windows of Carlton
House he looked sombre, threatening even. The dark blue
eyes were shadowed, the beautiful mouth set in harsh
lines. A chill went down her spine and she shivered. His
hold tightened.

'Tell me what happened to put you in such a panic.'

'I. . .I can't. And I must not stay here like this. Please
let me go, Marcus.' He did not immediately release her
and with a sudden flare of spirit she wrenched herself out
of his arms and said angrily, 'This won't do! I must be
mad! I don't intend to escape from one seducer, merely
to fall into the arms of another!'

'Damn you, I'm no seducer!' he said fiercely. 'Of all
the pig-headed, obstinate women—'

Francesca interrupted what promised to be a notable
loss of temper by turning away to start back to the house,
but she stopped short when she saw the tall figure of Lord
Coker in the middle of the lawn. It was impossible to
avoid discovery. Her pale blue dress was luminous in the
darkness.

'Well now, what have we here? The lovely Miss
Beaudon, no less.' The words were harmless enough but
the tone was malevolent. 'Running away was very foolish,
my dear. It only arouses the hunter in every male. Or did
you know that already, you witch? Did you expect me,
perhaps? You have certainly chosen a delightfully
secluded spot.'

Lord Coker advanced towards her, and Francesca felt caught in a snare, unable to move. 'Shall we continue our highly interesting conversation, Miss Beaudon? Or shall we move on to other delights? Payment, let us say, for my injuries.' His white teeth gleamed in the darkness as he smiled. 'I promise you, I shan't let you get away so easily this time.'

Marcus took a step forward, though he was still in shadow. The movement caught Lord Coker's eye, and he said softly, 'The devil! So it wasn't modesty alone which caused you to flee my arms with such drastic determination, but an assignation in the garden. Well, well, well! The virtuous Miss Beaudon has more of her father in her than I thought!'

'Coker!' said Marcus curtly. Francesca put her hands to her cheeks. The confrontation she had feared was about to take place, and it was bound to prove disastrous for Marcus. Physically he was more than a match for his lordship, but he had nothing like Coker's political power and influence.

'What the devil——?' Lord Coker stopped in his tracks and stared in surprise, not unmixed with annoyance, at the tall figure before him. His eye turned to Francesca, then back to Marcus. 'I see! Not without protectors, you said. With some justification. No wonder you appeared so indifferent to my charms, my dear. This is a conquest any young lady would be pleased to flaunt.' Turning to Marcus, he drawled, 'I congratulate you on your turn of speed, my dear fellow. When was it you got back from Paris?'

'A few hours ago,' said Marcus curtly.

'One wonders when you've found the time to fix your interest with Miss Beaudon here. But one quite sees why. She has little idea how to behave but she's reasonably handsome—and so is her fortune. . .'

Marcus said softly, 'I don't think I understand what you mean, sir.'

Francesca was chilled by the menace in his voice.

The two men stared at each other for what seemed an eternity, then Lord Coker gave a laugh. 'I meant no harm. You must forgive my very natural chagrin at being denied a chance of furthering my acquaintance with one of the most desirable young ladies in London. Especially at being cut out by a man who hardly needs Miss Beaudon's. . .assets. You're as rich as a Nabob yourself. But what a stir this will create! The Nonpareil indulging in secret meetings in the gardens of Carlton House!'

'If I hear anything said linking Miss Beaudon's name with mine, you will hear from me, Coker. So guard your tongue.' This was said so peremptorily and so coldly that Francesca gasped and looked anxiously at Lord Coker. Had Marcus no sense? To address one of the the Regent's favourites in such a manner was to court disaster. But to her complete bewilderment, instead of threatening Marcus, as she would have expected, Lord Coker remained silent. What was going on?

Marcus offered her his arm and continued, 'Now I will finish what I was doing, which was to find Miss Beaudon and escort her back to her chaperon, before her absence from the ballroom is remarked on. As a close friend of her host, you will no doubt be shocked to hear that the behaviour of some villain or other forced her to seek refuge in the garden. . . Certainly the Prince would be furious at such an insult to a guest of his. Indeed, if he knew who the culprit was, he might even withdraw his favour from the fellow. Silence all round is called for, I believe.'

'Quite!' snapped Lord Coker.

'Good. Now, you will excuse us, I am sure, Coker.'

'I shan't forget this, Carne!' Then, with a lowering

glance at Francesca, Lord Coker gave a cursory bow, turned on his heel and strode up towards the house.

Marcus watched him go. Then he looked at Francesca, who had withdrawn her arm from his and now stood staring at him, a frown on her face.

'Did you wish me to challenge the fellow, Francesca? I'm sorry if I disappointed you, but I thought you would prefer to avoid the inevitable scandal if I did. Coker won't harm you again.'

'No, no! The matter is best forgotten. But. . .'

'But what?'

'Lord Coker called you Carne!'

'Yes, he did. Why are you surprised? It is my title.'

'B-but. . . That is impossible! Lydia talks of Lord Carne all the time! She cannot sing his praises loudly enough.' The incredulity in Francesca's voice was too much for Marcus.

He laughed out loud, then said solemnly, 'You must make allowance for Lydia's partiality. She adored her father and I was his friend. She will learn the truth in time.'

'But it's not only Lydia! Mrs Canfield. . .my father. . . all the rest. They all speak well of you! Indeed, they all admire you!'

'Mrs Canfield cannot think more highly of me than I do of her. Your father. . .I haven't yet met him, I believe. And as for the rest. . .' He shrugged his shoulders, and looked at Francesca with one eyebrow quirked. She was still shaking her head in disbelief.

His lips twitched and he went on gravely, 'I assure you that I am Carne. I inherited the title somewhat unexpectedly a few years after we first met.'

'But Lord Carne is rich, and you. . .you—'

'I was poor. Quite right. I inherited wealth together with the title. One doesn't normally mention such things, Francesca but, since we are talking so very openly, I will admit it—I am an extremely rich man. Rich as a Nabob, as Coker said.'

'I...see. That would account for some of it, I suppose...'

Marcus sighed and said ruefully, 'My popularity, you mean? I am sure you are right, though I know of no one else who would point that out with such brutal frankness. You don't mince matters, do you?'

Francesca did not hear him. She was still struggling to come to terms with this startlingly new situation. 'But it doesn't account for the admiration of the rest. I have heard good people—people I respect—talking well of you, describing you as a man of character.' She shook her head again in bewilderment. 'I cannot understand it.'

Marcus found that he was enjoying himself immensely. His voice was unsteady as he replied gravely, 'I can't account for it myself. It is gratifying to hear of it, of course. But don't worry, Francesca. I shan't suffer from conceit—not while you are there to redress the balance.'

At this Francesca stiffened and said accusingly, 'You are laughing at me, Lord Carne!'

He smiled and said, 'Only a little. It is quite refreshing, believe me, to find a lady in London who does not hang on my every word, whether it makes sense or not. But it is time to take you back to Mrs Canfield. Coker won't talk, at least not for a while, but others may notice you have been out of sight for too long. Shall we go back?' He offered his arm again and, with some reluctance, Francesca took it.

As they walked slowly up the lawns to the house, Marcus said, 'There must have been some considerable change in your fortunes, Francesca. Am I to understand that you and Lord Beaudon are now reconciled? He acknowledges you as his daughter?'

'He never denied it. It was my aunt who...refused to

believe that he had married her sister, and the neighbourhood, including the Witham Court set, took its lead from her. But she was. . .mistaken.'

'Mistaken? I doubt that.' Marcus flashed her a sceptical look, but she didn't see. Her mind was in turmoil. She had to ask, even though the subject was painfully embarrassing. 'Lord Carne, when you came to Shelwood. . . after my aunt had died. . .and. . .and offered for me. . .'

'Yes?' His tone was not encouraging, but she struggled on.

'Were you as rich then?'

'I told you. I inherited everything about four years ago. Why do you ask?'

Colour rose in Francesca's cheeks. How could she explain, when she didn't even know herself why it was so important?

He waited a moment, then drawled, 'I am not asking whether you have changed your mind, Francesca. The moment for that is past. But would your answer have been kinder, if you had known I was rich? Would you have treated me differently?'

'Of course I would!'

The look of cynicism on Marcus' face increased, but Francesca did not see it. She was not only totally unaware of the effect her words had on him, she hardly noticed indeed what she was saying, absorbed as she was in her own thoughts. Her resentment, her anger, the manner in which she had rejected him, had all been based on the belief that he would be marrying her for her money. Now she had just discovered that she had made another mistake about him—a more disastrous mistake than any of the rest. Whatever his motives in coming to seek her out at Shelwood, acquiring her fortune had not been one of them.

She had not only been shamefully insulting, she had been grossly unjust to him. Though she could still hardly

believe it, this man beside her, whom she had called a
rake and fortune-hunter, a seducer and abductor, was in
fact a polished leader of society, universally spoken of as
a man of integrity and wealth. An offer of marriage from
him must be regarded as a signal honour. Mrs Canfield
had called him a target for all the matchmakers in London.
'You have a better chance of marrying the man in the
moon!' her father had said.

But, in that case, *why* had he come to Shelwood? Had
she been wrong about his feelings? Had he genuinely
been in love with her all those years ago? And had his
love been re-awakened when he saw her again on the
road to Witham? Her eyes softened as she stole a glance
at him, a tentative smile on her lips. But he did not
respond. If anything, his face grew colder.

She took herself to task for idly dreaming the impossible. How could he possibly have fallen in love with her
again? In her old clothes covered in mud and weeds after
clambering out of that ditch, she had hardly represented
any man's ideal. He hadn't behaved as if he admired her,
and he certainly hadn't spoken like a man in love when
he had asked her to marry him. Indeed, she had had the
impression that she had hurt his dignity, not his feelings,
in refusing him.

But, *if it was not to gain a fortune, why had he come
at all?* She *had* to know. She turned to ask him, but was
astonished to see that he was, in fact, regarding her with
an expression of tired cynicism.

'Why. . .what are you. . .? Why are you looking at me
like that, Lord Carne?' she stammered.

'I suppose I had hoped for something better.'

'Better? What do you mean?'

'You made your opinion of me perfectly plain when
you refused me at Shelwood. I was surprised at your
vehemence, but I accepted that you did not like me enough

to marry me. I was disappointed to hear you say just now that, if you had known I was rich. . . But it's of no consequence. I had thought you would be different, that's all. Come, let me escort you to Mrs Canfield.'

The colour rose in Francesca's cheeks, but, restraining her impulse to answer him angrily, she said in her coolest tones, 'You think I would have accepted you had I known you were rich, whatever my opinion of your character?'

'Have you not just said so?'

'Indeed, no! You asked me if I would have *treated* you differently, had I known you were rich, Lord Carne, not whether my answer would have been different.'

'Aren't you splitting hairs?'

Francesca was losing the battle to stay calm. She said with a snap, 'Do you find it so impossible to believe that any woman could refuse an offer from the great Lord Carne? Allow me to tell you, my lord, that I find you impossibly conceited!'

'You have found me so many things in the past, Francesca, none of them flattering, that your insults now have very little power to offend me.'

His words reminded her that she owed him some apology. She took a deep breath and said formally, 'I have behaved very badly on several occasions, I know, and I have been at fault in jumping to conclusions about you. I now regret many of the things I have said, especially in the library at Shelwood, and I hope you will forgive me.'

He looked at her impassively, then nodded. 'Let it all be forgotten.'

'Not. . .not quite yet. There is something I still do not understand. I now know that your motives for coming to Shelwood were not what I thought. But. . .I am still puzzled. Why. . .why did you ask me to marry you after my aunt died?' Francesca held her breath, as she waited for his reply. It was not immediately forthcoming, so she went on, 'You did not appear to be in love with me—indeed, you said as much at the time.'

Marcus hesitated. He had broached this conversation impulsively, cynically almost. His pride had been badly hurt by her scornful refusal of him, and he wanted to hear her admit that she had been wrong to refuse such a splendid offer. So far she had not obliged him, and he now regretted opening the subject at all. His innate honesty compelled him to answer truthfully. 'Your situation seemed so hopeless. I cannot say that I was in love with you, but I was not in love with anyone else, either. I remembered our past association and thought we could build on that—'

'You were sorry for me,' said Francesca, cutting him short. She had known in her heart that he was not in love with her, but his words nevertheless had given her a pang. But no sign of this appeared as she said, 'Pray say no more, sir. Whatever the misunderstandings were—on either side—it was fortunate that they prevented us from entering into a marriage which could only have led to misery for both of us.'

She took a deep breath. It was all too painfully embarrassing. This conversation should never have started in the first place. He had been sorry for her! Sorry! The great Lord Carne willing to perform another of his charitable acts, to make a lovesick, idiot of a girl happy at last! Oh, no! There was no going back. She had been a fool to think otherwise. And if she wished to have any self-respect, any peace of mind, she must avoid him in the future, as far as that was possible.

'You still haven't told me what your answer would have been, Francesca.'

'You can hardly expect me to do so.' They had nearly reached the garden doors. 'I can't—I don't—' She was stammering like a schoolgirl! Francesca took a deep breath and began again. She said coolly, 'Lord Carne, pray let us forget what has been said tonight. I hope you will excuse my behaviour in the past. I have clearly misjudged you. In future. . .' She stopped, unable to continue.

Marcus regarded her with another slightly cynical smile. 'You will be kinder? Would like us to meet in order to explain how you have changed? Perhaps often?'

'What do you mean?'

'You are quite right, of course. "Marcus" was not good enough for you. But it cannot do you any harm at all to be seen in the company of Lord Carne, an eminently eligible member of the *ton*, the object of every match-making mama in Society!'

Francesca felt another surge of rage, but her training stood her in good stead. They were now in sight of other people. Her expression was calm and her voice low as she said, 'You were wrong, Lord Carne. It seems that even I cannot redress the balance of your conceit, nor, sad though it is to see it, have I any wish to do so.

'I was about to thank you for your protection tonight, and to say that I am ashamed of the things I said to you on that memorable day in the library. And, though your enormous self-esteem makes it unlikely you will believe me, I was also about to say that having made our peace, we should avoid each other as far as possible in the future. Because of the past I could never be easy in your company.'

They were now at the foot of the stairs. She raised her voice and said politely, 'Thank you for fetching me from the garden, Lord Carne, but pray do not let me keep you from your friends any longer. I am sure I can find Mrs Canfield for myself.' Then she gave a small curtsy and made her way up the stairs.

Chapter Nine

Marcus watched her go with a slight smile on his lips. Francesca wished to avoid his company, did she? He was not all convinced that he wished to avoid hers. You could say what you liked about Francesca Shelwood—or Beaudon, as she now was—conversation with her was never dull. Stimulating, appealing, infuriating—but never a bore. From what she had said, there was no danger that she regarded him as a prospective husband.

That was as well, for though he had sometimes been tempted to take a bride for the sake of the Carne name, the thought of marriage bored him beyond measure. The closest he had ever come to being in love—deeply in love—had been with Francesca herself all those years ago. But he had forgotten her in the time that followed, and he was now a very different man from the callow youth who would have thrown everything away for love.

His rash and quixotic gesture in offering for Francesca when her aunt died had resulted from a remnant of feeling for her, a sense of responsibility for her welfare. It had been very ill-judged. Thank God she had refused him! As she had said, they would both have regretted it.

But perhaps, for old times' sake, it would amuse him now to cultivate her a little, introduce her to his friends—

she might well find a reasonable match among them. The Beaudon fortune could not be very great, but not all the members of his circle were on the hunt for an heiress. One of them was sure to find her suitable—but who?

Marcus frowned. Some of them were sticklers—would they be put off by Francesca's behaviour? She could be very impulsive. . . But how could she know how to behave? Her training at Shelwood had not prepared her for life in Society. She was intelligent, she would learn. . . And she had been upset tonight by Coker's treatment of her. . .

Marcus's frown deepened. Coker might be one of the Prince Regent's gambling cronies, but he was a scoundrel all the same. What had he been up to with Francesca? It was out of the question, even for Coker, to think of making her his mistress, but the Beaudon fortune was hardly large enough to tempt him into marriage. His two previous wives had both been considerable heiresses.

Marcus shook his head decisively. Whatever lay behind Coker's interest in Francesca, he was certainly no fit companion for her; if no one else would stop the connection, then it was up to him to do so. . .she was much too good for Coker! The frown on Marcus's face gave way to a smile as he thought of Francesca. How lovely she had looked, even in her agitated state! Yes, he owed it to the past to keep an eye on her interests in London. She might yet make a reasonable match.

But when Marcus began to review his circle of acquaintance, he was surprised to find that the thought of any of them marrying Francesca repelled him. They made excellent friends, but each one of them lacked some quality or other which he considered essential for her happiness. Richard Caughton was a steady, kind fellow and he certainly wasn't hanging out for a rich wife. But it had to be said that he sometimes was rather a dull dog—Francesca would be bored with him in a month.

Vincent Tatham was much more the type for her—amusing, witty, polished. . .but would he cherish her when she was ill or unhappy? It was doubtful—he could be a bit of an unfeeling brute.

Monty Banford? Never! His taste was for a full-blown, obvious sort of beauty, and his mental processes were equally unsubtle. He would never appreciate Francesca's elusive charm.

What about George Denver? Now he was a distinct possibility. Plenty of address, nice little property in Kent, a very good fellow all round. . .but no, it wouldn't do! George simply wasn't up to her weight—she would walk all over him, and despise him for allowing it. He couldn't submit poor George to that. Who else was there? More names occurred to him, but each had something amiss. Devil take it! There wasn't one of them fit to marry her! Not one!

Irritated with his lack of success, Marcus decided to consult his sister. He had asked her once before to help him with Francesca without much success, but the present situation was very different. Francesca was now perfectly respectable. Her fortune might be only moderate, but she was worthy of any man's consideration as a wife. Lady Chelford was bound to think of someone—her circle of acquaintance was wide and comprised some of the most respectable families in England. But when he broached the subject, his sister's reaction was not what he had expected.

'My dear Marcus!' she exclaimed. 'Where have you been all these weeks?'

'In Paris—as you very well know. Why is that to the purpose?'

'Why should you imagine that Miss Beaudon needs

any help from me to find a husband? The idea is absurd!'

'Come, Sarah! You can surely help me this time! Miss Beaudon is no longer a penniless nobody. She is perfectly respectable now, with the Beaudon name and fortune behind her. It shouldn't be that difficult to think of someone who would be prepared to marry her.'

Lady Chelford's eyes narrowed. 'I am positive I can find at least a dozen, if not more! But. . .before I go any further, Marcus, tell me why you regard Miss Beaudon's future as your concern?'

'Damn it, I feel responsible for the girl!'

'I know you do, Marcus. But what puzzles me is *why*! You said you were sorry for her in the past, but Miss Beaudon no longer has the slightest need for your pity. She is a very fortunate young woman.'

'Sarah—'

Lady Chelford swept on. 'And unless you are about to declare a directly *personal* interest in her, Marcus—'

'You know I don't think of marrying anyone at the moment.'

'Then I suggest that you leave Miss Beaudon, together with her father and Maria Canfield, to sort out her future for herself. Good heavens, man, Francesca Beaudon could take her pick of London society!'

'That is surely a trifle exaggerated? She is beautiful enough, but the Beaudon fortune is modest—'

'Modest! Marcus, you have been out of London too long! Did you not know? The girl was her grandfather's heir. She has a personal fortune of seventy thousand pounds, and a large estate in Buckinghamshire. There isn't an eligible man in London who wouldn't give his eyebrows to capture the Shelwood heiress!'

'Her grandfather's heir. . .' Marcus was stunned. 'The devil she is!' There was a pause, then he said slowly, 'She said something about it that time in the library, but

I ignored it. . .I thought she was telling me a tale. . .' He fell silent again. 'An heiress. . .'

'A considerable one. She is, of course, courted and flattered wherever she goes. In fact, it is perhaps as well that you are not considering her for yourself, Marcus. You might find it difficult to get near her!' This was said with a touch of malicious amusement.

Marcus felt unaccountably irritated. 'I had no idea. . . Well, you're right for once. She certainly doesn't need my help to find a husband. What a ridiculous idea! Quite mad. I'm glad I spoke to you, Sarah—I was close to making a fool of myself.' He went to the door, then stopped. 'I don't know why it is,' he said angrily, 'but that girl has the knack of causing trouble wherever she goes!'

'What on earth do you mean?'

'She rushes about knocking me into streams, falls into ditches, reviles me for trying to help her, romps through the forest interfering in my concerns, and now—'

'We cannot be talking of the same person, Marcus! Miss Beaudon has charming manners! What is more, she is known for her detachment and poise. As far as I know, she has never put a foot wrong in matters of propriety.'

'Ha! You don't know her, Sarah!'

'No, I obviously don't. Nor, if what you say is true, does the rest of society! Tell me more about this creature.'

But Marcus recollected himself. Charlotte had willingly agreed to say nothing about what had happened in the forest, and now he had very nearly revealed the ridiculous story himself! 'No, no! It's of no consequence. It all took place in the very distant past, when. . .when she was still a child. Though I cannot believe she has changed as much as you say.'

'You will see for yourself. But if you have no wish to marry her, then you must leave her alone!'

'You need not say anything more, Sarah. I will certainly

leave her alone! I wash my hands of her. Completely. The rich Miss Beaudon can choose a husband whenever she will without my aid!'

He left at that point in what seemed remarkably like a fit of temper. Lady Chelford stared at his departing figure in astonishment. Marcus was the soul of patience and calm. She could not remember when he had last slammed a door like that. What had got into him?

Then she raised an eyebrow, and started to smile. Perhaps. . .just perhaps, her brother might be deceiving himself. How delightful that would be! Marcus was a very dear brother, always ready to help in any difficulty, and she was truly grateful to him. But there was no denying that, since he had come in to the title, he had been disgracefully spoilt. He had had his choice of Society's beauties for far too long. It would do him no harm at all if he was attracted to someone who did not fall over herself to win him.

Marcus may have washed his hands of Francesca, but he could not help observing her as she danced and conversed, as she took part in all the many events which made up the London Season. And, to his surprise, he soon saw that his sister's account of Francesca's conduct in society was perfectly correct. Francesca knew how to behave rather better than most her contemporaries, in fact. In spite of the persistent attention of so many members of the *ton*, she bore herself with dignity and grace. And in the face of their flattery and obvious admiration, she remained detached, even politely amused.

He could never find anything in her manner to fault. He was amazed. Her collapse into tears, her agitation and loss of temper in the garden at Carlton House—these had been completely out of character for the Honorable Francesca Beaudon as Society knew her. He had never liked Coker, but now he found it difficult to address the man with any degree of civility, for he was sure Coker was to blame.

In this he was wrong. Lord Coker's behaviour had merely set the scene. Marcus remained unaware that he himself had been the real cause for Francesca's distress. It did not occur to him that few people would ever be permitted to see her as he had seen her that night, that he was one of only two people in the world who could break through the wall of reserve to the vulnerable, passionate girl behind. London society approved of Miss Beaudon, but would have laughed to scorn the idea that her heart was not always ruled by her head.

The longer Marcus studied Francesca, the more puzzled he became. She was an enigma. It was not that she was beautiful in her fine dresses and fashionable hairstyles— that came as no surprise to him. He had always seen beyond the shabby clothes and the wilful refusal to attempt any personal adornment. The fineness of her bone struc- ture, the clarity of her gray-green eyes, even the gleam of dark gilt hair—he had noted all these on their first acquaintance.

Her beauty was less obvious than those of vivacious charmers such as Lydia Canfield—or in her different sphere, Charmian Forrest. Francesca Beaudon's attrac- tions were for a connoisseur's eye, someone who appreciated a more subtle play of colour and line. Her beauty was wasted on the general herd, yet he had seen it from the first.

But he had always been aware of a mysterious line of communication between them. It was there whether they wished it or not, something quite out of their control. He had known when she was worried and distressed, what- ever she actually said to him—it had produced an

irrational desire to help her. But now this ability to read
her mind, to know her true feelings, had vanished without
trace. Francesca had closed him off, and Miss Beaudon
was as proper, as reserved with him as she was with
everyone else—a pattern of decorum, grace and charm.

He had not been aware how much he valued the
warmth, the freedom that had previously existed between
them, until they were no more. Damn it, she could be
what she liked with others—they did not know what she
was truly like. But he—he missed the laughing,
impetuous. . .*real* girl he had fallen in love with on the
hill above Shelwood!

Then there was the question of her fortune. At first,
Marcus was strongly irritated by the thought that
Francesca was rich. He had made a fool of himself that
day at Shelwood with his offer of marriage. Mistress of
a large fortune and with her own father to look after
her, Francesca could well manage without Lord Carne's
solicitude then—and now. She was far from needing
his help.

But, as Marcus watched Francesca dancing, walking,
driving with some of the most eligible bachelors in the
town, he began to change his mind again. However little
Francesca realised it, she *did* need him! Her fortune was
a very real source of danger to her, putting her at risk
with all the sharks and self-seekers at loose in the polite
world. Lord Beaudon, much as he loved his daughter, had
been away from London too long to recognise all the
pitfalls, and he was quite clearly not in the best of health.

The obvious fortune-seekers were soon chased away,
it was true, but one or two more apparently respectable
characters, friends of the Prince Regent such as Lord
Coker, or charmers, such as Sir Anthony Perrott, whose
engaging manners hid their cold-hearted ambition—men

such as these were cultivating Francesca. She even seemed to be enjoying their company!

It became obvious to Marcus that something more was needed. And who better was there than Marcus himself? He had the entrée to all levels of society, from the Prince Regent down. He knew Francesca and he knew both the world she had moved in in the past, and the world she moved in now. However little she would thank him for it, protecting her from her own folly, until she found the right sort of man, was the least he could do. Marcus was filled with a sense of satisfaction at this clear call to duty. Perhaps on the way he would find that missing girl.

It was not long before Francesca realised that avoiding Marcus was impossible. His close friendship with Mrs Canfield and Lydia made meetings between them inevitable; to her annoyance, she soon saw that Marcus was making no attempt to avoid her—on the contrary, he seemed to regard her as part of the Canfield family, to extend to her his patronage and protection. He did nothing to single her out, made no special effort to engage her in other than general conversation, but she was conscious all the time of his presence, and frequently of his eye on her.

The Canfields were delighted when he accompanied them to balls and concerts. They accepted with pleasure his invitations to rides in the park, excursions into the country, expeditions to places of interest, and Francesca was always included. However reluctant she was, she found herself forced to accept more often than she wished.

'But why will you not come, Francesca?' cried Lydia on one occasion. 'Hampton Court is delightful. You will enjoy it much more than staying in town!'

'Lydia, do not press Miss Beaudon. Perhaps she has the headache and wishes for a little peace and quiet. Your chatter can be very tiring.' Mrs Canfield's voice was calm, but she was looking anxiously at Francesca.

'Oh, no, ma'am. I like to hear Lydia talking.'

'Then do come!' Lydia put a pleading hand on Francesca's arm. 'Lord Carne's carriage is extremely well sprung, and I shall see to it that you have all the cushions and parasols necessary to keep you comfortable. And I shall not say a word more than you wish to hear, I promise. Please, Francesca! It isn't the same without you.'

'But Lord Carne is an old friend of yours. He cannot wish to see me making a fourth on every excursion you make!'

'Nonsense! He likes you.'

'Lydia!' Mrs Canfield's voice held a warning and Lydia said no more.

But later, when they were alone, Mrs Canfield said quietly, 'Francesca, forgive me for what I am about to say. I only wish to spare you difficulty or embarrassment. Though you have not acknowledged it, I. . .I have the impression that you and Lord Carne knew each other in the past. Am I right?'

Francesca hesitated. She owed her friend the truth, but was reluctant to reveal the extent of her previous acquaintance with Marcus.

'Believe me, I do not wish to pry, but if it distresses you to be in his company, you have only to mention it. I shall perform the impossible and find a way of silencing Lydia.'

Francesca smiled. 'You are very kind, ma'am, but I truly enjoy Lydia's conversation. She is so. . .so artless, and so loving. How could I not enjoy her company? But you are right—I have met Lord Carne before. Briefly. In Buckinghamshire.' She paused. 'It was many years ago, before he succeeded to the title, so his name meant nothing to me when Lydia spoke of him. I only recognised him when he came back from Paris. I hope you don't think that I deliberately deceived you?'

'Of course not! And you are not disturbed to meet him now? I sometimes have the impression. . .'

Francesca had confided as much as she was prepared to. 'It is kind of you to be concerned. But I was a mere child when we first met, so our acquaintance was. . .was not important.' Her tone was so casual that Mrs Canfield was satisfied. No one could have guessed from Francesca's demeanor then or later how much she resented Lord Carne's constant attendance.

His presence agitated her, roused feelings which she preferred to forget—how could she conquer this stupid weakness for him, when he was always there, his dark blue eyes watching her, his voice a constant reminder of those hours on the hill? But once again, she had cause to be grateful to the hard school of her earlier life, which enabled her now to reveal nothing of this as she walked and talked, listened and smiled with every appearance of serene enjoyment, though her famous reserve was a trifle more apparent.

The presence of Marcus was not the only cause for unease. Francesca was becoming increasingly concerned about her father. His decision to support her during her London Season had delighted her and, since the news of her wealth had spread, she had been grateful for his protection from the worst of the fortune hunters. But he was not robust, and his exertions were having an effect on his health.

However, he dismissed her concern with a laugh. 'Nonsense, child! Watching your success has taken years off me! And though there are not as many old friends left in London as I would have wished, I manage to have a very pleasant time of it. I like that fellow Carne, by the way. Not at all the dull sort of stick I expected from Maria

Canfield's eulogies. You could do a lot worse for a husband.'

It said much for Francesca's control that though the rose in her cheeks increased a fraction, she reminded her father calmly that, as he himself had once said, Lord Carne was out of her reach.

'I'm no longer so sure of that. He's forever in your company.'

'He is a close friend of the Canfields, as you very well know, Papa.'

'But it's my impression that his eyes are on you a good deal of the time, not the Canfields. Perhaps you've caught his fancy—should I sound him out, d'you think?'

'No, Papa! Believe me, that is the last thing I want you to do.' The vehemence in her voice caused Lord Beaudon to raise an eyebrow.

'Protesting too much, Francesca?'

Francesca pulled herself together. 'The truth is, Papa, that Lord Carne and I do not. . .are not. . . The fact is, we have little in common. I have too much regard for Mrs Canfield to express this openly. It would hurt her, I know. And I am also aware that his. . .patronage is valuable to all of us. But I have to confess that my feeling towards him is best described as indifferent.'

Lord Beaudon regarded her in silence for a moment. There was more to this than met the eye. Once he would have taken her words at face value, as deceived by her cool control as the rest of the world had been. But now his instinct told him that, whatever she felt for Lord Carne, it was not indifference. Could Carne possibly be the man she had been in love with? Surely not! Carne was no rake, and he was a most unlikely crony of Charlie Witham. But there was something. . . Lord Beaudon resolved not to pursue the matter with Francesca, but to wait and observe.

'Is Carne to be at Lady Huntingdon's tonight?' he asked.

'I believe so. Why do you ask?'

'She usually sets up some card tables for those who don't wish to dance—I thought I'd invite him to a game, that's all. Nothing like a hand of cards to get to know a man.'

'Papa—'

'Oh, I won't mention your name, girl. Why should I, if, as you say, you have no particular interest in him? No, Carne seems to me to be a sound fellow—I'd enjoy making his better acquaintance. You surely don't wish for my company in the ballroom, do you? You'll be safe enough at Bella Huntingdon's—and Maria will be with you.'

'Are you sure you wouldn't prefer to rest this evening? I have no particular wish to go out—we could have a peaceful time together. . .'

'Francesca, it is my dearest wish to see you happily settled with a man you can respect. You won't find a husband if you sit at home keeping company with your papa!'

'I'm no longer so sure that. . .that I want to marry anyone. I seem to have met most of the eligible men in London, and there isn't one with whom I could spend the rest of my life. . .except you, Papa,' she added with a twinkle.

'Nonsense, girl. You must just keep on trying! Now off you go—put on the new dress I saw arriving today. Another from Fanchon, wasn't it? What colour is it this time?'

'White and green—I think you'll like it. Lydia was in raptures over it. Papa, I cannot begin to tell you how well your choice of sponsor has suited me. Maria is so very kind, she and I seem to agree on practically everything.

And Lydia is a darling. It is *my* dearest wish to see *her* safely established!'

'Young Tom Endcombe seems very attentive.'

'He does!' She paused. 'He's pleasant enough, I suppose...though...in my opinion, Lydia needs someone more mature, someone who would look after her. Still, Maria seems to approve of him. If I could see Lydia happily settled, I wouldn't care about the rest of the Season. You and I could return to Packards and enjoy some country air—and some country hours. You may not need a rest, but I'm certain that I do!'

'Rubbish, Francesca! In any case, I must return to Paris some time soon.'

'To Paris? I had rather forgotten Paris. You...have responsibilities there?'

'I must talk to you about Paris. We'll have a chat tomorrow—there's something I've been meaning to tell you.'

'What is it?'

'Tomorrow,' said Lord Beaudon firmly. 'Tonight we both have to change for Lady Huntingdon's ball. I am expecting to be stunned along with the rest of London by my daughter's new dress.'

Francesca's appearance in the doors to Lady Huntingdon's reception room caused many a man's heart to beat faster. Tall and slender in a simple slip of white silk, with an overdress of delicate green gauze draped with all the cunning of London's foremost dressmaker, she was a vision to take one's breath away. Her hair was wound with pearls and pale green ribbon, its dark gilt coils echoing the gold and pearl embroidery of her dress. Her eyes were silver-green in the candlelight, and she was smiling at Lydia as they entered the room a little way behind Lord Beaudon and Mrs Canfield.

She was quite unconscious of the impression she was making. Her attention was on Lydia, and her smile was full of affectionate warmth, very different from the polite mask with which she fended off her suitors. And at least one man found himself suddenly, disconcertingly, so stunned that he forgot everything else—much to the irritation of his companion.

'I say, Carne, old fellow—you might answer when a friend asks a perfectly civil question!'

'What was it, Monty?'

'I asked you if you was thinkin' of dancin' tonight. Lady Huntingdon usually sets up a damn good card room. Care for a game later?'

'I. . .don't know. Ask me later. I have to give the Canfields some of my time tonight. I promised Lydia a dance.'

'Nice little girl. A bit young for you, though.'

'There's nothing to it. You know that, Monty. Her father was a friend of mine, and I like to please Lydia and her mother for his sake.'

'He was a friend of mine, too, but that don't mean I have to dance attendance on his widow. Not at a ball! Anyway, Beaudon was asking if you'd be in the card room tonight. He wants a game.'

He had his friend's full attention. 'Beaudon? I wonder why?'

'I expect he likes picquet. I see the divine Miss Beaudon has arrived. By Jove, she's in looks tonight—it's almost enough to make me change my mind about blondes. I've always thought her a touch insipid.'

'Insipid!'

'Yes—Lydia Canfield is usually far better looking than the Beaudon girl. But tonight. . . Let me know about the cards, won't you?'

'Yes, yes. Excuse me, Monty.'

Not without difficulty, Marcus made his way over to the Canfields, who were surrounded by a crowd of admirers.

'Lord Carne! There you are! You remember your promise?'

'Lydia!' Mrs Canfield shook her head as she greeted him. 'You must forgive her, Marcus. She is a little excited tonight.'

'Her high spirits do her no harm in my eyes, Maria. She looks delightful. A new dress?'

'Yes! And I think it is the prettiest I have ever possessed. Francesca helped me to choose it.'

Marcus looked at the white dress with its coquelicot ribbons. 'Miss Beaudon chose well.' Then he turned to Francesca and bowed. 'Miss Beaudon.'

The smile which had so enchanted him from across the other side of the room had disappeared. Francesca's face expressed polite interest, nothing more. She looked beautiful, but remote. Marcus felt a sudden surge of impatience. He wanted to pick up the woman and shake her until her eyes sparkled with feeling again, until she smiled at him with the same affectionate warmth, until her lips parted to laugh with him, talk to him, revile him even, with her old passionate involvement. . .

Damn it, he wanted her to show some feeling towards him, some acknowledgment of their old bonds! This. . . statue was not the real Francesca. What had happened to her? But his own face revealed none of these thoughts.

He said calmly enough, 'Lydia, I have been looking forward all week to the dance you promised me. May I?'

He possessed himself of all three ladies' cards and filled in his name. Lydia was delighted, Mrs Canfield protested but was overridden, and Francesca found herself unable to object without appearing rude. That would show her—she couldn't escape waltzing with him tonight! And he'd written his name down twice. Satisfied, he offered Lydia his arm and took her in the direction of the music. As they went along, he noticed that Francesca was already surrounded with eager partners.

'Do you really like my dress, Lord Carne? It's from Fanchon.'

Marcus suppressed a smile at the awe in Lydia's voice, and assured her that he thought it very charming.

'It's a present from Francesca. She is so good. I love her dearly. People often say she's cold, you know. But I have never found her so, and nor has Mama. You don't find her cold, do you?'

'I think Miss Beaudon is very fond of you, Lydia. And who would not be?'

Miss Canfield laughed and blushed and for a while their conversation turned to other things. But just as they were leaving the floor, Lydia said suddenly, 'I wish she was happier—I sometimes wonder if she is in love.'

Marcus was startled. 'In love? Who?'

'Francesca, of course. Well, people often seem to be unhappy when they're in love, don't they? But I've watched her very closely, and have never had the slightest hint as to who he might be. I suppose she spends more time talking to Lord Denver than to anyone else. He's very kind, of course, and certainly very handsome. Mama likes him a lot, I know. But Francesca. . .I don't know. She certainly doesn't seem to encourage him—nor anyone else, which is strange when everyone knows that the object of the Season is to meet and marry someone you like.'

'It isn't always that easy, Lydia.'

'I suppose not. You haven't found anyone yet, have you? You know, I once hoped that you and she would become attracted. But it would never have done. I've given that idea up.'

'I'm relieved to hear it. But what makes you say so?'

'Well, most ladies of our acquaintance fall over themselves to attract your attention, Lord Carne. No, don't smile at me, you know it's true. But Francesca seems so reluctant to talk of you that I sometimes wonder if she doesn't like you. She's always very. . .quiet when I mention your name. I suppose she could hardly admit to me that she doesn't like you. And yet. . .'

'Yet what?'

'Oh, I don't know. Tell me, do you know Lord Endcombe's son, Tom?'

Marcus had been more intrigued by that 'yet' than he could show, but he had to drop the subject of Francesca, and exert himself to show interest in the present object of Miss Canfield's volatile affections. He did this to such good effect that Lydia returned to Mrs Canfield, very well pleased with her distinguished partner.

Marcus then turned to Francesca, who was just joining them. Ruthlessly stepping in front of a gentleman who was about to claim her hand, he said with a charming smile, 'I think you promised this one to me, Miss Beaudon. It will be the first time we have enjoyed a waltz together, I believe.'

Chapter Ten

They walked towards the ballroom together, and many who saw them thought how well-matched they looked— Lord Carne, tall and distinguished, and the elegant Miss Beaudon. No one could have guessed from their air that Marcus was far from feeling as assured as he looked, nor that Francesca was bracing herself to put other, less conventional, occasions in Marcus's arms out of her mind. She had always known it would be difficult and for this reason had always avoided dancing the waltz with him. But now she had to face it.

The music began, the couples swept on to the floor. Francesca concentrated with determination on the steps of the dance and stepped into Marcus's arms. They circled once, twice, with utmost decorum, the correct distance set and scrupulously maintained between them.

Marcus eventually said in a carefully polite tone, 'The orchestra is, I believe, excellent.'

'And the floor not excessively crowded,' responded Francesca, with equal care.

There was another silence while they negotiated the corner of the room. Then, 'Lydia looks well, I think.'

'It is a very pretty dress.'

'Very pretty.'

Another silence, while they each searched for something unexceptionable to say. Marcus could bear this artificiality no longer. He said abruptly, 'Do you dislike me so much, Francesca?'

Francesca missed a step. 'What did you say?' she asked in astonishment.

'I asked if you disliked me so much that you cannot bear to talk to me even as much as ordinary courtesy would demand!'

'How can you say that? I have talked as much to you as I would to anyone else!'

'Then I can only pity your partners. Perhaps they are so dazzled that they find nothing to criticise.'

'By my wealth, you would say. They are at least civil, Lord Carne.' Francesca's voice was cool but perfectly calm. In the old days she would have flared up to challenge him.

'But I claim the privilege of an old friend to speak the truth.'

'Truth is a double-edged weapon, Lord Carne. It is better not unsheathed without good cause. Tell me, is it your opinion that Lydia and Lord Endcombe's son will make a match of it?'

'Lydia is still very young. It's early days yet for her to be making her choice, but I find nothing to object to in young Endcombe. He's harmless enough. You, on the other hand, seem to be very reluctant to make any man happy—or am I behind the times?'

She stiffened, but still remained perfectly calm as she said, 'Mrs Canfield has told me much of your generosity to her family since her husband was killed. This must give you some right to take an interest in their future. . .'

'Let us say nothing of that! Peter Canfield was a very good friend to me.'

'But you have no privilege as far as I am concerned.

Nor do I propose to discuss my future with anyone who has so little claim to an interest in it, Lord Carne!'

'For God's sake, Francesca, stop this Lord Carne business! You called me Marcus once. Let me ask you again. Do you dislike me so much that you refuse to recognise any bond between us at all?'

'There isn't one. Not any longer.'

'Then I am simply another member of the crowd to you? Look at me, Francesca, and tell me it is so, if you can.'

Francesca's hand trembled in his. She was pale, but her calm air did not desert her, and she looked at him fearlessly as she said, 'You ask too much. It would be uncivil to tell you that I dislike you, and I have already been too uncivil in the past. In any case, how could I. . . dislike you, when you have been so attentive to all of us? But I will not feed your vanity by confessing to anything but a memory.'

'Of what?'

'Of. . .of someone in another life, a man called Marcus, who once said he loved me. I am not sure he even existed, except in a girlish fantasy. Now I would prefer either to talk of something else, or to go back to Mrs Canfield.'

The waltz had come to an end, but neither of them was aware that the music had stopped. They stood staring at one another, each challenging the other, unheeding of the curious looks they were attracting.

'This will not do!' said Marcus with determination. He took Francesca's arm and led her off the floor. But at the doors of the ballroom he turned away from where Mrs Canfield and Lydia were waiting, and marched her in the direction of the garden. Francesca pulled herself free. She was pale, but still calm.

'I do not wish to go into the garden, Lord Carne. Please take me back to my friends!'

'But I want to talk to you, Francesca.'

'I can imagine what you wish to say and have no desire to hear it. In any case, Lady Huntingdon's ball is not a fit place for such conversations.' Her tone was still measured, her air still remote.

It was the last straw. Marcus took her arm and walked her willy-nilly further into the garden. They would not be overheard here. Then he took both her hands in his. He said angrily, 'Francesca, I cannot bear to see you like this. I have seen statues who have more animation! You may deceive Society with your touch-me-not airs, but you cannot deceive me. I know you too well. What has happened to you?'

'When will I manage to convince you that you do not know me any longer? You take too much on yourself. I am not, and never was, your responsibility, Marcus.' Her voice rose as she spoke, and he could see that she was breathing less steadily.

'Ah, a touch of emotion at last! And you called me Marcus!'

Francesca bit her lip, and turned away from him. He was absurdly pleased to see it—the first round was his. There was a long way to go before she would smile at him with the same unguarded, affectionate warmth which Lydia had evoked, but he would not rest until she did. And he had at least cracked her unnatural composure. He exulted in the thought. He, of all the men in London, still had the key to that other Francesca—one which the polite world had never seen or even suspected, but a girl he had once loved.

'Francesca,' he said softly, seductively.

She tore herself out of his grasp. 'No! I won't listen to you!' she cried. 'I don't know why you are doing this— amusement, curiosity, pique—but whatever it is, it is not kind! You broke my heart ten long years ago, Marcus—

you see, I am not afraid to confess it. I understand your reasons—better now than I did then. But you left a lonely and unhappy girl behind you, and there were times when I was not certain I would survive the treatment. But I managed.

'It has taken me all that time since to learn common sense, but I have done it, too. I will not now throw all those lessons aside! I will not go back to what I was, not for you, not for any man in the world! I tell you, I *will not* listen to you!' Francesca dashed a hand across her eyes, turned abruptly away from him and head bent, went back into the house.

He would have followed her, but was stopped at the door by a familiar figure.

'Marcus, old fellow! Well, upon my word—still pursuin' the fair Francesca, eh? More worth the effort now, ain't she? My word, what a difference a few years can make.'

'Freddie! What are you doing here?'

'M'cousin brought me. Respectable chap, and devilish dull, but he got me an invitation, so I suppose I have to be grateful. The wine's not at all bad. Have you had some?'

It was clear that Freddie had indeed enjoyed the wine. His face glowed with good humour.

'Freddie, you must excuse me. I have to—'

'I'll come with you, Marcus. Truth to tell, there aren't many familiar faces in the crowd. I'm not sure I'm all that *grata* to most of them.'

The last thing Marcus wanted was Freddie Chantry's company, especially at this moment, but it was like trying to get rid of a puppy who wants to play. The years, he thought grimly, had done nothing for Freddie's sense.

'As a matter of fact, I was a touch surprised to see you with Miss Beaudon, Marcus. Especially coming in from the garden,' he added with a knowing look.

'I had something to say to her in private.'

'Of course you had! Talking all the way through that waltz, too. We all wondered what was going on. If you don't mind my saying so, old chap, the ballroom ain't the sort of place to try that sort of thing. Bound to set the tabbies miaowing. I shouldn't be a bit surprised if the odds on Denver didn't lengthen even more after tonight. . .'

'Odds on Denver? What do you mean? What has George to do with anything?'

Marcus spoke so brusquely that Freddie took a step back. 'Sorry, Marcus. Thought you'd have known. They were saying in the clubs that Denver's the most likely man to succeed with our heiress.'

'Denver!'

'Oh, it was never by any means a sure thing. The lovely Miss Beaudon don't show much by way of feeling, do she? But there's no one else she showed any preference for at all. Till tonight, that is.'

'Denver! She'd never have him!'

'Why not? Denver's very presentable. Plenty of address with the ladies, knows how to please, easygoin'. . .not short of the dibs—nice little estate and an income to go with it. She could have done a lot worse. What's wrong? A friend of yours, ain't he? But of course, if you and the charmin' Francesca have decided to take up where you left off at Shelwood, that's a different matter. . .'

Marcus' face darkened. 'Forget about that time, Freddie! You don't know what you're talking about.'

'Silent as the grave, old chap. But if you don't want gossip now, you shouldn't appear so dead to the rest of the world when you're dancin' with her. And you shouldn't make off into the garden and upset the famously self-possessed Miss Beaudon!'

There was no difference in Marcus's manner as he made his escape, but he was disturbed. He did not really believe that Francesca was attracted to Lord Denver. Of course she wasn't! He had been frequently in her company in the past weeks, with and without George. There had been nothing to indicate any special affection between them. It had been an unwelcome surprise to hear what the clubs were saying, though. . . And the new Francesca did not wear her heart on her sleeve. . .but George Denver? Impossible!

He made his way slowly through the ballroom, where he was less than delighted to see Francesca, apparently quite recovered, dancing with the same George Denver. He watched them, somewhat sourly, for a few moments, then went on into the library, where card tables had been set up. Here he found Lord Beaudon in an otherwise empty room.

'Carne! You couldn't have come at a better moment. I've just won handsomely from Standish, and am ready for another victim. Care for a hand of piquet?'

Marcus agreed readily enough but, as they played, the mind of neither man was totally on the game in hand. They talked, casually, about the West Indies, the politics of Europe, and Paris, but each was interested in learning more about his companion than the state of the world. They had an enjoyable game, which Lord Beaudon won by a narrow margin, then by common consent they wandered on to the small balcony that overlooked the ballroom. Francesca was dancing again with Lord Denver.

'Your daughter appears to be enjoying life in London, sir,' said Marcus.

'What? Oh, Francesca! Yes, yes, I believe she is. Though she sometimes finds the fuss and attention a touch tedious.'

'Tell me, Lord Beaudon, do you find London much changed after your long absence?'

'Society never changes, Carne. The mixture is very

much as before.' There was a slight pause, then he added, somewhat deliberately, 'I am surprised to see Chantry here tonight, though. I'd have thought our hostess more discriminating.'

'Oh, Freddie's harmless enough.'

'Friend of yours, is he? In that case I apologise, of course. He's generally seen with the Witham crowd. You a friend of Charlie Witham's, too?'

'I. . .I know him, let us say.'

'Ever been to Witham Court?' Lord Beaudon asked idly.

'Yes.'

'Lovely place—at least, it was in my day. Is it still?'

'The place itself is lovely, but it has deteriorated a lot in recent years. It badly needs some attention.'

'Is that so? You know it well, then?'

'Hardly,' said Marcus. 'I've only stayed there twice.' He looked at his companion with a slight frown. 'It's next door to Shelwood, of course. I expect that's why you take such an interest in it? Surely your daughter could tell you more about it than I?'

Lord Beaudon looked back at him blandly. 'She seldom talks about her life at Shelwood, and I haven't questioned her, Carne. But it's never a good thing to have a neglected estate on one's doorstep. I am quite certain that Shelwood itself is in perfect condition. My late sister-in-law would not have permitted otherwise.'

'I am certain she wouldn't. I hear it is in the hands of a manager at the moment. Does. . .does Miss Beaudon intend to return there at the end of the Season?'

'I suppose that depends. . . She might decide to live with me—or she might take a husband.'

'Yes, of course.'

The eyes of the two men followed the graceful twists and turns of the throng below.

'She seems to be difficult to please, my Francesca. She doesn't say much, but I rather think she's had any number of offers.'

'She's a beautiful woman.'

'I agree, though we needn't beat about the bush, Carne. She wouldn't be half as beautiful to some eyes if the Shelwood estate wasn't in the frame, too.'

'That's inevitable, I suppose. But she need not concern herself about them. There are many other, more honorable men,' said Marcus, adding casually, 'George Denver for one.'

'Yes, Denver. He seems quite taken. And she certainly seems to spend more time with him than with most of the others. Except yourself.'

'Me? I enjoy Miss Beaudon's company, of course, but it would be more true to say that I spend time with the Canfields. And since they share a house with her, it is natural. . .'

'Of course, of course. Quite natural. Another hand of piquet?'

'I am promised to Mrs Canfield for the supper interval. Perhaps later?'

'I'll come with you, Carne. Perhaps Francesca will be free to accompany her father.'

'I doubt it.' The two men watched as Lord Denver escorted Miss Beaudon off the ballroom floor. She was smiling as they disappeared through the doors and Marcus suddenly frowned and turned back to the library. Lord Beaudon was standing in the doorway, and Marcus was surprised to see him looking rather stern. He looked as if he was debating something in his own mind, but in the end he smiled and said, 'Shall we go?'

Though he badly wanted to speak privately to Francesca again, Marcus was given little opportunity that evening.

During the supper interval she kept close to her father, or talked to Lord Denver. And when he returned to claim the second set of dances he had written in to her programme at the beginning of the evening, she was not to be found. When he finally tracked her down, she was talking to Lady Clayton, who was regaling her with tales of her father's exploits in London twenty-five years before.

'Lord Carne! You must forgive me,' Francesca exclaimed brightly. 'I had to repair my dress, and by the time I had finished the dances had started. I am afraid I assumed you must have found another partner. You will think me very uncivil, but I assure you the repair was necessary.'

'In that case, how can I not forgive?' He bowed. 'Lady Clayton.'

'I suppose you've come to take this charming young woman away from me, Carne?'

'I am sure Lord Carne will excuse me if I do not go,' said Francesca. She turned to Marcus. 'Lady Clayton has been telling me such stories about my father.'

'My attractions apparently outweigh yours, Carne!' said the dowager with a malicious smile. 'What will you do?'

'Give in gracefully, I hope, ma'am,' said Marcus. 'Your stories are renowned. May I hear some, too?' He sat down on the chair at Francesca's side.

Lady Clayton's black button eyes took note of the colour rising in Francesca's cheek, then switched to Marcus, whose countenance was impassive. 'Of course you may, Carne,' she said. 'Though what the younger generation is coming to I cannot imagine. A ball is an occasion for dancing, not listening to an old woman's tales!'

'But since my present dancing partner is at your side, I shall be forced to spend the next half hour alone—

unless you take pity on me. Or are your tales unfit for my unsullied ears?'

Lady Clayton cackled with pleasure. 'I could tell you tales that would make your hair stand on end, Carne... but I won't. Indeed, I've just about come to the end of my repertoire.' She turned to Francesca. 'I'm a touch tired. I hope you won't mind, my dear—you must ask your father for the rest. Take her for some refreshment, Carne. The child looks flushed.'

'I... I... What about you, Lady Clayton?'

'I shall be perfectly happy here, Miss Beaudon. Look, here comes my son—he'll take care of me. Thank you for listening to my tales.'

'I enjoyed them. May I hear more another time?'

'Of course, of course. Call on me whenever you have the time. Bring your father! I wasn't allowed to have much to do with him in the old days.'

As they walked away, Francesca said, 'I do not need refreshment, Lord Carne. I should like to find my father, if you please.'

Marcus looked at her determined face. 'Very well. It seems I shall have to wait for a more suitable opportunity to continue our discussion.'

'I have told you! I do not wish to discuss anything with you. Why will you not leave me alone?'

'I cannot. I cannot let matters rest as they are at the moment. I will not let you shut me out, Francesca. But there's no time now to pursue the matter—I will call on you tomorrow or the next day.'

There was no time for more. Lord Beaudon was just a few yards away. Marcus bowed and left her.

Francesca spent a sleepless night. For some mysterious reason of his own, Marcus was determined to reawaken feelings in her that she thought she had conquered. And, in the small hours of the morning, she faced the unwelcome truth that, if Marcus chose to exert the inexplicable power he had over her, she would be powerless to stop him. The thought filled her with dread. She had sworn that she would never again be as impulsive, never as subject to her emotions, that no man would ever hurt her again! Never! She had made herself invulnerable. But not to Marcus, seemingly.

What should she do? Was flight the answer? Madame Elisabeth had returned to her cottage in Shelwood after Francesca and the Canfields had come to London—perhaps she should do the same? The idea was appealing. She could occupy herself running the Shelwood estate—there was much she would like to try. Marcus would hardly pursue her there.

But. . .what would her father say if she fled to Shelwood? They had learned to love each other again during these months at Packards and in London. He had sacrificed his comfort, his life in Paris to be with her. What would he think if she abandoned all their plans?

In the end she decided to go back to her original plan of finding a husband and an establishment of her own. It was undoubtedly what would most please her father. But marriage was a solemn step—one she could not undertake lightly, and for all the offers she had received, there was not one which had tempted her.

Francesca threw up her hands impatiently and took herself to task. This was absurd! At least three or even four of the men who had offered for her were men of honour and consideration. And now there was George Denver. . .more than moderately well off, handsome, quite amusing. Why was she being so difficult to please? She was a fool! She shivered. Unless she did something soon, Marcus would make an even greater fool of her!

On this frightening thought, Francesca lay down and finally fell asleep.

The next day, Francesca's desperate desire to find a way out of the trap that was closing round her, assumed even greater urgency. In the afternoon, Lord Beaudon arrived, demanding to have a talk with her. But he had not come, as she thought, to talk of Paris.

'I've been thinking about Carne,' he began abruptly. 'He's Freddie's friend, isn't he? The one you fell in love with years ago. The rake.'

Francesca was too startled to put up much of a defence. 'How. . .how can you say so?' she stammered. 'Everyone knows that Lord Carne is the pattern of honour and decency. No rake.'

'Don't prevaricate, Francesca. I am right, aren't I? Aren't I?'

'Yes, but—'

'Then he shall marry you!'

'No!'

'He won't need much persuading. I had a word with him last night at the ball. He's very intrigued with you. He could hardly take his eyes off you. He'll marry you after I've had a word with him. You still love him, don't you?'

'Papa, you mustn't! You don't know what you're saying. No, I don't love him!'

'It's my belief you do. And you obviously haven't anyone else in mind for a husband. Carne would be an excellent choice.'

'I could not possibly marry Lord Carne, Papa. The idea is absurd. I won't let you approach him.'

'Couldn't stop me if I've made up my mind.'

'Please, Papa, please do not say anything to Lord Carne!'

'Why not, Francesca? Are you afraid he will refuse?'

'Yes. But I would be even more afraid if he agreed.' The words had slipped out before she could stop them.

Lord Beaudon regarded her for a moment. 'I find that very curious, Francesca. I can't believe he's a monster. He seems a very civilised sort of fellow. . .why should you say a thing like that? Unless. . . My child, I want to help you all I can, but I must know the truth. What is it about Carne that frightens you?'

Francesca gave a little shrug of resignation. Then she took a deep breath and said stiffly, 'Lord Carne has already asked me to marry him.'

'Well, then. . .?'

'Last year. At the time I thought he was hoping to make his fortune by marrying me, and I refused him. I told you about it.'

'But that's ridiculous. He's a very wealthy man himself.'

'I. . .I didn't know that at the time.'

'But now you do know.' Lord Beaudon frowned. 'But I don't understand—if he was rich, why did he want to marry you? He must have been in love with you, Francesca!'

'No. He was sorry for me. He felt some lingering sense of responsibility because he had abandoned me all those years before.'

'Rubbish! No man chooses a wife because he is sorry for her!'

'You're wrong, Papa. It's just the sort of thing Lord Carne would do. He is very involved in charitable works of every kind.' Francesca's tone was bitter.

'Well. . .it's just possible, I suppose.' Lord Beaudon sounded far from convinced. He went on briskly, 'But even so, that is no reason to reject him now. He's no fortune hunter, and you no longer need his pity or his money. Your pride wouldn't be hurt. It's perfect!'

'I *will not* marry Lord Carne, even if you managed to persuade him to make me the offer,' said Francesca fiercely.

'He would make a kind, considerate husband, Francesca. Isn't that what you were looking for?'

'Papa, don't you understand? I once loved Marcus to distraction. I could not now marry him for less. Kindness, consideration, friendship even—these are what I might seek in any other man. But not Marcus! Never Marcus. . .I could not be content with so little from him!'

'I see.'

'If it will make you happy, Papa, I will marry someone else—of your choosing, if that is what you wish.'

Lord Beaudon shook his head. 'I think you would be making a grave mistake, my dear. I must consider. . .'

'But I have your promise that you will not approach Lord Carne?'

'Oh, yes. That wouldn't answer. Not at the moment.'

He was still looking preoccupied when he left a few minutes later. Neither of them had thought of mentioning Paris.

Francesca's next visitor was Lord Denver. When he came in to the saloon, she was standing at the window, staring down into the street.

'Miss Beaudon! I hope you are well?' His voice, cultivated, resonant, with a pleasant timbre, expressed concern.

Francesca pulled herself together and turned to welcome him. 'Lord Denver—how pleasant to see you. I am quite well, thank you.'

'You look a little pale. . .'

'That is because I was too idle to go out for my walk this morning. And you?'

'Oh, I'm always perfectly fit. I rather hoped you would

come for a drive with me. I have the carriage outside.'

Francesca was about to refuse, but then changed her mind. 'I'll get my bonnet,' she said.

Lord Denver handled the horses with considerable skill through the crowded streets, then they drove out to pleasantly green parts of the town that Francesa had not seen before. His conversation was undemanding, but revealed facets of his personality she had not previously noticed.

He made her laugh with his account of the difficulties in running a family home that had its origins in a Norman castle, and had hardly been improved since, and she was impressed by his love of the countryside and his considerable knowledge of its flora and fauna. He was attentive without being obvious, and they returned to Mount Street perfectly in charity with one another. Francesca's spirits were considerably improved, as she thanked him.

'You. . .you mentioned that you had sketched some orchids near Shelwood,' Lord Denver said. 'May I see the sketches some time?'

'Would you like to see them now? I have them in my room here. You must not expect too much of them, Lord Denver—they have no great artistic merit. But I tried to capture the main characteristics of the plant.'

He made some complimentary response and she left him in the saloon while she fetched her drawings. When she returned he was speaking to Lydia, who had just come in from her ride. Her hat and veil had been discarded, revealing dark curls and glowing cheeks. Her eyes sparkled with laughter as she described some event at the previous night's ball. She was a picture of life and animation.

'Francesca! Lord Denver here swears that I must be teasing him. Tell him, if you please, what happened to

Lady Portman's wig! Did it or did it not catch in Sir Rodney Forrester's coat button?'

'I assure you it did, Lord Denver.'

'You see?'

'I was wrong to doubt you, Miss Canfield. I wish I had been there to see it.'

'Francesca had to take me away before I disgraced her by laughing out loud. But I think she was just as hard-pressed. And now you must excuse me. I have to change my clothes. Mr Endcombe is taking me to Somerset House, and I hardly think these will do.' Lydia curtsied and left them.

'A charming girl,' said Lord Denver, still smiling.

'She's a darling.'

Lord Denver looked at Francesca quizzically. 'You speak with rare warmth, Miss Beaudon. Miss Canfield is fortunate to have aroused such affection.'

'She deserves it.'

'And I? Could I hope in time to deserve a little of your affection?'

Francesca was unprepared for such a direct approach. She was still holding her sketchbooks and fingered them nervously as she replied, 'You have been very kind to me, Lord Denver. But I. . . I. . .'

He smiled. 'I spoke out of turn. Forgive me. Dare I hope you will come to the Lady Marchant's with me tonight? You did say you would.'

'Of course. I shall be pleased to.' She spoke warmly, relieved at avoiding a tender scene.

'I will call for you. Till tonight.' He took his leave without any further attempt to approach her.

And that evening he was once again the charming, considerate man she was growing to like. They left Lady Marchant's early. When they arrived at Mount Street,

Francesca was so much in charity with him that she
invited him in.

'You left the sketches behind when you went this afternoon. They are still on the table—I told the servants to
leave them.' They went into the salon. 'Here they are!'
As she held the book out to him, the cover, worn with
age, gave way and the contents fell to the floor. They
both bent to gather them up, but Francesca froze as she
recognised one of the sketches—a small orchid that had
been flowering just ten years ago up on the hill above
Shelwood. Sunlight on water, leaves against a blue sky,
happiness such as she had never known before or since. . .

'Miss Beaudon! Francesca! You are not well! Let me
help you!'

Francesca did not hear. She was staring at the sketch,
overcome by a feeling of such pain and loss that she could
not move. Then she became aware that someone was
gently raising her and helping her over to the sofa by the
window.

'Shall I ring for a maid?'

She looked up. Lord Denver was at her side. 'No. No,
thank you. It was only a moment's weakness.'

'You were pale when I first called this morning. I have
overtired you—the drive was too long.'

Francesca forced herself to speak normally. 'No, it was
not that. I probably over-exerted myself at Lady
Huntingdon's ball. I am perfectly well again now. Thank
you for your concern, Lord Denver. You are very kind.'

'I should like to be much kinder to you, Francesca.
Indeed, it is my very ardent wish that you would give me
the right to cherish you for the rest of your life.'

The pain in Francesca's heart eased a little at the sincerity of his tone. 'Cherish' was a comforting word. She
even managed to smile.

'Francesca? Would you. . .could you ever consider marrying me?'

She looked into the brown eyes so close to her own. True, faithful, kind, considerate, honourable. . .the temptation was very strong. If she married Lord Denver, she would be safe forever from Marcus, and the torment he could cause, safe from herself. Why did she find it so difficult to take the final step?

'You are very kind. I am honoured, Lord Denver. But I. . .I'm not sure. . .'

'Say yes, Francesca! I know I could make you happy.'

'I. . .I would need time to think. . .'

'But you will at least give me leave to hope?'

'I. . .yes, I will.' He snatched her hand and kissed it fervently.

'You have made me the happiest of men, my darling!'

'But—'

Neither of them had noticed that the door was open, nor that a tall figure was coming through it.

'Forgive me for interrupting you like this. The matter is urgent, or I would not have intruded on what is evidently a private moment.' Marcus was very pale, and he spoke in clipped tones. 'Your father is ill, Francesca. I have come to take you to him.'

Chapter Eleven

Francesca put her sewing down and looked over to the bed. Her father was restless. She went over, and gave him a sip of water, speaking to him softly. But he did not respond, and eventually she sighed and laid him back against the pillows, which were piled high behind him. She went back slowly to her chair by the window and picked up her sewing again. Dr Glover had assured her that his patient was making good progress, but it was difficult to believe him. For three days now, ever since he had been taken ill at White's, Lord Beaudon had been lying helpless, unable to talk or move without assistance.

'But he hears you, Miss Beaudon!' Dr Glover had said. 'He may not always understand the words, but a familiar voice is a lifeline to him. You must talk to him, let him know you are there.'

This Francesca had done. She had spent most of each day in her father's room and at night she had the room next to his, ready to be fetched at a moment's notice. The outside world had not existed for her. All her attention and energies had been directed towards the figure on the bed, willing him to recover. She had talked to him often, dredging her memory for details of their life on St Marthe and the people there—her mother, Maddy and the rest.

Talk of London had seemed to distress him, and Francesca had avoided mentioning it, though she had wondered what the cause was—her father had always seemed so content with his life in the capital. Mrs Canfield, when asked, had seemed to think it might have something to do with the events at White's immediately before Lord Beaudon's collapse, but had not been able to tell her more precisely. Francesca had not pursued the matter—there would be time for that later. For the moment, she was content to concentrate on ensuring her father's recovery.

There was a gentle tap at the door and Mrs Canfield came quietly into the room. 'You have a visitor, Francesca. I'll sit with your father while you see him.'

'Who is it?'

Mrs Canfield shook her head and put a finger to her lips. 'I think you should go down and see for yourself.'

Puzzled, Francesca got up and after a quick glance at her father she went downstairs. Marcus was waiting for her in the salon. Shocked, Francesca turned to go back upstairs.

'No! Francesca, wait! I have to know how your father is.'

'You could have asked Mrs Canfield.'

'She thought I ought to see you.'

Francesca looked at him in astonishment. 'Maria wanted me to see you? Why?'

Marcus did not immediately reply. He strode about the room, looking most unusually ill at ease. 'Damn it, I don't like this,' he said savagely. 'I don't like it at all. Why the devil couldn't Maria have dealt with this?'

'What are you talking about? I don't underst—' Francesca drew in her breath and gripped the chair in front of her. 'It's about my father, isn't it? You were with him at White's. You know what happened. Were you the cause of his attack—is that it?'

'No, on my honour! But. . .but I was involved.'

'*What happened,* Marcus?'

'Your father was very angry at something he heard. He was about to challenge someone when he. . .when he fell ill.'

'Go on,' said Francesca. 'I want to hear everything, Marcus. Was it you he challenged?'

'No. It was Coker.'

'*Coker*!'

'We were all there at White's—your father, myself, Monty Banford, some others, and. . . Coker. And the Witham crowd. You don't want to hear this, Francesca.'

'Yes, I do!' she said fiercely. 'My father is lying upstairs helpless. He might even die. I want to know it all!'

'We'd all been drinking, but Witham and Freddie Chantry more than most. They hadn't seen your father— he was at a corner table. They started talking about the old days, about the parties at Witham, and how your grandfather had tried to stop them. One thing led to another and Freddie mentioned you. . .and me.'

'What. . .what did he say?' Marcus looked uncomfortable, and she added bitterly, 'No, you needn't tell me— I can guess. I know what he thought of me—he made it plain enough at the time.'

'But how could Freddie have said anything to you? He never saw you.'

Francesca looked at him derisively. 'Oh, but you're wrong, Marcus! He sought me out a few days after you left. On the bridge where I first met you. I think you must have given him a false impression of my. . .availability.'

'*What*?'

'Freddie and the others were very impressed with your account of my charms. The night after we met. I suppose you had to tell them? Anyway, he thought he could console me for your defection.'

'Good God—I never knew! Francesca, I swear it wasn't like that at all!'

'I deserved it. I had behaved like a w-wanton.' Her voice revealed self-condemnation. 'I deserved it all. But now my father has suffered because of it.'

'How could you possibly have deserved anything like that? What happened?'

'With Freddie? I was shocked and frightened, of course. Whatever impression I may have given you, I was. . .very innocent. My life had been rather isolated. He tried to kiss me, and I couldn't get away from him. That was when my aunt found us. She thought the worst, of course. I was in disgrace for a considerable time.' She gave him a twisted little smile. 'Wasn't that an ironic turn of Fate? The right punishment for the wrong man.'

'By God, if I'd known that I'd have throttled him! You have to believe me, Francesca, I had no idea of all this! Not till this moment.'

'No,' she agreed. 'How should you? You were away fighting for your country, weren't you? I expect you had already forgotten me. But why are we talking of this? It all took place a long time ago. Are you going to tell me what happened at White's? Was that when my father came into it, when Freddie told his tale?'

'Not then, no. I lost my temper and knocked Freddie down. I realised afterwards it was the wrong thing to have done. It only made the whole affair more public—it would have been better to take him outside quietly and deal with him there. But. . .I was in a rage. Freddie apologised when he came to, and withdrew what he'd said. Even then, if it had been left there, it would have been forgotten. No one takes much notice of anything Freddie Chantry says.'

'But Lord Coker was listening.'

'Yes. He sneered at Freddie for apologising. He never forgets an injury. He said he had seen us in the garden at Carlton House, and that anything Freddie had said was perfectly true. You can imagine the rest.'

'And?'

'I turned on him, but your father just swept me aside. He went up to Coker and demanded he withdraw his words. By God, Francesca, your father was impressive! I've never heard Coker so spoken to before.'

'But getting in a rage is bad for him! He shouldn't have done so. Why didn't you stop him?'

'I couldn't. No one could. And he didn't seem to be in a rage. He was cool. Icy. Very much in the grand manner. Coker couldn't bear it. He lost his head and went for your father.'

'Good God!'

'I hauled Coker back, but your father had already fallen. When I got to him he was unconscious. I thought. . .I thought at first he was dead.' He paused. 'You know the rest. Tell me, how is he now? I hear Dr Glover gives some hope?'

'I believe he is improving. There are more signs of consciousness than there were. What happened to Lord Coker?'

'He. . .er. . .nothing.'

'Tell me, Marcus! I shall ask someone else if you do not.'

'He objected to the way I had handled him. He was right. I hadn't been gentle. He challenged me.'

'To. . .to a duel? But they're no longer allowed!'

'I said I'd meet him wherever and whenever he wished. And I'd have been glad to. But the Prince got to hear of it, and Coker's now in disgrace. I hear he's talking of going abroad for a while.'

Francesca got up and walked about the room. Marcus's eyes followed her.

'And now?' she said finally. 'What are they saying now? About us?'

'It's forgotten, Francesca. And you needn't worry about Denver. I've seen him and made it clear that there's nothing in it. He. . .he was with you when it all happened, of course. I'm sorry I had to interrupt you.' He paused. 'I must wish you happy. I suppose this business with your father has delayed any official announcement?' Francesca looked blank. 'Of an engagement.'

Francesca hesitated. Then she said, 'Yes. Nothing can be settled until I am sure Papa is on the mend. What did you tell Lord Denver?'

'That he was a lucky man.' Their eyes met. Then Marcus looked away and walked to the window. 'A very lucky man.'

There was silence in the room. Francesca broke it.

'I must get back to Papa,' she said nervously. 'I'm sure he misses me when I am not there.'

'I should like to see him when he is fit to receive visitors. I'd like to reassure him that all is well.'

'Of course. I'll send you a message. And. . .thank you for telling me. Maria was right to insist.' She went to the door, but stopped, the handle in her hand as he said,

'Francesca!'

She turned slowly but stayed where she was, her back to the door. 'Marcus?'

'Do you love him?'

Francesca flushed painfully. 'He is a good, kind man—'

'Good God, I know that! But it wasn't what I asked. Are you in love with him?'

'There are different kinds of love, Marcus—'

Marcus muttered something incomprehensible and strode over to her. He looked at her for a moment, then swept her into his arms and kissed her hard, a passionate, deep kiss which made no concession to propriety or

feminine weakness. Her response was instinctive—
immediate and overwhelming. He grunted with satisfaction and kissed her again, more deeply than before. When
he finally released her, she would have fallen if he had
not supported her. He said with grim satisfaction, 'Is that
the kind of love you feel for Denver?'

Francesca's eyes filled with tears. She lifted her arm
and hit him as hard as she could. Then she opened the
door and ran up the stairs as if all the demons in hell
were after her.

As Marcus left the house and strode down the street, his
cheek was burning from Francesca's blow. But he was
unaware of it. His feelings were in turmoil. He felt
anger—with himself, with Francesca, with his long-dead
uncle, with the world at large. He felt regret—bitter
regret—for the pain and humiliation he had caused
Francesca all those years ago. It had been all so much
worse than he had ever suspected. Even more bitterly did
he regret his carelessness in throwing away something he
should have cherished beyond everything else.

But above all, his overmastering feeling was desire—
a passionate desire to return to Mount Street, to take
Francesca in his arms once more, to feel again her total
response to his kiss. Why had he never before realised
that Francesca was the one woman in the world for him?
The one woman in the world with whom he felt complete?
Why had he deceived himself for so long—complacently
seeking suitable husbands for her, smugly protecting her
from fortune hunters, when he should have been claiming
her triumphantly for his own? He had been stupid
beyond belief.

But recognition had come too late. Because of his own
wilful, incomprehensible blindness, Francesca now
belonged to someone else. To one of his best friends, in

fact. It was too much to bear. He shouted for a bottle of brandy when he arrived home, and spent the rest of the day in his room, completely failing to drown his sorrows. However, Marcus was made of stern stuff.

The next day, in spite of a bad hangover, he recovered a measure of reason. Though Francesca appeared to be lost to him, he could still be of service to her. His position in Society gave him power to protect her, to stifle any remarks which foolish gossips might venture. His friendship with the Canfields gave him every excuse to visit Mount Street, and once Lord Beaudon was well enough, he could visit him, keep him entertained during his convalescence. There might well be business that needed attention, matters which could not be entrusted to an unmarried female.

He grew happier at the thought that he could still help Francesca in all sorts of ways. It did not occur to him that these services might be better performed by her betrothed. When the thought did occur to him, he dismissed it. Denver was a good fellow, but simply not up to it.

The next time Marcus visited Mount Street he was told that Miss Beaudon was unable to receive him. And the next. When he asked Mrs Canfield to help him, she looked extremely uncertain.

'I don't know what was said the last time you were here, Marcus. But Francesca was very upset. I think you cannot have presented the affair at White's as tactfully as you should.'

'I know she was distressed. That's why I must see her—to put matters right.'

'She's with her father. I'll go up and ask her. But don't place too much confidence in my efforts. She is very determined.'

'How is Lord Beaudon today? Is he well enough to receive visitors?'

'He will be very soon. He still cannot speak, but he understands what we say, and can now nod or close his eyes in reply. It is a great improvement.'

She went away, but returned a few minutes later, shaking her head. 'I cannot prevail upon Francesca to see you. I have never known her so obstinate. I am sorry, Marcus. Perhaps in a little while. . .?'

Marcus set his jaw. 'Will you let me know when Lord Beaudon is ready to see people? I might at least be permitted to visit her father. Does Denver come often?'

'He is very attentive. But Francesca really does not have a great deal of time, you know. She is with her father most of the day, and rarely sees anyone other than myself and Lydia.'

'Is she getting fresh air?'

'I do my best to persuade her. She occasionally consents to go for a drive with Lord Denver, but it is not enough.'

Marcus looked at her curiously. She seemed unaware of any official link between Francesca and Denver. And though he had spoken to Denver himself several times, there had been no further mention of a betrothal. Damn it, he thought irritably, what was wrong with the man? He ought to have been here all the time, shouldering Francesca's burdens, making sure she had enough rest, exercise, fresh air and generally exerting his right to take care of her! What was the man made of?

Or—his heart gave a great leap at the thought—was it possible that he had been mistaken in what he had heard that fateful evening? Was there still a chance of winning Francesca, after all? Somehow or other, he must, he would find out. But to do that, he would have to see her, and at the moment that was apparently impossible. He would wait. She couldn't refuse forever.

None of these thoughts showed, however, as he said in his usual calm manner, 'I see. Well, I place my confidence in you, Maria. You have said you will let me know when Lord Beaudon is well enough to see me. Francesca need not be there if she does not wish. Is she. . .is she well?'

'She looks pale and tired, I'm afraid. It's natural—her nights are frequently interrupted. Once or twice I have found her sitting in her father's room wide awake, even in the small hours. It isn't at all necessary for her to do so—he sleeps quite well now, and, in any case, the nurse is always present. I think she herself finds it difficult to sleep.'

Marcus nodded. The sooner he sorted out this business of Francesca's engagement, the better. It was clear that she was urgently in need of someone to look after her.

The summons to Lord Beaudon's bedchamber came a few days later. Marcus set off for Mount Street in a frame of mind that was a good deal happier than on his previous visit. He had used the time to good effect. A convivial evening with Denver had established that the engagement was a tenuous one—more an agreement on the lady's part to consider an offer, rather than a commitment to accept.

Lord Denver was sanguine about the outcome. Francesca had treated him with more kindness than any of her other suitors, and, what was more, she had assured him that no one else, not even Marcus with whom her name had been linked, had a right to greater hope.

Marcus listened, filled up Denver's glass, and pitied him from the bottom of his heart. If his friend had succeeded in winning from Francesca a firm committment to marry him, then Marcus would have been forced to step aside. But as it was. . . Denver had no idea of Francesca's true nature. Her passion, her laughter, even the strength of her character were unknown to him. If he

ever did manage to discover them, they might even come
as an unwelcome surprise. No, there was no doubt whatsoever—Francesca would be wasted on this kind,
conventional. . .ordinary man.

So Marcus went back to Mount Street, determined to
set about persuading Francesca that she was his and his
alone. His plans suffered a setback when he was told once
again that Francesca would not meet him. Undaunted, he
asked to see Lord Beaudon and was conducted up the
stairs to a large bedchamber on the second floor.
Francesca was nowhere to be seen, but Lord Beaudon
was awake and watching with a fierce eye. Marcus greeted
him fearlessly, then sat down and proceeded to give him
a clear account of what had happened since the evening
at White's. Lord Beaudon nodded once or twice, but still
seemed unhappy.

'What is it, sir?'

The pale lips mouthed, 'Madeleine. P-Paris.'

'I don't understand. Can you repeat it?'

'Mad-M-Madeleine. Want you to go.' He moved restlessly when he saw that Marcus was still looking puzzled.
'Francesca. Fetch Fran. . . Francesca.'

Marcus went to the door and told the servant to bring
Miss Beaudon. She came a few minutes later. When she
saw Marcus, her step faltered, but her eyes went to her
father. Marcus was shocked at her appearance. She looked
as if she had not slept for a week.

'He was asking for you,' Marcus said. 'I'll leave you
with him.'

There was a grunt from the bed. Francesca hurried over.
'What is it, Papa?' she asked urgently. 'Are you in pain?'

'Ca. . .arne. Stay.'

Marcus came back to stand on the other side of the
bed. 'I'm here, sir. What can I do?'

'Pa. . .aris.' Lord Beaudon's eyes went to Francesca.

'Mmm-eant to tell.' He frowned and said suddenly, 'Madeleine.'

'That's what he was saying before,' Marcus said softly. 'Do you know what it means?'

'Madeleine. . . I don't—Papa! Do you mean Maddy?'

Lord Beaudon nodded, a smile of relief on his worn face.

'Do you know where she is?'

'Paa. . .ris.' Exhausted with his efforts to speak, Lord Beaudon closed his eyes.

'Papa! Papa!' There was no response. The eyelids did not even flicker.

'Leave him, Francesca. Let him rest.'

'But you don't understand! It's Maddy! He wants to tell me about Maddy.'

'He can't tell you anything more for the moment. Look at him.'

Lord Beaudon was lying perfectly still, eyes shut, his face pale and sunken. He was sound asleep.

'He'll tell you more when he wakes up. You'll have to be patient. Who is Maddy?'

'My nurse. On St Marthe. She came with me to England, but my aunt sent her away. I have always wondered what became of her.' A tear rolled down her cheek. 'He's known all the time, and never told me.'

'Come and sit down. Your father won't wake for a while. He's exhausted.' He led her to her chair by the window and sat her down. He looked at her white face, the dark shadows under her eyes, saw that her hands were trembling, and had some difficulty in stopping himself from taking her in his arms to give her comfort. He would almost certainly be rejected. Instead, he called the servant and ordered some wine to be sent up. When it came, he persuaded her to drink some. A little colour came into her cheeks. Then he drew another chair up and set himself to soothe her shattered nerves.

'Now tell me about Maddy. Her real name is Madeleine? It's a pretty name. My nurse was called Mrs Rolls. My sister and I called her Roly-Poly. And she was.'

'Maddy wasn't fat. She was a beautiful woman.'

'Tell me about her.'

Francesca seemed to have forgotten their last devastating meeting. She sat passively while he held her hand and encouraged her to talk about her life on St Marthe.

'Mama was ill after I was born. I don't know what she had, but it meant she had to rest a lot. Maddy was engaged to look after me, when I was just a few weeks old.'

'She took the place of your mother?'

'Oh, no! I spent a great deal of time with Mama—and Maddy was there, too. Mama had a huge bedroom with a veranda overlooking the sea. It was full of white draperies. I remember thinking how pretty they looked fluttering in the breeze—the Trade Winds, I suppose. No, Maddy and Mama were friends. They laughed a lot.'

'Who was Maddy? Where had she come from?'

'I'm not sure. I think she had lost her own family in a hurricane. She was a Creole. They were both so beautiful, Mama and Maddy. Mama was blonde and little, with dark brown eyes, but Maddy was quite tall. She had black hair and a skin that looked like the petals of the magnolias that grew at the side of the house.'

Marcus blinked. Privately he wondered how Lord Beaudon had dealt with the problem of an invalid wife and a raven-haired beauty as his daughter's nurse. It was as if Francesca could read his mind.

'I expect you're wondering about Maddy's position in our household. She was my nurse, of course. But later, when I got older and used to think about the time on St Marthe, I often wondered how my father viewed her. At the time I had no high opinion of him, so I assumed the worst. But one thing I was always sure of, even as a child. My mother and Maddy loved one another. Whatever happened, they were friends. And Maddy was as unhappy as I was when my mother died.'

'Whatever the truth of it, your father must have placed your comfort above his own. He sent this Maddy to England with you.'

'Yes, he did, didn't he?' She sat for a moment in thought. 'I didn't see a lot of him on St Marthe—or at least, I don't remember seeing him much. But since he came back, I have talked to him a great deal. I am quite sure now he was devoted to my mother.'

'When did your mother die?'

'When I was five. More than twenty years ago.'

'And you have never seen or heard of Maddy since she left Shelwood.'

'Not till today.'

'Then we must find out where she is. Your father clearly knows.'

'I think. . .I think she might have gone back to stay with him. Which would mean that she was in Paris now.'

'We shall see.' He took her other hand in his and bent forward. 'I'll help you all I can.'

Francesca looked up at him, then seemed suddenly to realise who he was. She snatched her hands away from him and jumped up. 'Thank you, but I don't need your help. I can send for Maddy myself as soon as I know for sure where she can be found.'

'Your father seems to regard me as necessary.'

'He is sick.'

'And therefore not to be listened to?'

'I told you, I don't need anyone!'

'What about Denver?'

'Oh. Oh, yes. He'll help me. If I need him. I must

ask you to go now. My father will soon wake.'

'In that case I must stay—to take my leave of him.'

Francesca said nothing, but moved away to the side of the bed. Once again Marcus stood on the other side. Their eyes met.

'Can't you forgive me?' he said.

'I. . .find it hard. I find it hard to forgive myself.'

'Don't say that! You have nothing, nothing at all, to forgive yourself for! Let me start again, Francesca. I've been all kinds of a fool, but you must believe me when I say that I've come to my senses at last.'

'I. . .I owe something to Lord Denver.'

'George Denver isn't the issue between us. You know that. Can you compare what you feel for him with your feeling for me? Can you forget what happened the last time we met?'

Francesca shut her eyes. When she opened them again, they were full of pain.

'Yes,' she whispered. 'Yes, I can. I will. I won't let myself remember. I don't want any part of it. Please go, Marcus!'

'I know I hurt you in the past, and I cannot say how much I regret it. But can't you bring yourself to trust me now? Please, Francesca!'

She started to shake her head, then looked at him uncertainly, confusion in her eyes. The sincerity in his voice had had an effect. 'I. . .I. . .I don't know,' she said at last. 'I don't know. I can't think at the moment. It's all been too much. You'll have to excuse me.'

He saw that she was at the end of her tether and grew angry with himself for pushing her too far, too quickly. 'It's all right, my dear,' he said swiftly. 'I'll wait. At least you haven't refused to think about it. But don't shut me out completely. I'll leave you to say my farewells to your father. I'll come again as soon as he wishes.'

He took his leave of her and went out. Francesca watched him go. Neither of them had noticed that Lord Beaudon's eyes were wide open, and that he was studying them both, straining to hear what they were saying. By the time Francesca turned back to the bed, his eyes were shut.

Chapter Twelve

Marcus cancelled most of his engagements and came back at an early hour the next day, without waiting for a summons. Lord Beaudon had made it clear that he was to help Francesca in the business of 'Maddy'. That 'Maddy' was important to both of the Beaudons was reason enough in Marcus's mind to abandon any obligations to the rest of Society.

When Mrs Canfield saw him arrive, she shook her head and intercepted him before he had set foot on the stairs.

'May I have a word with you, Marcus?'

He hesitated, then good manners prevailed. They went into the salon.

'Why are you here?'

'To see Lord Beaudon.'

'You are very good, I know that. Who should know better? But do you not think you are being a little. . . unwise, Marcus?'

'Unwise?' he asked with a touch of hauteur.

'The gossip has been silenced for the moment. But do you not think your frequent visits—your very frequent visits—might provoke more? You know what London is like. I am venturing to speak to you like this, Marcus, because I am very fond of both you and Francesca. She has enough to bear at the moment without becoming the topic of more speculation.'

'Lord Beaudon has conveyed that he wants my help in some way, Maria. I am here to see if he can make his wishes clearer. I shall probably not even see Francesca.'

'Is there no one else who can aid Lord Beaudon?'

'Apparently not. Not even Denver.' This was said with a certain degree of satisfaction.

'You realise that your readiness to help may lead others to read more into your relationship with Lord Beaudon's daughter than you might wish?'

'That is not possible.' Mrs Canfield's eyes widened. He smiled ruefully and said, 'I had not intended to say as much to anyone yet. Certainly not to Francesca herself—but I think I may rely on your discretion, Maria. You are the first to know that when all this is over, I intend to ask Francesca to marry me.'

'Marcus! This is very sudden. I had no idea—'

'Do you think she will?'

He waited for her answer with more anxiety than he was willing to reveal. Maria Canfield must be more in Francesca's confidence than most.

'I. . .I don't know,' she said slowly. He had the impression she was choosing her words carefully. 'You have a powerful effect on her, of that I am certain. I know you two met in the past, but Francesca has never talked about it to me. I suspect she has painful memories of it.' He would have spoken, but she went on, 'That must remain between you. I do know that she has set her mind on marrying someone. . .less dangerous to her peace of mind than you appear to be.' She paused, then added, 'Lord Denver is devoted to her.'

'He would never make her really happy, of that I am sure.'

'How can you say so? It is my opinion that Lord Denver

is everything a young girl could hope for. Indeed, I could
have wished. . . But no matter.'

'That's just the point, Maria! George Denver is the best
of fellows—a man couldn't ask for a better friend. He
would make an excellent husband for a young girl—
someone like Lydia, for example. But Francesca is not a
young girl! She is an intelligent, strong-minded woman.
In a very short time they would each be disappointed in
the other. Francesca would be stifled, burdened by his
concern, his desire to protect and indulge her. She could
not maintain the image she presents to Society throughout
years of marriage. Not without doing violence to her true
character. And, ultimately, Denver would be made
unhappy by her desire for independence, her strong views,
her appreciation of a good argument—her passion, her
impulsive ways. . .'

'Francesca? Impulsive?'

'You see? Even you, who have lived with her all these
months, do not know the real woman.'

'And you do?'

'I know Francesca as I know myself. She is part of me,
as I am sure I am part of her.'

'These are strong words, Marcus,' said Mrs Canfield,
looking at him as if she had never seen him before. 'And
I think I know you well enough to know that you do
not use them lightly. But. . .have you considered this?
Francesca may well not wish to be the real woman you
claim to know.'

'What do you mean?'

'From the time Francesca Beaudon first came to
Packards, she been single-minded in the pursuit of one
ambition.'

'To find the sort of husband she thinks she wants. I
know that, Maria.'

'That is not what I meant. Finding that sort of husband—a man like Denver, for example—is merely a symptom. Her real ambition is to protect herself from the kind of hurt she suffered in her earlier life. Her aunt's treatment of her was, from all accounts, unbelievably cruel. And, though I cannot imagine you meant to, I suspect you, too, hurt her—badly. Now she seeks calmer, kinder waters in her relationships. She allows herself affection—look how fond she is of Lydia. And her love for her father has deepened over the months. But strong, passionate feeling? I doubt if she will ever allow it to rule her.'

Marcus frowned and swung away to the window. He was silent for a minute. Then he said harshly, 'What you say merely makes me more determined. Given time, I know I could make her love me—as she should love someone. Anything else would be a denial of her true nature.'

Mrs Canfield looked at him thoughtfully. Then she smiled and said, 'In that case, I wish you success. I am quite sure that, if Francesca allowed herself to fall in love with you, she could not be in better hands. Will you take a little advice?'

'Of course.'

'Do not press her at the moment. She has enough to cope with. Act as the good friend I know you can be. This business with Lord Beaudon gives you an excellent opportunity.'

'So you've changed your mind—you approve of my visits?'

'You are always welcome, you know that, and now that I understand your real feelings, I will do all I can to promote your interests—we shall ignore gossip and speculation. And now I think Lord Beaudon has waited long enough.'

Marcus kissed her hand. 'If you can help me in this

matter, Maria, you will have more than repaid any trifling service I may have done you in the past—ten times over!'

'I have to say that I never thought to see you in this state, Marcus. I had quite given up hope that you would ever marry.'

'Oh, I shall! And Francesca Beaudon will be my bride. You will see!'

When Marcus entered the bedchamber, Lord Beaudon was once again alert. He was looking at the door, an expression of anxiety on his face. When he saw Marcus he relaxed visibly.

'Good morning, sir.' Lord Beaudon inclined his head and lifted his hand—shakily, but a movement all the same. In response to the gesture, Marcus sat down by the bed. He wasted no time on niceties—Lord Beaudon's strength was limited and must be used on more important matters. 'You were telling me about someone called Madeleine— Maddy. Is she in Paris?' Lord Beaudon nodded, looking at him anxiously, and Marcus continued, 'She was your daughter's nurse?' Another nod. 'You have been. . .looking after her since she was sent away from Shelwood?'

A slight grin twisted Lord Beaudon's mouth as he nodded, then the worried look descended again.

'You wish me to send a message to her. Should she be sent for?'

This time there was a distinct frown.

'Fetch her myself?'

Another frown. The wrinkled hand on the cover clenched in a gesture of frustration, as Lord Beaudon tried to speak.

'Easy, sir, easy. It will come. Don't force it.'

'Don't understand. Hu. . .hurr-rry. Age—' Marcus was puzzled again, but waited patiently. After a moment, Lord Beaudon tried again. 'Age. . .nt!'

'Your agent? In Paris?' An impatient shake of the head.
'In London? You wish me to speak to your agent in
London.' Lord Beaudon sank back with a sigh of satisfaction. 'I'll do it at once. Does Francesca know who it is,
where he is to be found?' A tired nod. 'I shall find her
and ask. Ah, here she is.'

Francesca came in with an older man, obviously a
doctor. She was very formal as they greeted one another.

'Your father has requested me to visit his agent, Miss
Beaudon. Could you give me his direction?'

Francesca looked at her father, who nodded slowly. 'Of
course. I have it downstairs.'

'Then I shall wait downstairs. Do you wish your agent
to come to see you, sir?'

The doctor intervened. 'If I may interrupt? I think that
would be most unwise. Lord Beaudon should not exert
himself as much as he has done already. He should not
have any visitors at all.' His look at Marcus was severe.

Marcus smiled charmingly back. 'I am a family friend,
sir. I venture to suggest that Lord Beaudon will be easier
in his mind if someone he trusts is looking after his daughter, and his business affairs.' Ignoring a small gasp of
indignation from Francesca, he turned to the figure in the
bed. 'May I see the agent on your behalf, sir? I will report
what he says.'

Lord Beaudon nodded. A close observer would have
said that he was smiling.

Marcus returned later that day, but asked to see Miss
Beaudon rather than her father. She came into the salon
reluctantly.

'Don't look like that, Francesca. My reason for wishing
to see you is perfectly legitimate. How is your father? I
thought he looked brighter this morning.'

'He fell asleep again after you left. But in general he

seems to be improving by the hour. His ability to speak
is slowly coming back to him. Why did you wish to
see me?'

'I sent for Loudon, the agent, and your father's affairs
are all in hand. There are a few papers for him to put a
mark to when he is ready. But the news I was initially
sent for—the news of Maddy—is not very satisfactory.'

Francesca sat down. 'What is wrong?'

'Your father rents a house in a fashionable quarter of
Paris. Maddy lives with him there.'

'What is wrong with that? I'm sorry he concealed
Maddy's presence for so long from me, but there's no
reason to condemn—'

'I have made no such comment. Your father's affairs
are his own. Don't jump down my throat, Francesca. I'm
trying to help.'

'Well, what is wrong, then?' she asked, less than
graciously.

'The house in the rue du Luxembourg has been closed.
Maddy has disappeared.'

'What?'

'I wasn't able to make a great deal of sense out of what
Loudon said. But it appears that when your father decided
to spend the Season here in London, he sent a large sum
of money to Maddy, care of his steward in Paris. This
was for household expenses, including the rent on the
property, which fell due last month. It, apparently, wasn't
used for this purpose. The owners' agent has been trying
to get in touch with your father for the past week.'

'But what has happened to Maddy?'

'Loudon doesn't seem to know.'

'But this is terrible! She must be found. I couldn't bear
to lose her again after all these years. And my father. . .
what will my father say?'

'That is precisely why I am consulting you. He must

be told, but gently. You must calm yourself, Francesca.'

'Yes, yes, of course. We must not alarm him. I will be calm.' She took several breaths, then said, 'It would be better if I had a plan of action to suggest to him. What can I do?' She paused again, then said with decision, 'I shall go to Paris.'

'You! Don't be absurd! What could you do in Paris? No, I must be the one to go.'

'It is you who is being absurd! Maddy doesn't know you, you have no connection with the Beaudons—what would the world think if Lord Carne were to race off to Paris in search of Miss Beaudon's former nurse?'

'It's better than having them wonder why you were allowed to go in search of Rake Beaudon's mistress!' He looked at her with a flicker of amusement in his eyes, asking her to share the joke. Her lips trembled into a reluctant smile, but she soon grew sober again.

'I'm serious, Marcus. I must be the one to go. I had already sent for Madame Elisabeth to help us with Papa. She should arrive any minute. I think I could persuade her to come with me, and I shall find a reliable courier to look after us.'

'You are still talking rubbish, Francesca. If you insist on going, I shall accompany you, of course.'

'You will not! How could I possibly allow it? What a field day that would make for the gossips!'

For a moment Marcus was tempted to declare himself. As Francesca's acknowledged fiancé, he could escort her, suitably chaperoned, on her father's business without arousing too much censure. But a moment's thought put a stop to the impulse. If Francesca refused him, as she well might, there would be an end to all communication between them. And she needed him at this moment more than ever before. He must find a way round the problem, not meet it head on.

'Your father will be wondering what has become of you. And of me. Francesca, shall we declare a truce for now? Before we launch into any schemes, it might make sense to find out exactly what your father wants.'

Francesca looked at him as if her mind were only half on what he was saying, and he wondered what she was plotting. But he was pleasantly surprised when she said, 'I agree. But I think we must tell Papa the truth. Evasion or pretence would only worry him more. His speech may be impaired, but his wits are as sound as ever.'

They went up to Lord Beaudon's bedchamber.

'I'm that glad you've come, ma'am. His lordship has been fretting this half-hour!' The nurse sounded and looked flustered. It was obvious that Lord Beaudon had been a difficult patient.

'Papa! I'm sorry I wasn't here. I. . .I was delayed.' Lord Beaudon made a dismissive movement with his hand. His eyes went to Marcus. As usual, Marcus wasted no time on formality, going straight to the point, as he knew Lord Beaudon wished.

'Good evening, sir. You are looking better. I've done as you asked. Loudon and I have sorted out most of your outstanding business, as you asked—and there are papers for you to sign.'

'Madeleine?' Lord Beaudon's speech was distinctly clearer.

'What is it you wish to do about Maddy, Papa?'

'Want her to know. . .I haven't forgotten. Haven't seen her. . .three months. . .more.'

'Does she know about me?'

He nodded. 'Proud of you.'

'Why didn't you bring her?'

'Gossip. Didn't want. . .to spoil. . .your début.'

'Oh, Papa! Why didn't you tell me? How could you leave her?'

'Francesca.' Marcus had put a warning hand on Francesca's arm. Lord Beaudon's eyes followed the gesture.

'Fetch her now. With his help.'

'Whose?'

A smile lit the tired face on the pillow. 'Carne's, damn it.'

'I cannot do that!'

'Course y'can. Get engaged. Time anyway.' He closed his eyes and slept.

The stormy expression on Francesca's face was confirmation enough that Marcus had been right to be cautious. As soon as they were outside the door of Lord Beaudon's room, she turned on him.

'I know what you are thinking, but I assure you that I have never encouraged my father to believe that I wished to marry you! Indeed, it is the last thing I want!'

He glanced round expressively. 'Shall we discuss this in private, Francesca?'

'There is nothing to discuss! I have no intention of becoming engaged to you, Lord Carne!'

'You force me to tell you in something less than privacy that I have at the moment no intention of asking you to be my wife, Miss Beaudon!'

They were both so absorbed that they were not aware of Mrs Canfield until she said gently, 'Francesca, I'm surprised. What sort of discussion is this to be having on the staircase? Take Lord Carne into the salon.' Unseen by Francesca, she raised an eyebrow at Marcus as she passed them.

Marcus was fighting for survival. He said more calmly, 'Your father's interests are surely more important than our own for the moment. We can talk more easily downstairs.'

Francesca, still looking mutinous, allowed herself to be led into the salon. Here she marched past him and sat down defiantly in the window seat.

Marcus said carefully, 'Whatever my feelings, I should not have indulged in that piece of discourtesy upstairs. I apologise.'

Francesca said stiffly, 'I provoked you to it, Lord Carne. You have no need to apologise.'

'Very well. Now, can we forget it and continue with our efforts to solve the problem of Maddy?' His even tone and casual air were designed to reassure. Francesca relaxed a little. 'It is now clear that someone has to go to Paris, and that your father will not be content unless we go together. Whatever our own views on the matter, his are quite clear. He wishes us to be engaged.'

'And that would suit neither of us,' said Francesca with determination.

'Quite. But may I suggest that we do not tell him that? I am sure we could travel to Paris together without arousing comment if I went on official business and merely acted as your courier. I do have some unfinished Foreign Office business in Paris. Perhaps Mrs Canfield and Lydia would come with you?'

'Mrs Canfield has agreed to supervise the care of Papa. And Lydia should not be dragged away from London at the moment.'

'True. I had forgotten. Madame Elisabeth? I heard you say she was already on her way here?'

Francesca looked at him. Once again, he had the impression that he had only half her attention. 'It might work, I suppose,' she said slowly. 'How long would it take to arrange?'

'A few days.'

'Good!' Marcus looked at her in surprise. He had been

delighted that she had agreed with so little resistance, but had thought she would object to the delay—short though it was. 'I mean,' said Francesca carefully, 'that it is good that we have managed to settle on a solution.'

'What shall we tell your father?'

'He will be happy to know that we have agreed to go. We need not go into great detail.' She smiled wryly. 'He trusts you, I am sure.'

'Do you?'

'Trust you? Why, of course!'

'Do you, Francesca? Really?' He moved closer to her, absurdly pleased at her words. But she avoided him and went to the door.

'Papa must know what we are doing,' she said, and went upstairs.

Marcus followed her in silence. Very well, my girl, he thought. We shall see how we progress when you and I journey to Paris together. There will be occasions when I shall have you to myself—I'll make certain of it! And then. . .we shall see.

Marcus visited Mount Street only fleetingly the next day, and not at all the next. He and Francesca had seen Lord Beaudon and told him of their decision. He had congratulated them both and expressed his delight, though it was clear that this was shadowed by his anxiety about Maddy. Marcus had felt some compunction at deceiving Francesca's father, but comforted himself with the thought that, if all went well, he and Francesca would, in truth, be engaged by the time they returned to London.

What Francesca made of it, he was not sure. She had recently been more open with him, but now she retreated once more into reserve, and he found it difficult to guess what she was thinking. He was content to wait. He would have all the time in the world on their journey to

France to find a way back into her confidence.

So though he sent messages to Mount Street, he did not have time to see the Beaudons himself. He had been speaking the truth when he said he had unfinished business in Paris, but there were people in London he had to consult first. He spent an energetic two days making arrangements and gathering papers, making sure that their journey would be as comfortable as man could make it, and sending couriers ahead to prepare their reception in Paris. It was a demanding time; if he had not been buoyed up by the hope of finally persuading Francesca to trust him, he would have found it exhausting.

He was shocked and furiously disappointed when he arrived in Mount Street and found Francesca already gone.

'Miss Beaudon isn't here? Of course she is!' he said sharply to the hapless footman who had taken his hat and cane.

Roberts, the butler, came to the rescue. Dismissing the footman with a nod, he said, 'Mrs Canfield left instructions that your lordship should be shown into the salon. Would you come this way, my lord?'

Containing himself with difficulty, Marcus allowed himself to be ushered into the salon. He refused an offer of wine somewhat curtly, and waited impatiently for Mrs Canfield to arrive.

'Maria, what's this nonsense about Francesca?' he demanded as soon as she came through the door. Mrs Canfield was in an unusual state of agitation.

'Francesca set off for Paris last night, Marcus.'

'You cannot mean it!'

'I'm afraid I do.'

'Does her father know?'

'No. We haven't told him yet.'

'Why the devil did you permit such a thing, Maria?' His tone was peremptory.

Mrs Canfield stiffened. She said, 'I knew nothing of the matter. Francesca took advantage of the fact that Lydia and I were at the Scarborough rout party to escape.'

'Did she go alone?'

'No. Madame de Romain arrived yesterday and I assume she accompanied Francesca.'

'Two women! When did you say she went?'

'Last night.'

'My God! Two women travelling through the night along some of the most dangerous roads in England.' He paced restlessly through the room, then he stopped and turned. 'You must have suspected something! Why didn't you stop such a mad escapade? Or at least send for me!'

'Marcus, I make every allowance for your sense of shock, but you are being unnecessarily rude. I repeat—I had no idea, no idea at all that Francesca would undertake such a foolhardy enterprise. Nothing about her behaviour in the past would have led me to suspect it.'

'I told you that Francesca was impulsive and head-strong, and you refused to believe me. Oh, this is exactly like her! I should have anticipated it. Past experience should have taught me.'

'I can still hardly credit what you say. But I have come to agree with you, Marcus, that she needs a stronger man than Denver to control her. This will be a most unpleasant surprise for him. I believe him to be sincerely in love with her, but he will be shocked beyond measure at her behaviour.'

'Denver? Bah! He's too gentle a man for Francesca. Even I couldn't control her. No, with Francesca, you merely try to guard her from the worst of her follies, and love her for them. And hope that, with time, she will trust you enough to allow you power over her!' He had been talking almost to himself. But now he went on, 'So you see, Maria, I have to rescue her. I'll leave straight away, though it's impossible to catch them up before the packet sails. I wish you had sent for me sooner.'

'I did try to find you, but you were not at home. I could hardly send round the clubs for you!'

'I was with Stewart's man in the Foreign Office. Oh God, I hope she's safe!' He made for the door, then stopped. 'What about Lord Beaudon?'

'There's a note for him. I wasn't sure what to do, so I waited for you to come before giving it to him.'

'I'll take it. He's pushed her into this. If he hadn't been so hasty, we'd have managed very well. You'd better warn Glover to be on hand.'

But Lord Beaudon took what the letter had to say with remarkable fortitude. It did not mention the name Carne, but Francesca's reluctance to be in his company was clear in every line. When Marcus grew pale and clenched his jaw, Lord Beaudon chuckled. 'Don't worry. She'll have you,' he said. 'Patience. I suppose you're going to follow her?'

'I must. Though she does seem at least to have had the sense to supply herself with plenty of protection.'

The letter had been intended to reassure Francesca's father about her safety. She told him that she had used a reputable agent and she and Madame Elisabeth had found companions and guards for their journey. And they had letters of introduction, together with the addresses of some of Madame Elisabeth's old friends to help them in Paris.

'This is ridiculous!' Marcus burst out.

'Then be off to Paris and tell her so. And bring Madeleine back with you!' was Lord Beaudon's response.

Marcus wasted no more time. He was forced to take the travelling coach he had prepared with such care, for it contained all his papers, but it meant that progress was not as fast as he would have wished. But it was too late in any case to catch Francesca's party before they embarked for France, and the next packet was not till the following day. But, all the same, Marcus chafed at the delay. In spite of Francesca's reassurances he wanted to see for himself that she was safe and sound. And preferably under his own protection!

As Francesca travelled the long road to Paris, she occasionally allowed herself to wonder what the journey would have been like in Marcus's company. In different circumstances it could have been. . .idyllic. But she did not allow her mind to dwell on this for long, and not once did she regret her hasty decision to come to France without him.

Lord Carne may be everything Society said of him— totally honourable, completely dependable, absolutely scrupulous. But the Marcus that was lodged so unshakeably in her heart was none of these. The admirable Lord Carne would never attack a helpless female as she had been attacked in the salon at Mount Street. And elegant Miss Beaudon would never respond to any man at all in the abandoned manner in which she had responded, returning kiss for kiss, meeting passion with passion.

But Francesca and Marcus. . .ah, that was different! Neither reason nor respect for propriety, no sense of self-preservation or fear of hurt seemed to hold back this overwhelming force which could flare into life between them. Time had not affected it—at twenty-five she was as vulnerable to Marcus as she had been when she had given in to his charm when she was not even sixteen. She had managed to survive the experience of a broken heart once. A second exposure might well destroy her. The only way to guard herself was to avoid as much contact with him as possible. . .as she would.

*   *   *

They arrived in Paris early in the evening after an uneventful journey and went to a hotel not far from her father's house, recommended to them by connections of Madame Elisabeth. It was too late to pursue the question of Maddy that evening, so the two ladies retired early to their rooms and tried to get some rest.

The next morning they set off, armed with a street guide and Lord Beaudon's address. Though the rue du Luxembourg took some time to find, Lord Beaudon's house was soon identified. It was securely locked up. They tried knocking, and pulling the bell, but there was no response. When Francesca looked all round for someone to consult, the street was deserted.

'We are too early, Francesca. No one stirs here till midday.'

'Surely there must be some servant. . .?'

'Not in the front half of the houses, not before noon. Haven't you noticed that there are no street vendors about, either? Their cries are not allowed to disturb the peace of this neighbourhood till later in the day. If we return this afternoon, I am sure we shall find someone.'

Francescsa had to agree, and they returned, somewhat tired, to their hotel, where they went to their rooms to rest. But when Francesca called for Madame Elisabeth later in the day, she found that lady stretched out on her couch looking very frail.

'I am sorry, Francesca. I cannot walk another step today. Could we try again tomorrow?'

'Of course! You make me ashamed of myself, Madame Elisabeth. I dragged you all the way here without pause or rest, and then got you up early. . . Of course, you need rest. I have been unpardonably selfish.'

'Oh, no, my dear! You are anxious to find your nurse, I understand that. I shall be perfectly fit tomorrow, you'll see.'

Francesca sent for a chambermaid to attend to Madame Elisabeth. 'You must not allow me to stop you, Francesca,' said Madame Elisabeth. 'It is a beautiful afternoon—I am sure you would find someone to ask if you went back to the rue du Luxembourg.' She spoke to the maid in rapid French, then turned to Francesca. 'The maid says the streets are quite safe round here, but you must take care if you go further afield.'

Francesca thought for a moment. Then she said, 'I think I'll take the carriage, Madame Elisabeth. It's here in the stables, and the grooms are in the yard—I saw them as we came in. I just might want to go further, if someone tells me where Maddy can be found.'

'Of course. I'm sure you wish to find your nurse as soon as possible. You must be worried about her.'

'Are you sure you'll be all right? I'll get one of the chambermaids to stay with you if you wish.'

'No, no, that won't be necessary. A rest today and I shall be quite well again. And I am happy that you will be safe with the grooms we brought from England to guard you. They seem to have their wits about them. Off you go, my dear. And—*bonne chance*!'

The street was full of activity when Francesca arrived there for the second time. Nursemaids were walking the children, footmen were delivering notes and parcels, and next door to her father's house an elegantly dressed lady was just setting foot in her carriage. Francesca sent one of the grooms to knock at the door of her father's house and waited, aware of curious glances directed at her from all sides. The groom knocked once more, but there was still no response. Her heart sinking, Francesca left the carriage and went up to the house. The groom shrugged his shoulders and shook his head.

'It's no use trying there. They've gone.' Francesca's

French was far from perfect, but it was adequate enough to understand these words. She turned round. The speaker was about eight years old, and looking up at her with a child's curiosity. '*Tais-toi, Virginie*!' The nursemaid with the little girl took her hand and hurried her away.

Francesca looked helplessly round. The elegantly dressed lady, who had stopped to stare, got into the carriage and gave an abrupt order. The carriage moved off before Francesca could speak to her. A small crowd of footmen, other servants, street vendors and children had gathered at the bottom of the steps, gabbling rapidly. Francesca regretted that Madame Elisabeth was not with her. Her own French was not equal to this.

'*C'est la maison de Milord Beaudon*?' she asked hesitantly.

They all stared, then one of the footmen, taking pity on her, said, '*Oui, mais. . .* the little one is right, *mademoiselle*. The English milor' has not been here for months. More. And *Madame* was taken ill.' Francesca caught this last word—*malade* was ill.

'Where is *Madame* now?' she asked. The footman shrugged his shoulders. There was a discussion. At one point they eyed her uncertainly, then shook their heads.

'Please,' she cried. 'I must see *Madame*!'

They only shook their heads again. One woman—a street vendor from her looks—obviously disagreed with the rest. She harangued them in a French which was totally incomprehensible to Francesca's untutored ear. They replied in kind, and the footman ended the discussion with a decisive '*Non*!' Then he turned again to Francesca.

'I regret, *mademoiselle*, we cannot help you. Perhaps the embassy will advise you?'

Francesca thanked him, pressed a few sous into his hand and turned away disconsolately. She had the impression that they knew what had happened to Maddy, but

had decided not to tell her. The speed with which they
disappeared seemed to confirm this notion. She started
back towards the carriage, and was just getting in when
she heard,

'Psst! Psst, *mademoiselle*!'

Francesca turned. The street vendor was sidling up
behind her. The groom attempted to push her away, but
Francesca stopped him. The woman clearly had something
to tell her. She was talking in some kind of patois, but
when she saw that Francesca did not understand a word,
she tried again, more slowly.

Francesca gathered that she was trying to give her an
address, and eventually, after many false starts and failed
repetitions, Francesca managed to say the address to the
woman's satisfaction. She beamed with pleasure and held
out a dirty hand. Francesca gave her some money, and
they parted on good terms. As she hurried off down the
street, the woman shouted something in a warning voice,
but Francesca did not heed her. She was sure that *La
Maison des Anges* in the rue Giboureau was where she
would find Maddy. It sounded like a hospital of some sort.

Chapter Thirteen

After studying the street map one of the grooms had procured, Francesca saw that the rue Giboureau was some distance away in what looked like a prosperous district not far from the Bois de Boulogne. It should be easy to find. It was still early, so Francesca decided that, if she went straight there, she could see Maddy, find out how she was and still have time to get back to the hotel before it was too late. Then the next day, if Maddy's health permitted, she could set about making arrangements to convey her to England. Francesca gave the orders, and the carriage set off in the direction of the Bois de Boulogne.

The journey took longer than Francesca had anticipated, and it was almost evening before they reached the rue Giboureau. The road was lined with high walls, interrupted occasionally with tall, elaborately decorated iron gates. Francesca marvelled at tantalising glimpses of opulent houses set in lawns and flowerbeds behind them. If Maddy was in one of these, she was clearly being comfortably looked after—these mansions were like no hospital Francesca had ever seen.

'Miss Beaudon! Look!' One of the grooms was pointing at an elegantly discreet board set outside an open gateway which bore the legend *Maison des Anges*.

They drove up a short drive, lined with statues of nymphs in various graceful poses, to a beautiful house, built in the days before the Revolution. Broad steps led up to an imposing portico and intricately carved doors, and again there was an elegant board at the side which gave the name of the house. This time the board was surmounted by the head of a beautiful girl, her long, curling locks forming a frame for the whole.

Francesca rang the bell and then studied the board more closely as she waited. Flowers and leaves formed a background to the girl's head, all beautifully carved, and looking very lifelike—there were even a few insects on the flowers. Francesca saw that they were mostly bees— in fact, they were all bees. How strange!

'Madame?'

An exotic figure in Turkish costume was standing impassively at the door. He was at least six and a half feet tall with huge shoulders and a swarthy face half hidden by an imposing moustache.

Francesca blinked, checked the board, which still said *Maison des Anges*, and cleared her throat. In her coolest manner she said, 'I have come to see Madame Madeleine. . .' She stopped. What name would Maddy now be using? 'Madame. . .'

'Je regrette. Madame Madeleine est malade.' The deep voice expressed nothing but a detached finality. He started to close the door.

'Yes, I know she is sick,' said Francesca, raising her voice and speaking with all the authority at her command. 'I have come to see her. Please tell her that Miss Beaudon, Miss Francesca Beaudon, is here. Meanwhile, I should like to see your. . .your *directrice.*'

'Pas possible!'

'Of course it is possible! Kindly let me in!'

'Qui est-ce, Hassim?' Hassim's tall figure completely

blocked the view into the hall, so Francesca did not see the owner of the voice until she appeared at her servant's side.

The man bowed. *'Une anglaise, Comtesse. Elle veut voir Madame Madeleine.'*

Though the Countess was in her fifties, she was still a beautiful woman. Her hair was grey, but fashionably cut, and her dove-grey dress, though sober in hue, was of heavy silk and trimmed with white lace. The figure revealed by the superb cut of her dress was still elegantly slender.

Francesca was impressed, but did not disguise her annoyance with this cavalier treatment. 'My name is Beaudon,' she said coldly. 'Until recently, Madame Madeleine was living in the rue du Luxembourg, in my father's house. I am one of her oldest friends. It surely cannot be that difficult for me to see her. Even if. . .' Francesca hesitated. 'Is she so very ill?'

The Countess looked disconcerted. 'Miss Beaudon? The daughter of Lord Beaudon? But you should not be here, mademoiselle! Please go at once!'

Francesca set her jaw. 'I have come from England to see my friend, and I am not going until I know how she is!'

'But you don't understand. . . Oh, *mon Dieu*, you mustn't stand here on the doorstep where anyone could see you. It is most unfortunate. Please go!'

'If you do not take me to see Madame Madeleine, *immediately*, I shall return with someone from the British Embassy.'

The Countess had been looking distinctly agitated, but at these words her lips curved into an ironical smile. 'It wouldn't be the first time one or two of them had visited me, *mademoiselle*, but they wouldn't bring *you* back here, I assure you.'

'What do you mean?' Francesca was growing angrier

by the minute. 'Surely even in Paris one may visit a sick friend in hospital?'

'A *hospital*! Is that what you think? Ah! Now I understand. . .a hospital! That explains a lot.' The woman turned her head away, but Francesca could have sworn she was laughing. It was too much! Exasperated, she turned on her heel and started down the steps.

'No! Wait, Mademoiselle Beaudon. I have changed my mind. You can see Madame Madeleine, if you promise not to stay too long. I think you are right. Your visit might do Maddy some good.'

Francesca swung round and stared at the Countess. *'Maddy?'*

'I, too, am a friend of Maddy's. An even older friend than you, I think. But please come inside. We can talk more comfortably there. If you will permit, Hassim will show your groom where to put the carriage. But you must be away from here before. . . Please do come in, Mademoiselle Beaudon.' When Francesca hesitated, the Countess said with a charming smile, 'You shall be perfectly safe, I assure you. Believe me, my sole object is to protect you. Let Hassim speak to your groom. We cannot leave the carriage in the drive for all to see. Come!'

Somewhat doubtfully Francesca allowed herself to be escorted inside.

Francesca had an impression of velvet and gilt, painting and statues, ormolu and boulle, as she walked into the grand entrance hall. Spacious rooms could be glimpsed on each side, and a broad staircase swept up in a wide curve to the first landing, its balusters supporting candelabras in the form of nymphs on either side. The house obviously belonged to someone of enormous wealth, though the furnishings were too opulent for Francesca's

taste. What sort of hospital was this? She looked doubtfully at her hostess.

'I shall take you straight away to Maddy. I think you
will be reassured when you see her. She has been ill, but
will soon be well again.'

Francesca tore her fascinated gaze from one of the
nymphs, on whose scantily clad bosom rested a small
carved bee, and said, 'But. . .why is she here, *Comtesse*?'

The Countess had started up the stairs, but now she
stopped. 'Do you not know? Your father has sent no
money to Maddy for the past three months—since he last
visited her, in fact.'

'But, indeed, he has! His agent in London. . .'

'Swears he has sent it? I thought as much,' said the
Countess, looking satisfied. She started up the stairs again.
'I said so to Maddy. Richard has not forgotten you, I told
her. And if she had not been ill, I think she would have
had more confidence in him, and pursued the matter.
There has been some trickery, I think. I never trusted her
steward, I'll swear he's to blame. But. . .why are you
here, *mademoiselle*? Why has your father not come in
person?'

As Francesca explained the circumstances which had
led to her visit, they reached the top of the stairs and
started walking down a wide corridor with beautifully
carved and painted doors on either side. Once again the
theme was that of nymphs, bees and flowers, though here
some of the nymphs were disporting themselves with
more exuberance than decorum. Francesca blinked at one
spectacularly improper scene and hastily averted her eyes.
They passed a smaller passage leading off to the left,
which was hung with diaphanous rose and gold draperies.
The air here was scented with roses and a heavier, more
exotic perfume.

Francesca wanted to ask the Countess what it was, but

her attention was caught by a deep semi-circular alcove a little way beyond the side passage. The walls were covered in dark red damask and in the centre was a small fountain. A white marble nymph was bathing herself in abandoned grace in the basin at its foot. Francesca felt the colour rising in her cheeks. The statues Lord Elgin had brought from Greece had been positively *chaste* compared with this. She hurried to catch the Countess up. 'I had no idea where Maddy was, otherwise I would have written to her long before this, *Comtesse*. Where. . .where are we?'

'You know where you are, Mademoiselle Beaudon. You are in *La Maison des Anges*.'

'Yes, but. . .' Francesca looked back doubtfully at the marble statue, but said no more. They turned into another side passage to the left, an altogether simpler affair with no doors, no draperies and only a faint scent of lavender.

'Maddy talks of you frequently. She loved you and your mother.'

'You have known her long?'

'We were children together.' They had now reached the end of the passage. The Countess turned and started to mount a narrow staircase. The scent of lavender grew stronger. 'We married more or less at the same time, had our babies more or less at the same time. Then the hurricane came to the island. . . We both lost everything. . .everything. We left the island after that— we could not bear to stay.'

'Maddy came to St Marthe. She was my nurse.'

'I know. And I came to France. But here is Maddy's room, *mademoiselle*. Wait here one moment.'

They had been talking so busily that Francesca had had no time to look around. She saw that they were now in a much plainer part of the house, and the door that faced them was uncarved and unadorned. The Countess went in and Francesca could hear her speaking rapidly, then an exclamation of joy in another voice—a well-loved voice from years ago. Questions and answers followed. She could make out none of the words, though there were echoes of the patois she had learned on St Marthe in her childhood. Then the Countess came out again.

'She is overjoyed to be seeing you again, but still weak—do not overtire her, Mademoiselle Beaudon. I have much to do, so I hope you will excuse me now. But. . .I *beg* of you, do not leave this room until I come to fetch you.' She led the way into a simply furnished room and then went out again. Francesca did not see her go—all her attention was on the figure in the armchair by the window. Maddy held out her arms and Francesca ran to her with a cry of delight.

Marcus arrived in Paris a little less than twenty-four hours after Francesca. He drove straight to Francesca's hotel, and found Madame Elisabeth alone in her room. From there he went to the rue du Luxembourg, and discovered that the house was still shut up and deserted. There was no sign of Francesca, but one of the boys in the street told him he had seen an English lady driving off in a big coach earlier in the day. He had no idea where they had gone.

Marcus went back to the hotel to find that Francesca had still not appeared, and that Madame Elisabeth was beginning to grow anxious for her. After doing his best to reassure the old lady, Marcus then went to the British Embassy and spent some time with a certain Mr Percy Gardiner, one of his closest friends there. What he discovered appalled him.

'Good God! Are you sure? *La Maison des Anges*?'

'Only too true,' said Mr Gardiner, looking at him curiously. 'Why are you so upset? The lady mean anything to you? No, that can't be so—Madeleine Lachasse is nearly old enough to be your mother, Marcus old dear.'

'She's nothing to me personally. I. . .I'm acting for a friend.'

Mr Gardiner looked sceptical. 'Well, you'd do better to tell your friend to leave *La Maison* well alone. Good Lord, I don't have to tell *you* what goes on there—apart from serving as a high-class brothel with some very peculiar practices, that is.'

'I have to get her out of there.'

'You mustn't go near the place, Marcus!' exclaimed Mr Gardiner, dropping his casual air. 'What the devil can you be thinking of? Don't touch it! Can't someone else fetch the lady?'

A vision of Francesca arriving at *La Maison des Anges* flashed through Marcus's mind. He shuddered. 'That's just what I'm afraid of. Er. . .has anyone else been asking about Lord Beaudon's *petite amie*? Today, or yesterday, perhaps.'

'No. . .I don't think so.'

'It's important, Percy. Could you ask around?'

Mr Gardiner came back a few minutes later with the assurance that no one had even mentioned the lady for the past few months. Marcus breathed a sigh of relief. Francesca had not yet learned Maddy's address. But in that case, where was she?

'What is all this about, Marcus? You can't seriously be considering visiting that palace of corruption! Think what it would do, man, if you were found there!'

'I know. But I must get Madeleine Lachasse out of the place as soon as possible—before anyone else goes looking for her.'

'I think you'd better explain.'

Marcus paused, then gave Mr Gardiner an edited version of his mission. Francesca's name did not figure in it.

'But damn it all, you cannot—you really cannot—be

prepared to jeopardise all your work for the past year for the sake of this. . .this paramour! What is Richard Beaudon to you?'

'His daughter and I are betrothed,' said Marcus, stretching the truth a little.

'All the same. . . Wait here!'

Marcus spent the next few minutes arranging his thoughts. He was determined to go out to *La Maison des Anges* as soon as he was free of the Embassy, but knew that he was about to have a serious disagreement with people he had worked with in complete harmony over the last twelve months.

'What's this nonsense, Marcus? Don't be a fool, man. Of course you can't visit *La Maison*.' Marcus got to his feet and bowed to the distinguished-looking gentleman who now came in. Percy had wasted no time in bringing up the heavy guns. His friend gave him an apologetic glance, then went out, shutting the door carefully behind him.

'Good evening, Sir Henry.'

'Oh, good evening, good evening! No! It won't damn well be any sort of good evening if what young Percy tells me is true. Have you gone mad?'

Marcus gritted his teeth. 'No, but I can't see anything else to do. I have to get that woman out of *La Maison des Anges* as soon as possible.'

'The devil take it! Can't anyone else go instead?'

'No, sir. The matter is one of some delicacy. . .'

'To hell with that, Marcus! Look, if you are found anywhere near that hotbed of Napoleon supporters you'll. . .*we*'ll lose all credibility with the French government—you know that! Of all of us, you're the one man they really trust. An escapade like this would ruin months of work. I forbid you to go.'

Marcus grew pale. 'You'll have to forgive me, Sir

Henry. I am not one of your staff. And I intend to go, as soon as I leave you, to fetch Madeleine Lachasse.'

'But *why*?'

Marcus was in a dilemma. The last thing he wanted was to bring Francesca into the discussion. She was at present loose in Paris, searching for her old nurse, and his blood ran cold at what she might do if she found out where the woman was. He placed no reliance on her sense of self-preservation. Impulsive, headstrong Francesca would once more rush in where angels would never dare to tread, but this time the consequences could be disastrous. For all its name, *La Maison des Anges* was no place for any kind of angel!

If that happened, then it would need all the discretion, all the skill at his command, to save Francesca from a catastrophic scandal. If it were once known that the Honourable Miss Beaudon had been found in one of the most notoriously wicked brothels in Paris, nothing—not a thing!—could save her from social extinction.

'*Why*, Marcus?'

Marcus was not to be rushed into a reply. He had no illusions—Sir Henry was perfectly capable of restraining him by force from visiting *La Maison des Anges*. That would hardly benefit Francesca. He must persuade, not fight.

'First, I should tell you, Sir Henry, that Lord Beaudon's daughter has agreed to marry me. . .'

'So London's most eligible bachelor has been caught at last? My congratulations, Marcus. But we'll give this news the attention it deserves later. At the moment. . .'

'That is the point, sir. Why I have to reach Madeleine Lachasse—tonight, if possible.' He took a breath. 'Madeleine Lachasse was Miss Beaudon's nurse, and Miss Beaudon herself is in Paris in order to take her back to England.'

'Good, good. So why can't we send one of the embassy staff to fetch the Lachasse woman and deliver her to yourself and Miss Beaudon? I'd like to meet her while she's in Paris, by the way. She must be a real diamond to have trapped you, Marcus.'

'I. . .I don't know where she is, sir.'

'What the devil do you mean?'

'Miss Beaudon is devoted to her nurse, Sir Henry. She was in such haste to meet her again that she left London ahead of me. However, Madeleine Lachasse was not at the rue du Luxembourg house, so Miss Beaudon decided to seek elsewhere. My worst fear is that she will find out where the woman actually is, and visit her there. That is why I wish to get to *La Maison* as soon as possible. Why I will not trust anyone else with the mission.'

'But, good God, man! Surely no delicately nurtured female would go near such a place!'

'Miss Beaudon can be a touch. . .impulsive, sir.'

Sir Henry frowned. 'Are you sure she's the right girl for you, Marcus? Travelling alone to Paris, visiting all sorts of queer places—she sounds like a bit of a hoyden.'

Marcus stiffened. 'She is everything I could wish for, sir. She can be the soul of propriety. But where her loyalty is concerned, she simply doesn't heed the cost. I consider it my duty—and my deepest pleasure—to protect her from her own impulsive generosity. But you are right— her reputation is in some danger, and if it is to survive, she needs my help tonight. I know I can rely on your discretion, but the story is too dangerous to be trusted to anyone else.'

Sir Henry sat in thought for a moment. Then he said, 'I suppose most of the men who go to visit the "Angels" take care not to be recognised. It wouldn't be too suspicious if you were to muffle yourself up a little. Very well! But. . .for God's sake, don't get caught! If you do,

we'll have to disown you, you know that. It will be the
end of your work here.'

Marcus called again briefly at Francesca's hotel, only to
find no news of Francesca, and Madame Elisabeth in a
state of great anxiety. He refused all pleas that she should
accompany him on his quest, claiming that she should
remain where she was in case Francesca should return by
herself. He did not reveal where he feared she might be.

He hired a fiacre to take him to the rue Giboureau—a
slow business, but necessary to preserve his anonymity.
When he finally arrived at the house it was getting late,
though still early in the evening for its normal clientele.
Hassim received him and asked him to wait in the hall
till the Countess could be found. Marcus shook his head.

'I wish to speak to Madeleine Lachasse,' he said firmly.
'Take me to her, if you please.'

'*Madame Madeleine est malade.*'

'I know. Where is her room? Has she a visitor?'

Hassim glanced up. It was enough. Marcus leapt up
the stairs two at a time, ignoring nymphs, candelabras,
bees and the rest. At the first side passage he hesitated,
and Hassim caught up with him.

'*Monsieur*!' He took hold of Marcus, but was pushed
away so violently that he lost his footing and fell. Ignoring
him, Marcus strode on past the alcove to the second passage. He paused to listen, then found his way to the small
flight of stairs which led to the servants' quarters. At the
top he could see a figure in a wine-red silk evening dress
standing at an open door. She was speaking with emphasis
to someone inside the room.

'Miss Beaudon, I beg of you, come away now. You
have stayed far longer than you should. The evening visitors will be arriving at any moment. You *must not* be
discovered here. I shall send Maddy to your hotel as soon

as she is well enough, I promise you. That cannot be more
than a day or two. Meanwhile, you must wait in patience,
and not visit her here again.'

Francesca's back emerged from the room. For a
moment Marcus could hardly breathe, he was so relieved
to see her. Then he was overcome with sudden fury at
her foolhardy, stupid, potentially catastrophic behaviour.

'I shall see you soon, Maddy. Very soon, I hope.'
Francesca's voice was tremulous. The meeting had obviously been an emotional one. She went on, 'Then I shall
take you back to England. Goodbye.'

'Miss Beaudon! Come! Quickly!' Exasperated, the
Countess took Francesca's arm and ushered her out of the
room, shutting the door behind her. She stopped suddenly
at the sight of Marcus. He took a step towards her, but
Hassim, who had just arrived, seized him from behind.
With a roar Marcus turned on the Turk, glad to have an
outlet for his rage.

'Hassim! No!'

'Marcus!'

The two voices spoke together. Hassim stepped back
immediately and Marcus and Francesca faced one another.

'You fool, Francesca! What the devil do you think you
are doing now? You unutterable fool!'

'Lord Carne!' The Countess took a step forward, then
turned to her servant. 'Hassim, go back to the door. Don't
let anyone up here till I tell you. Keep them below. And,
don't say a word of this to anyone, you understand me?'

Hassim bowed and went in unruffled dignity downstairs.

'Lord Carne—this is a most. . .unexpected pleasure.
May I ask what you are doing here?'

'Saving that. . .that. . .' Marcus could not find a suitable
word. 'That idiot girl from her own folly.'

'It is no folly to visit a sick friend in hospital, sir!' said Francesca with spirit.

'*Hospital*!'

'That is what Miss Beaudon believes *La Maison des Anges* to be, Lord Carne.'

'Oh, God!' said Marcus.

'Quite,' said the Countess, her lips twitching in spite of her obvious concern. 'We are in rare agreement. Miss Beaudon must be removed from here as soon as possible. And you must go with her. It would not enhance *your* reputation to be found here, either.'

'I should have thought that would suit you very well, Countess Rehan. We have been enemies for long enough.'

'I do not regard you as an enemy, Lord Carne. My partners in this enterprise are your enemies.'

'I don't understand. What are you talking about?' Francesca looked from one to the other with a bewildered air.

'We haven't much time, Miss Beaudon. Lord Carne might explain—later when you are free of this house.'

'Why are you doing this for me, *Comtesse*?' asked Marcus abruptly.

'I am not a political creature. I may owe some loyalty to my partners, but my older loyalty—to Maddy and those she loves—must take precedence.'

'You have my thanks.'

The countess shook her head. 'We are wasting time, and we have none to waste. You must go as soon as you can. There is another exit at the back of the house, but you cannot reach it from here. We shall have to go back to the main corridor. Pull the collar of your cloak up round your face. Miss Beaudon, put this veil over your head.'

When Francesca appeared to be ready to argue, Marcus took the heavy veil and threw it over her. Then he took her firmly by the arm and said, 'Lead on, *Comtesse*.'

Sounds of conviviality could now be heard from some of the rooms, while others were silent. But the Countess hurried on, aiming for a small disguised door set into the wall at the top of the main stairs. They had almost reached it when she stopped short and uttered a cry of vexation.

Three men were slowly coming up the staircase. It was evident that they had dined—and wined—well. They held on to the baluster as they ascended, examining its decorations with exaggerated care and making bawdy comments on the nymphs. Though the Countess had cut off her cry as soon as she had uttered it, the men had heard her. They looked up.

She turned and pushed Francesca and Marcus back along the corridor. 'That idiot Hassim!' she whispered. 'Go back to the alcove. You can hide there. I'll see that they take the Harem passage.' Francesca and Marcus ran, soft-footed, back to the alcove, but just as Francesca was scrambling in behind the fountain, her veil caught in the statue's upturned fingers. Marcus swore and laboured frantically to release it. Then he joined her, pushing her further back into the niche. They heard the Countess greeting her visitors at the top of the stairs. 'Good evening, gentlemen. How may *La Maison des Anges* please you?'

'She's speaking English!'

Marcus whispered savagely, 'For God's sake hush, Francesca! Believe me, it's essential you keep quiet.'

'But—'

Marcus swore under his breath, then seized her and kissed her hard. Then he put his hand over her mouth and whispered, 'There are more of those if I can't keep you quiet any other way.'

'How dar—'

Marcus kissed her again. Then he said angrily, but still softly, close to her ear, 'This isn't a hospital, Francesca. It's a. . .a bawdy house!' Francesca gazed at him in shock.

He went on relentlessly, 'One of the most notorious in Paris. Now do you understand why you mustn't be found here?'

Francesca wanted to contradict him—wanted to reject the idea with horror, but she found that she couldn't. In a flash, she realised how well everything fitted—the Countess's anxiety to be rid of her, those nymphs, the rest of the exotic decor, even the name—a horrid irony. It was true! She hid her face in her hands in shame. No wonder Marcus was so angry. He put his arm round her.

'We'll come out of it,' he breathed into her ear fiercely. 'For God's sake, don't lose heart now.'

'I have a number of. . .temptations for the jaded palate.' The Countess was leading the men down the corridor. 'What is it to be?'

'We shall be guided by you, fair lady,' drawled a hatefully familiar voice.

It was as well Marcus had firm hold of Francesca. She jerked up in terror and clutched his arm. He nodded slowly. 'Coker,' he mouthed.

'Will it please you to come this way, milords?'

'Hold hard!' Another familiar voice. 'Am I dreamin' or what? Wasn't that Carne I saw just now, Countess?'

'You're drunker than I thought, Freddie,' said Lord Witham's voice. 'Carne? Here? Carne's a right enough fellow, but he's above being seen in a bawdy house—certainly not one with such a spicy reputation!'

'Well, that's what I would have said, Charlie,' said Mr Chantry with alcoholic dignity. 'But all the same. . .'

Francesca hid her face in Marcus's shoulder. Her hands clutched the cloth of his coat in fearful tension as disaster loomed.

The Countess said with the merest suspicion of censure in her voice, 'Is there something wrong, milords? Perhaps you would like to discuss the matter elsewhere? You must be disturbing some of my other guests. If you will follow me. . .?'

Her effort was wasted. Freddie said obstinately, 'I'm sure I wasn't mistaken. . .there's something about the set of Carne's shoulders. It was Carne, I'll swear.'

'Who is this Carne, milords?'

'A man of unimpeached virtue, my dear *Comtesse*— or so we've been led to believe.'

The Countess gave a low, delightfully incredulous, laugh. 'Unimpeached virtue is a rare commodity in *La Maison des Anges*. I doubt you'll find your friend here, milords. But come, I can find you something much more exciting—a rare beauty from Constantinople, three years in the seraglio of the Sultan, trained in all the arts. . . The story of her escape is itself a fantasy. She lives along this passage to the left of us. Come, breathe in the scents of the East, milords, and succumb to her enchantments. If you will follow me. . .'

But Freddie was not to be distracted. 'Later, Countess, later! You didn't know Carne in the old days, before he came into the title, Coker. Not nearly so respectable then, eh, Charlie? Remember those parties, what? I say! What a lark if it was Carne! I've got to see! He was standin' just down there somewhere. . . It almost looked as if he was tryin' to hide. . .' He suddenly shouted, 'Marcus! I say, Marcus, old chap!'

'Milords! Mr Chantry! You mustn't! This is an outrage! That part of the house is not for guests. Hassim! Hassim!'

The Countess' protests went unheeded. Freddie's curiosity had been aroused, and he was sufficiently intoxicated not to care for anything else. Charlie Witham joined in.

'Down there, you say, Freddie? Let's go and see. Excuse me, Countess.'

To Francesca and Marcus, the moment was one of undiluted horror. In the next few seconds they would be exposed, not only to Coker, who had no cause to love either of them, but worse, to two of the biggest scandal-mongers in London. Marcus pushed Francesca right back into the alcove. '*Stay here,*' he said softly, but fiercely. Then he opened his cloak, loosened his cravat and stepped out into the corridor.

'I heard the noise,' he said languidly. 'Is this the way to keep a house such as yours, *Comtesse*? I thought discretion was the keynote?'

'Milord, forgive me. I don't know what to say. . .'

'*Carne!* It *is* you! Well, I'm blowed! So this is what they call important diplomatic affairs? Affairs! They're affairs, all right!' Freddie gave a roar of laughter. 'Here to negotiate with the Sultan's favourite, are you?'

'Freddie. I wish I could say I was charmed to see you, but I really cannot do it. Do take yourself. . .and your two friends away. What a reputation you'll give the English!'

'Reputation! Well, that's cool! That's pretty cool!' said Witham.

'I hope you don't think that yours will survive tonight's revelation,' Lord Coker said, smiling unpleasantly. 'Even in London, one has heard of the infamous House of the Angels. It's a surprising place to find the noblest peer of them all.' His voice was full of malevolent satisfaction.

'Oh, come, Coker! Don't be naïve! We're men of the world, I hope? What will it gain you to chatter in London about what I get up to in Paris? It's not like you to be so childish.'

'It's hardly a matter for children. Or ladies—I wonder what Miss Beaudon would think of this?'

'You know my views—or you should by now—on hearing Miss Beaudon's name on your lips, Coker. I had hoped you learned your lesson. But surely not even you would soil any lady's ears with tales of brothels and the like! I'm sure the Prince wouldn't approve. Most ungentlemanly.'

'These things have a habit of getting around.'

'Well, well! I shall know who to blame if they do, shan't I? Freddie? Witham?'

The two gentlemen named responded to the sudden menace in Marcus's voice with eager assurances of their discretion.

'You can threaten them out of it, but not me.'

'You know, I've thought you many things, my dear Coker, but I never took you for a tittle-tattle before. Do your damnedest. The sticklers might disapprove of me for a while, but most of London will be amused—no more than that. Now, if you'll excuse me. . .'

'But why were you tryin' to hide, Marcus?'

'Freddie, you force me to be brutally frank. I didn't wish to meet you. I was on my way to some delightful, but unfinished, business. And now, if you'll excuse me. . .? *Madame la Comtesse* is no doubt anxious to provide you with some delights of your own. Goodnight, gentlemen!'

Marcus watched as the Countess ushered the three men down the Harem passage, then stepped back into the alcove. He let out a deep sigh.

'Marcus! Oh, Marcus!' Francesca clutched his arm.

'Wait! We're not quite out of the wood yet.'

'But I didn't know. . . What. . .what would happen if they found me here?'

Marcus's silence was eloquent. Then he said grimly, 'They won't. They mustn't. Let me help you put that veil on again. We must get out of here while we can.'

'I'm sorry, Marcus.'

He looked as if he was about to say something severe, but then changed his mind. 'The veil,' was all he said.

Francesca looked up at him and put her cheek against his. 'Thank you,' she said. 'Oh, Marcus, I do thank you.'

His arm tightened round her, but after a moment he put her away from him, and arranged the veil over her face.

'This is not the place,' he said. 'Let's get away from *La Maison des Anges*, and tomorrow I'll arrange for Maddy to come with us to England. Ready?'

Francesca lifted her head. 'Ready,' she said.

Chapter Fourteen

Francesca's carriage was waiting for them in the mews behind the house. They reached it without further incident, climbed in, closed the blinds and set off for the hotel. But just before they got there Marcus told the coachman to stop.

'I'll get out here,' he said. 'You mustn't be seen tonight in my company. Indeed, you should not be seen again in Paris. There's always the chance that Coker or one of the others might catch sight of you, and that would never do. Stay indoors till I get in touch with you.' He looked at her. His face was as stern as she had ever seen it. 'I will say nothing about tonight's escapade. Knowing you, it was fairly predictable. But I don't think I need tell you that the consequences could have been severe indeed.'

'I know,' Francesca said miserably.

His expression softened slightly. 'Don't look so cast down, Francesca. I think we have avoided detection. But you must now do exactly as I say until you are safe in England again. I shall not come to your hotel myself, but will contrive to send messages daily. And I will engage to have Maddy here as soon as she is fit to travel. Meanwhile, you will keep to the confines of the hotel. Do I have your promise?'

She nodded, unable to say a word.

'Good! Then I will bid you goodnight.'

'Goodnight, Marcus,' she said. Her manner was still subdued.

He sighed and said ruefully, 'You know, I find all this docility very alarming. I had expected at least a token resistance.'

'No doubt I shall eventually come about,' she said bitterly. 'But I begin to despair that I shall ever behave as I ought in any matter where you are involved.'

'The answer lies in your own hands, Francesca.'

'What do you mean?'

'Oh, no! I am not about to embark on any discussion or argument. Not here, not now. But some time you may like to reflect on our long acquaintance and perhaps view it in a different light. As I have. Goodnight.'

He bowed, had a short word with the driver and groom and was gone. The carriage started up again. Francesca pushed the blind aside and stared out, following the tall, lithe figure with her eyes until it disappeared into the darkness. Then she sat back, suddenly indescribably weary.

What had Marcus meant? Her behaviour tonight had been enough to give any decent man a disgust of her. She felt sick with horror at the thought of how Coker and the others would have behaved if they had seen her in that dreadful place. Thanks to Marcus, that danger had been averted, but what did he now think of her? His words had been enigmatic—in what 'different light' did he view her now?

These thoughts and others, equally tormenting, kept her awake for most of the night. Even the knowledge that she had found her beloved Maddy failed to comfort her. But the next morning, though her spirits remained low, she set herself to maintain a brave front before Madame

Elisabeth and to behave with all the circumspection that
Marcus had advised.

As Marcus walked back to the Embassy he was equally
heavy-hearted. He had saved Francesca from disgrace,
but only at considerable cost to himself and his mission.
His work in Paris was now irretrievably compromised,
and only one course remained open to him. He did not
relish his forthcoming interview with Sir Henry, but was
determined to seek him out and inform him of the night's
developments before anyone else could tell him.

The subsequent interview was every bit as painful as
Marcus had expected. Sir Henry was famous for his
patience and tact in dealing with representatives of other
nations, but he did not waste either on his subordinates.
Marcus was called every kind of fool in language that
was as forceful as it was picturesque. He knew better than
to offer any defence. Though in his own mind there was
no question that he had acted in the only possible way,
he could hardly expect Sir Henry to understand that.

'It's a damnable matter altogether! You know as well
as I do that if anyone hears of this visit to the Countess
Rehan's place, neither the French, nor any of our Allies,
will trust you again.'

'I have thought of little else for the past two hours, sir.
And though I did my best on the spot, it would be foolish
to hope that Coker and the others will not spread the
story—the tale of Lord Carne's lapse from virtue is too
tasty a morsel.'

'Your personal reputation is your own affair. You could
have visited all the bordellos in Paris every night for a
month for all I care. But one of the most notorious centres
for Napoleon's supporters in Paris! Why the devil did it
have to be *there*?'

'Unfortunately—'

'Unfortunately!' roared Sir Henry. 'You ruin some of the most delicate negotiations we've been involved in for years, and you call it *unfortunate*! It's catastrophic, man!'

Marcus gritted his teeth. 'The consequences for Miss Beaudon could have been catastrophic, too, Sir Henry. She had to be rescued. But I am not belittling the quandary you and the rest of your staff are now in as a result. I deeply regret the necessity for my actions, and hope you will accept my immediate resignation from the mission. You shall have it in writing tomorrow.'

'I'll have it in writing tonight, Carne! Tomorrow the vultures may well descend on me. But no resignation is going to save this situation. Unless. . . How would it be if I saw Coker and the others myself? Explained the situation. . .' When Marcus hesitated he said impatiently, 'Well? Don't just stand there, tell me what you think.'

'Witham and Chantry are amiable fools. I think you could persuade them to say nothing—for the time being at least. Long enough for the effect to be diminished. But Coker. . .'

'Coker's a gentleman. I've never heard that he's unpatriotic. Fought at Waterloo, didn't he?'

'With some gallantry. There's nothing wrong with his courage. But. . .he has a personal animosity towards me, which might impair his judgement.'

'Balderdash! I'm surprised at your suggesting such a thing, Carne! No man of Coker's standing would indulge his own feelings at the expense of his sovereign's best interests. D'you doubt my ability to put it clearly enough? Is that it?'

'Of course not, sir.'

'Well, then. That's it. I'll send someone to fetch the gentlemen concerned as soon as they are. . .er. . .free. What the devil are you looking so doubtful about?'

'I wish you every success, Sir Henry. But. . .if Coker won't cooperate—'

'I'm sure he will!'

'But if not,' said Marcus desperately, 'then there's only one thing left for you to do.'

'What's that?'

'You'll have to disown me, vilify me. Say I'm in disgrace.'

'Don't be a fool, Marcus! I can't do that to you! You may have acted quixotically, but you're not a double dealer! Dammit, boy! I'm not going to spread lies about you!'

'You won't have to,' Marcus said with a grim smile. 'Just say you've sent me packing, and refuse to discuss the matter. Rumour will do the rest.'

'I can't do that to you, Marcus.'

'If Coker or the others do talk, it's the only way you can save your own position.'

Sir Henry was clearly uncomfortable with the idea, but he, too, could see the force of Marcus's words. 'Let's hope for the best,' he said gloomily. 'Write out that resignation and go to bed. I take it you'll be leaving Paris tomorrow—or today, rather. It's past midnight.'

'I can't guarantee that, but I'll go as soon as I possibly can. I have my own reasons for wanting to be away from here.'

Sir Henry was a skilful and experienced diplomat. A cosy chat in the Embassy library, a few carefully prepared half-truths, with a glass or two of superb Burgundy, and in no time at all Lord Witham and Mr Chantry had been persuaded that it was in their own interest, as well as that of the country, that they forgot the episode in *La Maison des Anges*. As Sir Henry ushered them out he was well satisfied with his efforts. But when he turned Lord

Coker was regarding him with a cynical eye.

'They're fools,' he said, 'to be satisfied with so little. If I'm to keep my mouth shut I want to know a good deal more than you told them, Sir Henry! How directly is Carne involved in these mysterious negotiations? Why is he so important?'

Sir Henry gave him a bland look. 'Why are you so interested? Most people would regard the request as reasonable, without any further detail.'

'Ah, but I have never been "most people". I flatter myself that my friendship with the Prince Regent gives me greater distinction.'

Sir Henry filled Lord Coker's glass. 'This. . .friendship. Am I right in thinking it is at the moment under a slight cloud?'

Lord Coker smiled. 'His Highness is sometimes forced to act in public against his private inclination. I shall return to London in the near future and you will see—he will receive me as warmly as ever. I amuse him. You may have confidence in me, Sir Henry. I shall have the Prince's ear again in a very short time. Now, tell me why you are so anxious to protect Lord Carne. I should have thought he was well able to take care of himself.'

'Hmm. . .' Sir Henry paused for thought. It was obvious that Lord Coker was not to be put off. His claim that he would return to the Prince Regent's favour was convincing. And there had been no sign of the animosity Marcus had spoken of. He made up his mind to be frank.

'Confidence is at the heart of Lord Carne's recent work for us. . .' And Sir Henry went on to explain the delicate balance of the negotiations, the importance of Marcus's known integrity, and the significance to the pro-Napoleon faction of *La Maison des Anges*.

'But if Lord Carne knew all this, why was he in the place at all?'

Sir Henry was in a quandary. He could not possibly betray the girl Marcus had gone to such lengths to protect. He blustered, 'How the devil should I know? Some woman, no doubt.'

'And you are asking me to remain silent about a man who knowingly put all these important negotiations in jeopardy for the sake of a woman? A harlot? The story gets better and better, Sir Henry. You've dismissed him, of course?'

'I didn't have to. Carne resigned that very night. But if it were known that he had been seen in the *Maison des Anges,* the damage to our position could be enormous.'

Lord Coker's interest was not in the government's position. He said thoughtfully, 'You would have to repudiate him instantly and publicly.'

'Even that might not be enough.'

'And people are so uncharitable. They would be bound to assume that he was guilty of much worse—double dealing, even.'

'I sincerely hope not.'

'You are being quite amazingly forbearing, Sir Henry. I wonder at you.'

'My chief interest is in saving our reputation with the French. But Lord Carne has done much for us in the past. He does not deserve the universal condemnation which would follow if his. . .indiscretion were revealed. I think you can see the force of my argument?'

'Oh, I can indeed, Sir Henry! I can indeed!'

Sir Henry Creighton was not a devious man. He accepted these words as an indication of Lord Coker's good faith. But he would have been much less happy if he could have seen the smile of satisfaction on Lord Coker's face as he left. He could not have known that he had just given Lord Coker a long-sought weapon.

* * *

It was two days before the Countess sent word that Maddy could undertake the journey to England. Both Marcus and Francesca greeted the news with relief. Francesca had grown heartily sick of the hotel and its small garden, but she had not dared to disobey Marcus's orders. As for Marcus himself—he had spent two of the most uncomfortable days of his life, not excepting his experiences at Waterloo. At least during the battle he had been kept too busy to be aware of anything else. Here in Paris, he was forced to stand on the sidelines while others did what they could to save the situation. His patience was sorely tried as he suffered sidelong glances, conversations that stopped suddenly whenever he came into a room and, worse than the rest, ribald remarks from one or two who had themselves paid visits to the Countess Rehan, men he had till now held in some contempt. Sir Henry was keeping his distance, but Marcus gathered from the few words they did exchange that the diplomat thought Coker would keep quiet. Marcus himself remained doubtful.

It was without regret that Lord Carne's party, consisting of two travelling coaches and their passengers, left Paris early one morning before the rest of the city was astir. No one was awake to remark on the sight of Lord Carne escorting a sick lady and her friends to England, though one or two might have wondered at the noble lord's hasty and discreet departure from the capital. Later, of course, when Lord Coker's poison spread, they knew the reason—or so they thought.

The journey was uneventful but not particularly enjoyable. Marcus drove his own carriage and, since it was more comfortable than the one Francesca had hired, the three ladies travelled inside. The second coach carried servants and luggage.

Francesca spent a good deal of her time with Maddy, talking of the old days on St Marthe, holding her when they travelled over rough patches of road, and generally exerting herself to make the journey as comfortable as possible. She was glad to do it, but it was a strain—especially as she found she was not sleeping very well at night. At the last stop before they reached Calais, Madame Elisabeth looked at Francesca's pale face and heavy eyes, and had a word with Marcus. As a result, Francesca was invited to travel outside for a while.

The fresh air was welcome after the close confines of the carriage, but as they travelled the last few miles in France, Francesca grew ever more dejected. Though Marcus had been perfectly courteous, and had taken pains to make sure she was comfortable, he had hardly spoken to her on their journey, and now when she was sitting right beside him, he was behaving almost like a stranger.

For the first time in their acquaintance, he appeared to find conversation with her difficult. He seemed to have something on his mind that he was not prepared to discuss. Never before had she felt shut out of his thoughts in this way, and the feeling was very lowering to her spirits.

Why on earth had she gone to such lengths to avoid his company on the journey to France? If this was the way he would have treated her, her efforts had been a waste of time! To think she had been afraid to travel with him, unsure of her ability to resist his charm, his claims to the old, closer ties between them, had feared that her feelings would once again overcome her caution. But now she perceived that such concern had been totally unnecessary. Marcus hardly seemed to notice she was there!

Perversely, she found herself wanting to be provoked and challenged in the old manner. . .yes, even flirted with. But. . .she stole a glance at him. Far from regarding her with affection, or even interest, he was frowning at the road ahead as if it held all sorts of unknown dangers.

Francesca grew more and more despondent. It was clear that Marcus now regretted having followed her to Paris! She couldn't blame him for that, though what she would have done without him she hardly ventured to think. All the same, she had not invited him to follow her, she thought resentfully—she had done her best to avoid his company! And when her father had pressed them to become engaged, it was she who had rejected the idea, not Marcus.

But she became gloomy again as she remembered that Marcus had afterwards stated with some force that he had no wish to marry her! And now she came to think of it, he had only pursued her and kissed her *after* he had witnessed Denver's declaration. That was it! He didn't want to marry her himself, but he didn't want anyone else to, either. He was a selfish, arrogant dog in the manger! She stole a glance at him. He didn't *look* like a selfish, arrogant dog in the manger. He looked like a man with a load of trouble on his back.

'Marcus?'

He looked at her apologetically. 'Forgive me. I was woolgathering. I'm afraid I'm poor company at the moment.'

'What is wrong?'

'Wrong? Why, nothing! I think we brushed through that business in Paris pretty well, do you not agree?'

'Are you concerned about Lord Coker and the others?'

'Not in the slightest. I doubt they will say anything, you know. Freddie and Charlie Witham are featherweights. They'll have forgotten about me by the time they get back to England. And Coker. . . What has he to gain? No, you mustn't concern yourself about Coker.'

'I think he will talk about. . .about *La Maison*—'

Marcus interrupted her before she could say any more.

'Don't ever mention that name again, Francesca! Not even to me. You must forget that you ever heard of the place, and you must make sure Madame Lachasse doesn't talk of it, either.'

Francesca looked at him with scared eyes. Marcus had sounded. . .frighteningly authoritative. When she nodded, he said more lightly, 'You need not concern yourself on my behalf. Coker gave his word to Sir Henry—he won't talk.'

'Sir Henry? Sir Henry Creighton?'

'Yes—apart from its. . .somewhat unworthy day-to-day business, the place you chose to visit is also one of the chief centres of pro-Napoleonic activities in Paris. My being found there might have prejudiced Sir Henry's position vis-à-vis King Louis and his regime. But I think we have managed to prevent that—Sir Henry saw Coker and explained.'

'And you trust Lord Coker? He hates you, Marcus. If he can do you harm, he will.'

'He may hate me, but he will hardly break his word. And. . .if he does. . .there's nothing wrong, if you'll forgive my mentioning it, in a man such as myself visiting a. . .a place which is not normally spoken of in the company of the ladies of Society.'

'You mean a bawdy house.'

'Precisely.'

'Have you been in the habit of it, Marcus?'

'What a question to ask! Really, Francesca! No, it is not something I have indulged in, if you must know. Now, if you would care to change the subject?'

'If Lord Coker's gossip won't do you any harm, why are you so. . .so abstracted? You haven't spoken a word since I joined you.'

He looked at her with a frown. Francesca lifted her chin and held his glance, refusing to back down. A glint of humour appeared in his eyes, the corner of his mouth twitched in the old, familiar, endearing way. 'You mean you feel neglected? Dare I hope that you would welcome my attentions?'

'Of course not! That is. . .I would welcome some attention, perhaps. More than I have been receiving from you in the past half-hour.'

'This is not what I have been accustomed to hear, Francesca. What has happened to the young lady who ran away to Paris rather than face my company on the journey?'

'Yes, well, things have changed.'

'Indeed, they have!' His face grew sombre again. 'I've been thinking. When we get to England I think you, Madame Elisabeth and Madame Lachasse should go straight to Packards. In that way, we might hope to avoid comment on your return, and any connection at all in the eyes of Society with me. I can see to it that your father joins you soon after. Both Madame Lachasse and your father need time to recover, and I am sure Packards is the best place for them. It would be natural for you to stay with them.'

'But. . .?'

'Yes?'

Francesca shook her head. She was disappointed, but could not argue with such an eminently sensible scheme, particularly as the only objection that occurred to her was that Marcus would not be there. It was plain that he did not desire her company in London. Pride came to her rescue. She sat up straighter and said brightly, 'I think you are right. And it will give me an opportunity to renew my acquaintance with Maddy. With one thing and another, I feel I have hardly spoken to her. Thank you, Marcus.'

He looked at her quizzically. 'Will you miss me?'

'A little, I suppose,' said Francesca airily. 'But I expect

Lord Denver and one or two of the others will visit us.
It isn't far from London.'

He took hold of her chin and turned her face to his. 'I
have other plans for Denver. Leave him alone, Francesca.'

This calm order—not even plans for her, but plans for
Denver, indeed!—roused Francesca to challenge him. 'I
do not think what occurs between Lord Denver and myself
is any concern of yours,' she said somewhat coldly. 'I
shall invite whom I choose to Packards.'

He laughed and kissed her briefly. Then, as she opened
her mouth to speak, his eyes darkened and he kissed her
again. In spite of herself, her response was as complete
and unrestrained as it had always been. Even as her arms
went round his neck, as she clung to him as closely as
he was holding her, she had a fleeting moment of despair.
Why was it that no caution, no memory of her grief and
despair in the past, however painful, ever stopped her
from responding to this man with all her stupid,
unguarded heart?

Then she forgot everything as she abandoned herself
to the feelings of delight, of bubbling joy, of excitement
and desire which he could always evoke. The kiss went
on, the horses dropped to a walk as his arm went round
her, holding her more firmly to him.

He groaned, 'Francesca, Francesca! You've been
trouble since the moment I first met you, but. . .kiss
me again!'

For one glorious moment they forgot time and place,
lost once again in the enchantment which had always held
them in its spell. But then a plaintive voice coming from
inside the carriage brought them startlingly back to earth.

'Lord Carne! Why have we stopped? Has something
happened?' Madame Elisabeth's head was poking out of
the window. Fortunately Francesca was not in her view.

'No, no! There is no cause for alarm, Madame

Elisabeth. Miss Beaudon was interested in the spire of the church over there. Er. . .shall we go on, Miss Beaudon?'

Francesca had been hastily tidying her hair and putting her hat back on. 'Thank you, Lord Carne,' she said calmly, suppressing a wild desire to giggle. 'It was most. . .interesting.' Marcus lifted an eyebrow and Francesca went scarlet. 'That is to say. . .'

'Good,' said Madame Elisabeth. 'I am glad to hear that Francesca has not lost her eye for detail. One can always learn something.' She put her head in again.

'Indeed, one can!'

'Marcus! Please don't make me laugh. You are cruel.'

'I am delighted to see you in a more cheerful frame of mind. You've been a little hipped since we left Paris.'

'I didn't think you had noticed.'

'Oh, indeed I had. It was natural, I suppose. But to return to our conversation before that. . .delightful interlude—I've more than made my point, I think.'

'Which is?'

'If you marry Denver, you'll spoil more than your own life, Francesca. Don't let him persuade you differently.' He turned to look at her. 'You must know I'm right.'

How could he even think of Denver at such a moment? Francesca's chief feeling was one of hurt and bewilderment. She had thought him as oblivious to the rest of the world as she had been. She had clearly been wrong. 'A delightful interlude'. Was that how he regarded it? 'A delightful interlude' sounded uncomfortably like 'Nothing much!'—his words to Freddie all those years ago on the hill at Shelwood. Had he. . .had he kissed her merely to prove a point?

With considerable self-discipline, she put her hurt on one side and sat up more firmly. Two could play at that game. 'I know nothing of the kind,' she said calmly. 'I don't know what particular point you wish to prove, Marcus, but that kiss—'

'Those kisses,' he murmured.

'Those kisses proved nothing at all. There's more to a good marriage than gratification of the senses. Comfort, ease, friendship—these have an important share, too. Please stop the carriage again—no! I will not listen to any more. I wish to rejoin Maddy and Madame Elisabeth inside.'

He hesitated a moment. Then his jaw set, and he did as she asked without further protest.

It took over a week to reach Packards, by which time Francesca's nerves were stretched to their limit. The conversation with Marcus before Calais was the last she had of any consequence with him. Once they reached the port he insisted that she stayed out of sight, and while he escorted Madame Elisabeth and Maddy on a short walk round the deck, Francesca was made to stay in the cabin. In England, too, she stayed inside the carriage, and when they drove through London he made sure the blinds were drawn. His precautions seemed ridiculously elaborate, but when she protested Madame Elisabeth refused to sympathise.

'For you know, my love, that it would not do for you to be seen in Lord Carne's company on a journey such as this. It is not as if you were betrothed to him. I think Lord Carne is being truly the gentleman in his concern for your reputation.'

'But I have you and Maddy to act a chaperons! It is ridiculous!'

'It may seem a touch excessive, I agree. But I have every confidence in Lord Carne's judgement.'

'Francesca, my honey—you are in love with this Lord Carne?'

'Oh, no, Maddy! He. . .he is a friend of my father's.'

'It don't look as simple as that to me. And I never heard no mention of this "friend" before. Tell Maddy, child.'

'I can't! I don't know!' Francesca sat back against the cushions. 'Did Lord Carne tell you that, Madame Elisabeth?' she asked morosely. 'That we were not betrothed?'

'Well, not precisely. I believe his words were that you had to wait until you had spoken to Lord Beaudon.'

'I knew it!' Maddy cried softly, clapping her hands together. 'He's a wonderful man—and he'll make just the right husband for my little Francesca!'

'You don't know, Maddy! You just don't know. . .'

'I know enough. A man don't sacrifice his whole career for just anyone. It's proof of something or other, and if it isn't love, what is it?'

'Sacrifice? What are you talking about, Maddy? There's no danger of that. Marc—Lord Carne says those men have been silenced.'

'You reckon they will stay so? I never met a man yet that don't gossip with his friends worse than any woman.'

'Well, there may be a little talk. . .but that won't do Lord Carne much damage. He said so himself.'

'We'll see, child. We'll see. Just remember what I said when the time comes—about his loving you.'

Francesca was to remember Maddy's words just a few weeks later. They gave her courage at a time when it was badly needed.

When their little party arrived at Packards, they found to their surprise that Lord Beaudon was already installed there. He was looking considerably better, and greeted his daughter and Marcus with delight. Maddy was conveyed to a comfortable room which had been specially prepared for her, and his welcome to her was a private matter, and took place behind closed doors. When he came down he found Marcus ready to leave.

'You're not going, my dear fellow, are you?'

'I'm afraid I must, Lord Beaudon. There are matters which must be attended to in London. I only came in order to make sure that your daughter and. . .her friends arrived here safely.'

'But when shall you come again, then?'

'I. . .' Marcus hesitated. 'I am not sure. Do you plan to stay at Packards for the rest of the Season?'

'I shall do so, certainly. Madame Lachasse will need my company during her convalescence in a strange country. But I am sure Francesca will come back to town, eh, my dear?'

'I thought I'd stay here for a while, Papa.'

'Nonsense! You'll return to London just as soon as you've recovered from your journey, and had a chance to talk to Madeleine. There's very little of the Season left, and you can come down again as soon as it is over. Now take your leave of Carne, my dear, then you can go and see if Madeleine is rested. I'll see you to your carriage, Carne.' He walked to the door.

Marcus took Francesca's hand to his lips and bade her farewell. Francesca said stiffly, 'I am conscious that I owe you a great deal, sir—'

'Say nothing of that. You owe me nothing, Francesca, except. . .'

'Yes?'

His voice dropped. 'Be very careful what you say about Paris. To anyone at all. Your reputation will be in shreds if—'

'You have no need to warn me! I shall be careful.'

'And. . .remember what I said about Denver. He's not for you.'

She snatched her hand away. 'We have already said enough to each other on that score, Lord Carne. Your efforts to protect your friend from. . .from my wiles are ridiculous! If Lord Denver chooses to visit me here, I shall be delighted to receive him. You I shall no doubt see next in London.'

His face was grave. 'Perhaps. We shall have to wait on events. Till then, live well and be happy with your beloved Maddy. That at least is something good which came out of our Paris adventure. Goodbye, Miss Beaudon.' He bowed and she watched him as he joined her father at the bottom of the steps. Sudden tears started to her eyes; with an impatient sigh she turned and hurried upstairs.

Lord Beaudon stared soberly at Marcus. 'Well?' he demanded. 'Am I to send an announcement to the *Gazette* or not?'

'I'm afraid matters are a touch difficult at the moment, sir. Much as I honour your daughter, I cannot at the moment ask her to be my wife.'

'I thought you already had, Carne!'

'A ruse, merely, to ease your mind. There's still some way to go.'

'What the devil is all this about, Carne? I expected that you at least would behave as a man of honour!'

'That is precisely what I am doing my damnedest to do, Lord Beaudon!' Looking grimmer than ever, Marcus got into the carriage and gave a curt command. The carriage rolled away, leaving Lord Beaudon staring after it.

Chapter Fifteen

When Francesca finally came back to London after three weeks at Packards, the town had a slightly faded air. It was very close to the end of the Season—a few less fashionable couples had already left for their estates, preferring the freshness of the country to the dust and smells of London in summer. The Prince Regent was still at Carlton House, playing cards with his cronies, riding, driving and taking part in the normal activities his gregarious nature demanded, but his household was preparing for the move to Brighton.

However, there were changes that could not be ascribed to the end of the Season. The Prince was again much to be seen in the company of Lord Coker, who seemed to have made his way back into royal favour. On the other hand, Lord Carne, who had previously been held in such general high esteem, including that of his royal master, now seemed to have fallen from grace.

There was a change, too, in the atmosphere in the house in Mount Street. Before Francesca's departure for Paris the three ladies—Mrs Canfield, Lydia and Francesca herself—had lived in happy harmony. But now the two Canfields seemed reluctant to indulge in the pleasant chats and exchanges of gossip which they had all previously enjoyed, and Lydia seemed ill at ease, avoiding Francesca's company whenever possible.

Francesca was hurt. She had expected a certain amount of coolness from Maria Canfield—after all, she had deceived her friend about her plans to go to Paris. But she would have expected that Lydia, whom she had come to love, would admire her for undertaking what would seem to her such an adventure!

However, she owed too much to the Canfields to allow this situation to continue, so she set herself to coaxing Maria Canfield into a better mood, and in the interest of regaining her friend's confidence she was more open than she had ever been about her reasons for leaving for Paris so suddenly.

'You know, better than most, how hard it was for me to learn to give my affection—even to someone like you or Lydia. Lord Carne once broke my heart, Maria. I did not wish to risk another such experience. A man like Denver would be so much. . .safer.'

Even as she said these words, she wondered fleetingly whether George Denver would ever have risked as much as Marcus had to save her from her own idiotic actions in Paris. He was essentially very conventional. Would he have turned away in shock—disgust even? She pushed the thought away and turned to her friend with a smile. 'But I am truly sorry I had to deceive you. I hope you will forgive me. Indeed, I value our friendship more than I can say. And I regard Lydia as a sister.'

For a moment Francesca thought Maria was about to refuse this olive branch, for she coloured up and looked distinctly uncomfortable. But then she held out her hand and smiled. 'I am glad you are back, Francesca. And I am sure that Lydia will be, too, when. . .'

'When what?'

'When she is feeling better.'

'Has she been ill? Why didn't you tell me?'

'Not exactly, no. Please—I should prefer to leave this subject till later. Meanwhile, believe me, I am your very good friend still. Er. . .what if I were to tell you that Marcus loves you? Would you still be determined to refuse him?'

'There are times. . .when I am afraid. Someone like Denver would be so much easier to live with. And he, at least, has already asked me to marry him, whereas Marcus has not. I don't know, Maria.'

'I see.' Maria Canfield's voice had grown cool again. 'How is he?'

'Denver?'

'No, Marcus.'

'We have not seen a great deal of him. He came once to tell us you were safely back, but since then he seems to have avoided us. Lydia is quite distressed. But now. . .'

'What is it?'

'I am not sure. There are whispers. . . Did you see much of him in Paris?'

'I. . .I only saw him once. Then he escorted us home— but that is between ourselves, Maria. Marcus does not wish it to be generally known.'

'Francesca, he loves you and is trying to protect you. Something untoward seems to have happened while he was there. It seems to have been something unsavoury, so I don't expect he said anything about it to you. But it has undoubtedly done Marcus harm in the eyes of the world.'

'What. . .what can it be?'

'I think it's better not to ask. It's one of those things that gentlemen talk about in clubs, but ladies are not supposed to know. It is all very strange. The Foreign Office seems to be involved as well. Denver is certainly privy to what has been going on, but he wouldn't dream of mentioning it to us.'

'Denver?'

Again, Maria's voice was restricted as she answered. 'Lord Denver has been very kind while you were away. We have seen quite a lot of him. His attention is all the more welcome since Marcus has not been seen much in company.'

Francesca was worried. It was clear that something of the business in Paris had become known. She must find out how much, and how seriously it was affecting Marcus. She regarded her friend thoughtfully. It was useless to question Maria—she would never have been told the scandalous details, the very idea was absurd. Denver was connected with the Foreign Office, he would certainly know...but would he talk? Almost certainly not to her. It was all extremely frustrating, but she was determined to find out, somehow.

Meanwhile, it intrigued her that Maria's interest was clearly not with Marcus, but with Denver. This was a new development, surely? It appeared that Denver's visits had been as frequent as ever, even while she had been away. What had been going on here during the past month? Her eyes widened as a thought struck her. Lydia and Denver? Was that possible? Of course it was! And it would explain everything!

What was more, Denver was exactly the sort of man she would have chosen for Lydia herself, and, if Lydia loved him, she would relinquish her own claim without a second's hesitation. But she decided to say nothing for the moment. She would soon meet him—and observe for herself.

Sure enough, Lord Denver called that very afternoon. Francesca noticed with interest that Lydia, always so

open, so artless in her approach to visitors, gave him the
briefest of curtsies, then picked up her embroidery again
and stitched with unusual concentration. Maria was as
courteous as ever, but was obviously tense, and her conversation was uncharacteristically forced.

Francesca grew increasingly confident that her suspicion of an attachment between Lydia and Denver was
correct. She must act as soon as possible—Lydia's happiness was far too important to delay putting matters right.
While she waited for Lord Denver's call to come to an
end, she considered what she would say to him, and it
occurred to her that she might even put some of it to good
account.

So, when Lord Denver finally rose to take his leave,
she said boldly, 'Lord Denver, if you have a moment,
there's something I would like to discuss with you.'

The sudden silence was broken only by the small crash
as Lydia's embroidery fell to the ground.

'Of course, Miss Beaudon.' Lord Denver's tone was
gallant, but his smile was forced. Maria and Lydia bade
him farewell, and if Francesca had not already had a very
clear idea of what had been happening in her absence,
she must have seen and wondered at Lydia's pale face,
her haunted glance into Denver's eyes, her hasty and
unusually clumsy exit.

'Do sit down, Lord Denver,' said Francesca affably,
when they were alone.

'Thank you. . .I think I prefer to stand. You. . .you had
something you wished to say to me?'

'Yes. I wonder if you could tell me what it is that they
are saying of Lord Carne? I hear he is in some trouble.'
When he looked surprised, she explained, 'He was kind
enough to help me in France. I want to know what he is
accused of doing there.'

His face pokered up, as she had thought it would.

'There's absolutely no truth in any of it,' he said. 'His friends need not concern themselves with it.'

'I should still like to know what it is. What is he supposed to have done?'

'It is nothing fit for a lady's ears, Miss Beaudon,' Denver said dismissively. 'I could not possibly repeat it. Was there something else you wished to say to me?'

'I see.' Francesca saw that, as she had suspected, he was not prepared to discuss it—nor would anyone else. She would have to try other means. 'Well, it will probably soon be forgotten,' she said airily. She saw the look of doubt on Denver's face, but did not pursue it. Instead, she went to the sofa and sat down. 'If you will forgive my saying so, Lord Denver, you do not look as pleased to see me as I had expected.'

'Of course I am. . .er. . .I am delighted, of course, that you are safely back in England. I hear that you found your nurse.'

'Yes, she is at present resting. You might meet her some day. When you come down to Packards.' Francesca looked with some satisfaction at Denver's reception of this semi-invitation. She was sorry for his discomfort, but it was no part of her plan to make things easy for him.

'Miss Beaudon, I. . .' He stopped.

'Yes, Lord Denver?'

'I. . .I . . . nothing.'

'Mrs Canfield tells me how well you have been looking after them both while I've been away. That was kind of you.'

'On the contrary, it was my pleasure,' he said sincerely, if a touch uncomfortably.

'I've been thinking a great deal about your proposal, you know.'

'Really?' he asked, apprehension in his tone. 'And what. . .what have you decided?'

'Well. . .I think we should deal very well together.'

'Miss Beaudon, I. . .'

'On the other hand. . .I am beginning to suspect that you are no longer as devoted as you once were. Am I right?'

'How can you say so? I have asked you to marry me, and am bound in all honour—'

'But I don't want you to be bound, Lord Denver. Not to me. I value your friendship, I enjoy your company, but I am not in love with you. I never said I was. In fact, if you will do me one small favour—which you will not enjoy—I shall willingly release you from any promises you may have made me. Then you will be free to approach Miss Canfield with an easy conscience.'

He looked astounded. 'But. . .but. . . How did you know?'

'No one has said anything, but I have eyes and ears, you know. And I am even fonder of Lydia than I am of you. I will wish you happiness with all my heart, and think you will find it, too. Lydia will make you a much better wife than I ever would.'

He came over and kissed her hand. 'Francesca, you are wonderful! Noble!'

'I'm afraid I am not that. You did say you would do me this favour, didn't you?'

'Anything, anything!'

'Swear?'

'Of course!'

'Then you will tell me exactly what they accuse Marcus of doing. In detail. All of it.'

He took a step back, looking horrified. 'I couldn't do that! You would be shocked.'

'You did promise. And—' her voice grew serious '—it may help to put right a very grave injustice which is being done him. You are his friend, Lord Denver. Trust me.

This is no mere female whim. You will not shock me. You see, I know most of it already.'

'Forgive me, but that is impossible. How could you have heard of such things?'

'Never mind. Tell me!'

He was reluctant, but hers had always been the stronger character, and he eventually told her all he knew. It was far worse than Francesca had feared. Coker had obviously spread his poison far and wide. Marcus had told her that he might be regarded askance by the more stiff-necked members of Society if his presence in the *Maison des Anges* became known, but she had had no idea that there was a more serious, political dimension to the affair, one which would ruin Marcus' career and expose him to the severest possible censure.

She was not shocked, but she was furiously, royally angry. To think that Marcus, who had behaved with complete integrity throughout, was being ostracised, calumnied, on the word of a scoundrel like Coker! She was speechless with rage.

Lord Denver looked at her white face. 'It has shocked you,' he said miserably. 'I knew it would. Can you ever forgive me?'

'I am not shocked,' said Francesca carefully, her voice trembling. 'Not in the slightest. The only part of it that I did not know already was that they were accusing Marcus of double dealing. How dare they? How could they?'

'But how *could* you know?'

'I was there,' she said, forgetting all caution in her anger.

'In Paris? I knew that, but. . .'

'In the *Maison des Anges*.'

'No, no! That cannot be! Miss Beaudon! Please! You must not joke about such a dreadfully serious matter. If you were believed—'

'I am more serious than I ever was in my life before, Lord Denver,' she said, interrupting him without ceremony. 'How do you suppose I know the name of the place? You were careful not to mention it.'

He sat down and put his head between his hands. 'Oh my God,' he said, appalled. 'What can you have been thinking of? I regarded you—'

'Oh, it all happened very innocently! I am not the fallen woman you obviously think me,' she said bitterly. 'My nurse was ill and had taken refuge with her friend, Countess Rehan. She. . .she is. . .'

'Countess Rehan's name is known to us.'

'Really?'

'Because of the connection with Bonaparte.'

'Of course. Well, I went to her. . .house to find Maddy. I was completely unaware of its nature, though I realise that that will not help me in the world's eyes. Marcus came there purely to rescue me, though I gather that a more sinister interpretation is now being put on his presence there. He has kept silent to save my good name.'

'I see. I never thought for one moment that Marcus was capable of dishonorable conduct, but I had wondered why he. . . This explains it.'

Lord Denver came over to her. He spoke somewhat stiffly, but with obvious sincerity. 'Marcus is right. Miss Beaudon, you have been good enough to release me without reproach from my commitment towards you. I owe you a great deal. I will naturally say nothing to anyone of what you have just told me. And, believe me, I am speaking as your good friend when I beg you not to let a hint of it reach the ears of anyone else at all. No one. If the world were to learn of your. . .unfortunate adventure, no excuse, no reason, *nothing* would be enough to save you from complete ostracism.'

'And what about the man who risked everything for me?'

There was an appreciable pause. Then he said, 'Marcus will come about. Things may not be quite the same, but the world will forget. . .eventually. I expect he will live at Carne for a while.'

'But it's so unjust!' Francesca was getting angry again. 'He's a man of integrity, of honour. He enjoyed universal admiration and respect. And now they are accusing him of treachery, double dealing, hypocrisy and all the rest! How can he bear it?'

'He'll have to.'

'This is Coker's doing.'

'I think it must be. Though the rumour has not been ascribed to any particular source.' He cleared his throat. 'Mrs Canfield will be wondering what has become of us. May I. . .?'

'Take your leave? Of course. You have been honest with me, Lord Denver, and I appreciate it. I do not need to wish you luck, but I *will* wish you happy. May I make a suggestion?'

He looked as if he was wondering what further dreadful request she was about to make. 'What is that?'

'The decision is yours, of course,' she said reassuringly. 'But it might be a good idea to take Lydia and her mother to Kent on a short visit to your estates. They will be looking especially beautiful at this time of year.'

Relieved, he said, 'I think it an excellent idea. But. . . why do you suggest it? I assume you wish them to be out of London. Why? What are you planning to do, Miss Beaudon? Nothing rash, I hope?'

'That is my affair. But I will say that I cannot rest until justice has been done.' She held up her hand. 'No, do not argue. My mind is made up.'

Lord Denver regarded Francesca with a peculiar mixture of doubt and awe, as if she had suddenly grown two heads. Was this the stately, reserved Miss Beaudon, the woman of elegance and propriety whom he had admired for so long? He began to think he had had a lucky escape. A certain amount of liveliness could be very attractive, but Francesca Beaudon was suddenly revealing herself to be headstrong, imperious, passionate and foolishly scornful of convention—not qualities to be looked for, in his view, among the gentle sex.

But he softened towards her as she gave him one of her warm, enchanting smiles, and said, 'But my friends would be better out of it. So take them to Kent as soon as you can.'

'Are you quite sure I cannot persuade you to think again? I suspect that you are about to take a catastrophic step.'

'Lord Denver, I have to tell you that there is only one man who could ever have the slightest influence on my actions. And in this instance, though I am now certain that he loves me more than I deserve, and believes he is acting in my best interests, I will not listen even to him. I *must* do what I can to re-establish him in the world's eyes. Do not waste your time on me—you would do better to look after Lydia.'

'I think I will. She would be safer out of London for the moment. I'll see if she and her mother could possibly set off tomorrow!'

Mrs Canfield and Lydia were easily persuaded to leave London the next day. Lydia was over the moon with happiness—it simply did not occur to her to refuse Lord Denver's sudden invitation. Maria was a little surprised, but saw some reason in Francesca's argument that London would gossip less about the change in Lord Denver's affections if the happy couple were already out of town.

Once the Canfields had departed, Francesca sent a note to Marcus, requesting him to visit her. He sent a reply back with her man. It was unfortunately impossible for him to come to Mount Street in the near future. This was a setback, but one which Francesca had foreseen.

Undeterred, she set about preparing for the last great event of the season—a rout ball at Northumberland House. She dressed with unusual care. This would probably be her last appearance in Society, and she intended to bow out looking as lovely, as elegant as she had always looked. Her dress of silver-threaded gauze over a white satin slip, the diamonds in her hair and round her arms, the silver dancing slippers—all combined to re-create the image with which she had first impressed London, and to give her the courage she felt she might need.

Her final task before setting out was to write another note to Marcus to be delivered later in the evening. By the time he received it, she would already be at the ball.

At Northumberland House, she had a word with one of the footmen, who listened to her request impassively, received with lofty condescension the generous douceur she slipped into his hand, and only expressed his amazement much later to his particular crony in the back hall.

London was delighted to see Miss Beaudon in such looks, asked kindly after her father, and gave not the slightest indication that they knew anything of her sojourn in Paris. Everyone had assumed she had gone to Packards to prepare the place for her father. Francesca smiled, parried a few questions about the Canfields and Lord Denver, and danced a great deal.

The world had till now only seen the image Francesca had so carefully created for them—the image of an elegant, coolly disciplined cipher. But now, at long last free of the anxieties and fears of the past, as certain as she could be that Marcus loved her more than she had ever thought possible, she had decided to take the future into her own hands. She felt as truly rich, beautiful and powerful as she had ever wished to be—free to be more herself than ever before.

She glittered like a star, dazzling her partners with her wit and raillery, and seeming to float on the air, so graceful and carefree were her steps. Society was enchanted, and she was surrounded with eager admirers all competing for her favours. Francesca smiled at them, danced with them, bewitched them—and gave them not another thought.

As the hour advanced, all her attention was on the doors to the ballroom. A sigh of satisfaction escaped her as she heard sounds of slight altercation—Marcus had arrived, without, of course, an invitation. However, her footman friend soon intervened and within minutes Marcus was inside the ballroom, regarding her with a baleful stare. It was a quarter past eleven.

No sooner had the set of dances finished than he claimed her and, ignoring the protests of her partner, swept her off to one side. He began without ceremony, forced to keep his voice low, but sounding fierce, nonetheless. 'What the devil are you thinking of? I forbid you to do this!'

Francesca gave him a brilliant smile. 'On the stroke of twelve, Marcus. A dramatic time for a dramatic revelation. Appropriate, don't you think?'

'But it won't do any good. And it will do you irreparable harm! For God's sake, don't do it, Francesca, I beg of you!'

Francesca returned the nod of an acquaintance who was dancing by before she answered him. 'You didn't tell me everything, did you, Marcus? That you could be accused of betraying your trust, letting your country down, all for the sake of a night's indulgence at a brothel. You didn't tell me that.'

'Don't use that word in this company, for God's sake!'

'They can't hear us—they think I'm flirting with you. Why didn't you warn me what might happen?'

'Sir Henry assumed from what Coker said that he would remain silent. He was mistaken. And I did warn you that there might be some disapproval.'

'You didn't mention ostracism, social disgrace.'

'What does that matter? The important thing is that you should be saved from ruin.'

She put her head on one side and looked up at him. 'You keep trying to save me from ruin, Marcus. Why, I wonder?'

He hesitated, then said, 'We cannot possibly discuss such matters here in the middle of a ballroom. Let me take you home.'

'Oh, no! I've taken a great deal of trouble to get you here tonight. Leaving before I've done what I set out to do is out of the question. But I will let you take me on to the balcony here. For a minute or two.' Oblivious once again to the curious glances being cast in their direction, they moved out on to the balcony overlooking the gardens.

'Well, Marcus? Tell me why.' After a pause during which he remained silent she went on, 'Can it be that you love me? Really love me—enough to marry me? Or has my behaviour finally given you a disgust of me?'

'I love you,' he said wretchedly. 'You must know that. I think I've loved you ever since I first saw you on the hillside at Shelwood. But. . .marry you? I'm not sure I can.'

She lowered her head to hide the amusement in her eyes. 'I *have* given you a disgust of me,' she said mournfully. 'Impetuous, rash, foolhardy, found in. . .bawdy houses and the like, and worst of all. . .a wanton. I have never been able to behave as I ought when you kiss me.'

'Francesca! If you only knew what it does to me when we kiss. How could anything so wonderful give me a disgust of you?'

He took a step forward, but she turned away, shaking her head. 'You love me, you kiss me. . .but you won't marry me. Why not, I wonder? Are you a rake, after all? Surely not!'

He set his jaw and was silent. The new Francesca was not to be put off. She had a very clear idea of the situation between them and the knowledge gave her confidence to continue. She gave a sad little sigh. 'I see I shall have to abandon the last vestiges of maidenly behaviour. But after all, why shouldn't I? It will be of little consequence tomorrow. I have nothing to lose.'

'Don't say that!'

'Why ever not? It is true. And. . .though I cannot like it, Marcus, you have forced me into a most unconventional situation. I find myself having to ask *you* to marry *me*. You see, I'm giving up all pretence at behaving as Society expects. The Honourable Francesca Beaudon is about to disappear forever tonight. I hope she will be replaced with a besottedly happy Lady Carne. But if you. . .if you refuse me, then Miss Shelwood-Beaudon of Shelwood, spinster and recluse, will appear in her place.'

'Francesca, I love you. There is nothing I would desire more than to be able to marry you, but how can I? It is as you say—I am in disgrace. I cannot ask you to share that.'

'At last!' Francesca dropped her wistful air and said briskly, 'Marcus, you are being ridiculous. If that is the only barrier to our marrying, then the sooner I am in disgrace, too, the better. Thank you, that is all I wanted to know.' She started towards the ballroom.

He caught her arm. 'I will not let you do this!'

'You cannot stop me!'

'Oh, yes, I can—by force if necessary!'

Francesca wrenched herself free and ran into the huge room full of people. It was five minutes before midnight. Marcus followed and made his way purposefully through the crowds towards her. He caught her arm again.

'Carne!'

Francesca and Marcus, absorbed in their struggle, had not noticed the appearance of a number of personages in the double doorway. Foremost among them was the Prince Regent. At his side was Lord Coker.

'Sir.' Marcus released Francesca and bowed. The Prince's face was thunderous.

'What the deuce do you think you're doing here? Are you all right, Miss Beaudon?'

Francesca curtsied. 'Thank you, sir. Yes.' She found it hard to hide her satisfaction at this turn of events. Marcus could hardly stop her now.

'It seems that Carne finds it impossible to keep his hands off the ladies, sir,' Lord Coker said, with a sneer. Francesca turned on him in a flame.

'Lord Carne's attentions, however forceful, are more welcome than yours were on a similar occasion, Lord Coker! If I remember correctly, I had to break a vase over your head before you would leave me alone.'

A moment of stunned silence was followed by unmistakeable sounds of amusement among those present. Lord Coker turned sallower than ever, and said viciously, 'I can hardly believe that the Prince Regent is interested in the antics of someone who prefers the advances of a man such as Carne, Miss Beaudon. I must assume that you do not know the truth about the gentleman. . .'

'As it happens, I know the truth better than anyone here—'

'Francesca, I forbid it,' said Marcus urgently. 'Sir,

I beg you. . . Miss Beaudon is not herself. . .'

'And whose fault is that, Carne?' asked the Prince in a voice of ice. 'The behaviour we observed as we came in was not the sort to reassure a lady. A few weeks ago, we would have sworn you were incapable of such disgraceful conduct. As it is. . .you would be well advised to make your apology and go. Indeed, I am not sure why you are here at all.'

Marcus was white. The Prince's tone had been cutting, and the rebuke both public and powerful. It was the worst yet of the consequences of his Parisian débâcle.

'Sir, let me explain—' Francesca began.

'It is not at all necessary, Miss Beaudon,' said the Prince, smiling at her. 'You cannot be held to blame in this matter.'

'That's not what I meant, sir. I wish to make it quite clear why Lord Carne is innocent of the charges at present in circulation against him.'

'Francesca!'

'Really, sir, what can this woman know of such matters?'

Marcus's despairing cry and Lord Coker's contemptuous question came together.

The Prince looked at them both dispassionately. Francesca saw for the first time those qualities in him which made him royal. 'My lords, you will allow me to deal with this in my own way, if you please! I agree, Coker, that Miss Beaudon is probably not aware of the true nature of Lord Carne's. . .indiscretions—I am not prepared to call his conduct worse than that at the moment—but the lady's manner seems to me to carry conviction. It intrigues me.'

Marcus took a deep breath and approached the Prince. 'Sir, Miss Beaudon is overwrought. She does not know what she is saying. Send her home, I beg you.'

The Prince looked at him, a frown on his normally amiable face. 'You know, Carne, what intrigues me most of all is why you do not wish me to listen to the lady.'

'Miss Beaudon is impulsive and quixotic, sir.'

'Are you trying to save Miss Beaudon against herself? I find that hard to believe. And I have small inclination to listen to someone I should much prefer not to have to meet—at the moment.'

'Oh sir, please do not speak so, I beg you!' cried Francesca. 'You cannot know it, but you are being truly unjust to Lord Carne. He does not deserve your disapprobation.'

'Now why do you say that, Miss Beaudon? How can you possibly know why Carne is in disgrace?'

'I was in Paris at the time. Lord Carne escorted me back to England.' An audible sigh went up from the company.

The Prince looked grave as he said, 'I am not sure that you would be wise to go any further, Miss Beaudon.'

'I must! I went at my father's request to deal with some urgent business. He was unable to go himself—if you remember, sir, he was taken ill at White's a little while ago. I believe he was attacked there.'

With a glance at Lord Coker, the Prince said, 'Go on.'

'Lord Carne followed me there. He was of the opinion that I might do something foolish. And I did. I went, in error, to a place where no lady should ever be found. I will not mention its name, but Lord Coker apparently knows it well.'

Lord Coker laughed contemptuously. 'This is a farrago of nonsense, sir! The lady is clearly making this up in a ridiculous attempt to reinstate Carne. She must be besotted. Why waste your time with her?'

'I find myself for once in agreement with Coker, sir. Miss Beaudon is ill—let me take her home. Come, Francesca.' Marcus took her arm again.

Francesca shook him off and took a step forward. 'I *will* speak! The Prince deserves the truth.'

The Prince Regent regarded the slender figure in white and silver, who had just spoken with such passionate conviction. 'The situation is unusual. I think I'd like to hear what Miss Beaudon finds so important, that she risks her own reputation.'

Marcus groaned and turned away.

Francesca said, raising her voice a little so that everyone who wished could hear, 'Lord Carne came to rescue me from a place in Paris which was not only morally undesirable, but one which he knew to be politically dangerous. I had gone there in all innocence, but if I was seen there, particularly by anyone who knew me, my reputation would be soiled beyond repair. On the other hand, if he was seen there, his own reputation and his career in politics would be destroyed forever. He chose to take that risk. In the event he was seen. By Lord Coker, who has no cause to love him, and who, I assume, has been behind the campaign to blacken his name.'

'I still say this is nonsense! Carne has put her up to this! No lady would ever go near—'

'The *Maison des Anges*? But I was there, Lord Coker! I saw you and two others coming up the stairs, I heard the salacious remarks you made about the statues there, and I listened as the Comtesse Rehan offered you the... attentions of a lady who had once been a...a Sultan's concubine.' A scandalised gasp from those present, followed by murmurs of protest, caused her to pause. But she put up her chin and went on bravely, 'I was hiding in the alcove, trembling with fear of discovery when Mr Chantry and Lord Witham defied the Countess and came to look for Lord Carne. Is that enough?'

'Good God!' Lord Coker turned away from her. 'What sort of woman are you?'

There were more murmurs and a general withdrawal from Francesca's vicinity.

Marcus swept the crowd with a glance of scorn. Then he said, 'True, loyal and fearless. Strongminded to the point of obstinacy where the happiness of those she loves is concerned. Lord Coker would be fortunate indeed if such a woman ever stooped to do so much for him. Ask her to tell you why she was in Paris.'

'My dear Carne, I will do no such thing!' Lord Coker said loftily. 'The sooner Miss Beaudon realises her presence here is embarrassing us, the better.'

Francesca's public acknowledgement of her catastrophic mistake had taken more out of her than she had expected, and she was now suffering from reaction. She was trembling, but she faced the Prince Regent proudly and her voice was clear as she said, 'Sir, I assure you, it was always my intention to relieve Society of my presence after tonight—I have no wish to embarrass anyone.'

The Prince frowned, then said, 'Lord Coker was overhasty. I should like to hear why you were in Paris, Miss Beaudon, even if Lord Coker doesn't.'

'I had a nurse as a child whom I loved very dearly. My father sent me to find her and bring her to England. But when I went to her house, I was told she had been taken ill. She had sought refuge with her only friend in Paris, a lady who happens to be the *directrice* of. . .of. . . the place where Lord Carne found me. I had no idea of its nature. I cannot imagine what would have happened to me if I had been found there by anyone other than Lord Carne. He behaved throughout with integrity and honour.'

Her voice shook with the intensity of her feelings as she went on, 'And it is wrong, cruelly wrong, that he is being made to suffer for my folly, and another's malice.' She swallowed. 'Forgive me, sir, I. . .I cannot say any

more. It has been too much. Too much.' She curtsied
hastily and hurried out of the ballroom.

'Follow her, Carne. Look after her.' As Marcus turned
to obey, the Prince Regent added, 'And, Carne. . .I should
like you to come and see me as soon as you can.'

Marcus bowed and left the room.

He caught up with Francesca as she hurried down the
stairs to the entrance hall. 'You were magnificent!'
he said.

'Please. . .don't say anything. Now that it's all over, I
find I am not nearly so brave as I thought. The look on
some of those faces. . .'

Francesca's carriage was waiting at the doors. They got
in, and Francesca gave way to her tears. Marcus took her
in his arms.

'Hush, Francesca, my love. Why are you crying? You
must compose yourself—we have some unfinished business, if you remember. You asked me a question tonight,
and I still have an answer to give you.'

'Oh, what must you think of me?' she sobbed.

'If you will stop ruining my coat, I will tell you. Here,
let me.' He tenderly wiped her face with his handkerchief.

'How do I know that you're not just sorry for me?'
Francesca sobbed, tears breaking out afresh. 'You were
once before.'

'You're being absurd! Come, Francesca. Pull yourself
together. You must know that I love you beyond words.
More than my career, my reputation, my life! If I had
realised all those years ago what you would come to
mean to me, I could have saved us both a great deal of
inconvenience and unhappiness. Do I need to tell you that
you're the only woman in the world for me? Look at me,
Francesca. Did you mean it when you asked me to marry
you? Or were you just playing with my affections?'

'Oh, Marcus!' She looked up, laughing through her tears.

'We'll go down to Packards tomorrow. Then we shall marry as soon as it can be arranged. And after that I'll love you, and treasure you, all my life.' He tilted her face to his and kissed her gently. Then he looked at her; in the dark blue depths of his eyes was all the love, honesty, humour and passion that belonged to this man she loved— had loved for so long. She smiled at him. Then, as he kissed her again, less gently, she laughed for joy, and threw her arms round his neck, responding as she always did—and always would.

It was quite some time after the carriage had drawn to a halt in Mount Street before Lord Carne handed Miss Beaudon out and escorted her to her door.

'Till tomorrow,' was all she said as she gave him her hand. He took it to his lips.

'And all that it brings.'

'Disgrace, ignominy, rejection from Society?'

'Possibly, but why should that worry us? If the world does find it impossible to forgive us—though I suspect that sadly that will not be the case—then we shall have peace to enjoy each other, and more than enough to occupy us at Carne and at Shelwood. But you did your work too well tonight—I think the Prince Regent is disposed to be kind.'

'I could think of something else to shock them all, if that is your wish?'

Unheeding of the groom patiently waiting by the carriage, and of the butler standing in the hall, Marcus laughed delightedly and caught her in his arms again. 'I have no doubt that life with you will always hold shocks, my love—you seem unable to avoid them—but they should be confined to your long-suffering husband. He's used to them. Leave Society to shift for itself!'

Epilogue

It had been a beautiful day, and now in the early evening
a slight breeze had got up, bringing a welcome freshness
to the warm air. Shelwood glowed in the mellow autumn
sunshine, as the field workers returned to their homes.
The crops were in, the barns and granaries were full. They
could be reasonably certain of a safe, comfortable winter.
They knew themselves to be fortunate. Shelwood was not
only a prosperous estate, it was a happy one.

They smiled as they saw the little party approaching
them. On their way back from Madame Elisabeth's, no
doubt. Miss Fanny was hanging on her lord's arm like a
bride, not a matron of four years! And Lord Carne looked
as proud as any man could of his growing family—three
bonny young bundles of mischief as they were. Little
Miss Verity was the worst of the three of them, too, for
all her angelic looks! There were those in the village who
could remember Miss Fanny's mother in the old days.
From what they said, this one was just such another.

It had been a lucky day for Shelwood when Miss Fanny
had returned with a new and handsome lord for a husband,
though they could wish that the family spent more time
at the Manor. But Lord Carne had his own estates in
Hertfordshire to look after, and it was said they also usu-

ally spent a month or two every year in London, visiting King George that had been Prince Regent for so long. But every summer they spent two or three months at Shelwood, visiting, walking, catching up with the news in the villages and farms. A proper lady, Lady Carne was. And her husband was a very gentlemanly gentleman.

Yes, Shelwood was the happiest place to be in all England.

Historical Romance™

Coming next month

THE NEGLECTFUL GUARDIAN
Anne Ashley

Miss Sarah Pennington had taken matters into her own hands! If her guardian, Mr Marcus Ravenhurst, was not prepared to acknowledge her existence, then she would leave Bath and stay with her old governess. For propriety she became Mrs Armstrong, but her travels were cut short by snow and she found herself stranded in a wayside inn!

She didn't know that Marcus was hot on her trail. He might not have visited the chit, but he'd given her everything her companion had requested! Then the weather foundered him too, and he walked into that same inn, unaware that the delicious young widow called Mrs Armstrong was his missing ward—or that she had a marked propensity for getting into trouble...

THE BECKONING DREAM
Paula Marshall

When her brother Rob was held for seditious writing, the only way Mistress Catherine Wood could ensure his release was to accompany supposed merchant Tom Trenchard—pretending to be his wife!—to Holland on a spying mission. With roguish charm Tom made no bones about wanting Catherine in his bed—after all, Catherine was an actress!—but she was determined to hold him at bay. It surprised her to realise how hard that was, more so as they travelled into danger and depended upon one another, needing all their wits about them...

CAROLE
MORTIMER

Gypsy

She'd always been his one temptation...

Shay Flannagan was the raven-haired beauty
the Falconer brothers called Gypsy. They
each found her irresistible, but it was Lyon
Falconer who claimed her—when he didn't
have the right—and sealed her fate.

JAYNE ANN KRENTZ

Joy

When a couple win a mysterious emerald bracelet
in a poker game, their peaceful Caribbean holiday
becomes a rollercoaster of adventure, desire...and
deadly peril.

*"Jayne Ann Krentz is one of the hottest writers in
romance today."*—USA Today

AVAILABLE IN PAPERBACK
FROM SEPTEMBER 1997

DEBBIE MACOMBER

THIS MATTER OF MARRIAGE

Hallie McCarthy gives herself a year to find
Mr Right. Meanwhile, her handsome neighbour
is busy trying to win his ex-wife back. As the two
compare notes on their disastrous campaigns, each
finds the perfect partner lives right next door!

*"In the vein of When Harry Met Sally,
Ms Macomber will delight."*

—Romantic Times

**AVAILABLE IN PAPERBACK
FROM SEPTEMBER 1997**